Beyond the Storm's Reach

Adele Hewett Veal

Hewett Enterprises, LLC

To those who have carried the weight of of love that wasn't love at
all,
who have stitched their hearts back together with threads of hope,
only to wonder if love was ever meant for them.
To the ones who stayed too long,
who forgave too much,
who mistook longing for destiny
and sacrifice for devotion.
This book is for you.
For the moment you finally stood still long enough
to be truly seen.
To be loved without condition.
To be chosen without question.
May you never again settle for anything less.
Adele Hewett Veal

CHAPTER ONE

GRACE LEANED AGAINST THE kitchen counter, scrolling through her phone absentmindedly as the coffee pot gurgled softly in the background. Although it was unusual, Ethan's phone lay beside her, its screen lighting up with a notification at that exact moment.

Her eyes flicked to the message, and her heart plummeted. *Hey, I'm still replaying last night in my mind... and I definitely need more. Same time tonight? Don't make me wait. XO.*

The room seemed to close around her, the air thick and suffocating. Her hands trembled as she reached for Ethan's phone, the words burning into her vision.

This has to be a mistake, she thought, clinging to a thread of hope. But deep down, she knew better—had known for a long time. The late nights, the guarded phone, the growing distance. Each time she confronted him, he brushed her off, making her doubt herself.

Her pulse thundered in her ears as she tapped on the message and opened the thread. The sliver of hope shattered instantly. Text after text between her husband and a woman named Olivia. Flirtation. Secrets. Intimacy. It was all there, laid bare in glowing pixels.

Her knees weakened, and she gripped the counter for support. The dripping of the coffee pot mocked her with its normalcy, cutting through the turmoil unraveling inside her.

Ethan entered the kitchen, his footsteps casual, his expression neutral—until he saw her holding his phone. His gaze darted to the screen, then back to her face, his mask of calm cracking ever so slightly.

"What are you doing with my phone?" He asked, his voice sharp, defensive.

Grace held it out, her hand trembling. "Who's Olivia?"

His face paled, but he recovered quickly, his expression hardening. "Olivia? I don't know an Olivia." He shrugged, his tone dismissive. "Grace, don't jump to conclusions..."

"Jump to conclusions?" Her voice wavered with anger and pain. "Explain why she's thanking you for last night.

He rolled his eyes. "It's not what you think."

"Don't you dare say that to me!" Her voice cracked, overwhelmed by her emotions. "I want the truth. For once, Ethan. The truth."

He sighed, running a hand through his hair. "Fine. Olivia's... a friend. I didn't tell you because I knew you'd overreact."

"A friend?" Grace's laugh was cold, bitter. "I read the whole thread. Don't insult me by pretending I'm stupid."

He tried to give an intimidating look, but it faltered. Instead, he looked like a child caught in a lie for a moment. "What do you want me to say?"

Her eyes narrowed, blazing with fury. "You smug son of a bitch."

Ethan's jaw tightened. "Oh, so now we're name-calling? This is ridiculous. I'm not going to stand here and be scolded like a child. This is bullshit."

"Bullshit?" Her voice rose, raw and unsteady. "The past five years have been bullshit—lies and gaslighting. You've twisted everything, made me question my own sanity."

"Grace, it's not..."

"No, Ethan. It is." She stepped closer, her voice cutting like a blade. "Whenever I came to you with my suspicions, you called me jealous. Emotional. Said I was imagining things. You turned it all on me, made me doubt myself. Do you even realize how cruel that is?"

He opened his mouth to respond, but she cut him off.

"Don't. Just don't," Grace said, her voice breaking.

For a moment, his defenses crumbled. "What do you want from me? People make mistakes. Relationships aren't perfect."

Her laugh was hollow. "Forgetting an anniversary is a mistake. This—five years of lies and betrayal—is calculated. Deliberate. You can't fan this away like it's nothing."

He flinched, and silence stretched between them, heavy and suffocating.

"How long?" She asked.

His shoulders slumped. "Three years," he muttered. "But I didn't want you to find out like this."

Her laugh was sharp and still bitter. "Three years. You didn't want me to find out? We've been married for five, Ethan. Five years."

"I might as well tell you the rest," he mumbled, though his tone was defensive, not remorseful.

Her breath caught, her chest tightening. "There's more?"

His jaw tightened as he looked away. "Olivia's... pregnant."

The words hit her like a physical blow. Her hand flew to her mouth, her vision blurring. The room seemed to spin as the heaviness of Ethan's betrayal pressed down and crushed her.

"I can't... I can't do this," she whispered, brushing past him.

"Grace, wait..."

"Don't," she snapped, her voice fierce despite her tears. "You made your choice, Ethan. Now I'm making mine."

Her footsteps echoed as she walked away, each step tearing at the fragments of her heart.

CHAPTER TWO

THE HOUSE WAS UNBEARABLY quiet, broken only by the occasional clink of Ethan's coffee cup on the counter or the distant whir of the dishwasher. The stillness loomed in on Grace, amplifying the weight of everything she'd discovered. They hadn't exchanged more than a handful of words all week. She had nothing left to say to him. Ethan, meanwhile, moved through the house with detached indifference, splitting his focus between work calls and scrolling through his phone as if his betrayal hadn't shattered her world.

Grace wandered aimlessly from room to room, her thoughts clouded by a heavy fog. Every glance at him felt like drowning, and the absence of remorse in his demeanor only deepened the ache.

Her gaze fell on her phone lying face-up on the dining room table. She hesitated, her fingers hovering over the screen. She needed to talk to someone. But not her mother—she couldn't bear the disappointment or worry in her voice.

Her thumb scrolled to the top of her contact list. Zoe. Her best friend. The one person who would listen without judgment. Before she could second-guess herself, Grace tapped the call button.

The phone barely rang once before Zoe's warm, familiar voice answered. "Grace! Finally. I've been calling for days. Your phone keeps going straight to voicemail. What's going on?"

Grace's throat tightened. "Sorry," she whispered. "I didn't know what to say... I still don't."

"About what. What's going on?" She asked again.

Grace didn't know where to start.

"Hey," Zoe said gently, her concern cutting through Grace's numbness. "Take a deep breath. Start wherever you need to. What's happening?"

Grace closed her eyes, the pain swelling in her chest. She let out a shaky breath. "He's seeing someone else, Zoe."

A stunned silence filled the line before Zoe's voice sharpened. "Who? Ethan? I knew it. How did you find out?"

"I saw a text from her. Her name's Olivia. She thanked him for last night." Her voice trembled. "I read the whole thread. He couldn't deny it this time."

"Oh my God." Zoe's outrage flared. "Grace, no. Please tell me you're joking."

"I wish I were," Grace whispered, her voice cracking. "I confronted him. He admitted it... like it wasn't even a big deal."

"Son of a..." Zoe cut herself off, exhaling sharply. "What excuse did he give?"

Grace laughed bitterly, tears brimming in her eyes. "He just stood there with a stupid, smug look. He didn't even bother with an excuse. He said it wasn't serious. Like that makes it better. It's been going on for three years. How's that not serious?"

Zoe's voice turned fierce. "Three years? That's not just cheating—that's a whole damn relationship. I swear, if I were there, I'd slap that smug look off his face. After everything you've done for him, after all the crap he's put you through…"

"I don't know what to do," Grace interrupted, her voice barely audible. "My whole life just crumbled under me. How do I even begin to pick up these pieces?"

"You don't have to do it alone," Zoe said firmly. "I'm here. Whatever you need—space, a shoulder to cry on—a shovel—you just say the word."

Grace managed a shaky laugh. "A shovel sounds good right about now."

"Then I'm on my way," Zoe replied, her tone softening but resolute. "Let's get you out of that house. You need air. A plan. And to remember who you are without him dragging you down."

Grace hesitated; the gravity of Olivia's pregnancy was too much. She wasn't ready to share that truth yet.

"I feel like I'm drowning," she admitted, her voice breaking. "Ethan's here, in the same house, but it's like he's already gone."

"You need to get out of there," Zoe insisted. "Even for a little while. Come on a vacation with me."

"A vacation?" Grace laughed bitterly. "Zoe, my life is falling apart. I can't go sip cocktails on a beach."

"Why not? What's keeping you there? Ethan? Let him stew in his own mess for a while. You deserve a break."

Grace's chest tightened. "I don't know…"

"You do know," Zoe pressed. "I found a mini-cruise. Three days. Just you and me. No Ethan, no drama, no stress. You need this."

"Picture this," Zoe continued, her tone lightening, "a ship—no, not just a ship—a floating palace. Gourmet food, champagne that practically sparkles in your mouth, and towels so fluffy they'd put clouds to shame. And it's all-inclusive. Yes, all-inclusive, Grace!

You can eat, drink, kayak, and probably even learn to salsa dance if you feel like it. It's all covered. Every. Single. Thing."

Grace couldn't help but smile faintly. "Only three days?" she asked.

"Three days," Zoe echoed softly. "Say yes. You'll come back a new woman. Or at least a slightly tanner one."

Later that evening, Grace sat in the living room, staring at the cruise itinerary on her laptop. White sandy beaches. Blue skies. Freedom.

What's keeping you here? Ethan?

She clicked "Book Now." Relief washed over her, and her shoulders felt lighter for the first time in a week.

Grace stood at the edge of her closet, carefully folding clothes and placing them into the open suitcase on the bed. The soft rustle of fabric filled the tense silence in the room. Ethan walked in, his expression dark, his posture rigid. He stopped just short of the suitcase, his eyes narrowing.

He motioned toward the bag. "What's this?" he asked, his voice clipped.

Without turning to face him, Grace continued folding a blouse, her tone calm but firm. "I'm packing for my trip. I'm going on a cruise with Zoe."

Ethan's jaw tightened as he crossed his arms. "A trip? Seriously? You're planning a trip now?"

"Stop being dramatic. Like you really care. It's just a mini-cruise. I'll only be gone for three days. I need space—something this house doesn't seem to offer." She turned to the suitcase, carefully tucking the blouse and another swimsuit into a corner.

Ethan let out a bitter laugh, his tone dripping with disdain. "Really, Grace? You think running off for three days will magically fix our problems? That's just... pathetic."

Grace finished packing, zipped her suitcase, and slid it off the bed. She turned to face him, her eyes blazing with restrained fury. "What's pathetic, Ethan, is you standing here pretending to give a damn while all along making plans to be with her." Her voice was sharp, cutting through the tension like a knife.

His face tightened. "I don't know what you're talking about."

As if on cue, his phone buzzed in his pocket. He pulled it out, glanced at the screen, then turned away, lowering his voice as he answered. "Yeah... I can't talk right now... I'll call you back. Yes, of course, I'll be there."

Grace's fists clenched at her sides. The audacity of him making plans with Olivia right in front of her was too much. She took a deep breath, forcing herself to stay calm.

"Unbelievable," she muttered.

Ethan ended the call and turned back to her, feigning innocence. "What? She's pregnant. I can't just ignore her."

"I don't know why you bother pretending anymore," she said coldly. "Yes, I do. It's because Olivia can't give you the life I have."

"You're overreacting, as usual," Ethan shot back, his tone sharp as he crossed his arms over his chest. "But fine. Go. Run away. See if I care." His voice oozed condescension.

Grace stood by the kitchen counter with her suitcase. Her hands trembled enough to betray the calm she was fighting to maintain. "I'm not running away," she said, her voice steady. "I'm taking time to think. To breathe. Something you clearly don't think I deserve."

Ethan let out a bitter laugh, shaking his head. "Oh, right. Breathe. That's your excuse for everything lately. 'Take a break, Grace. Get some air, Grace.'" He waved a dismissive hand. "But hey, if a three-day booze cruise is going to fix things for ya, who am I to stop you?"

Grace clenched her jaw. "This isn't about fixing things, Ethan. I don't even know if it can be fixed. It's about finding clarity—something I can't seem to do with you constantly dismissing me."

His mouth opened as if to retort, but nothing came out. Grace tilted her head slightly. "You can think whatever you want. But here's the reality: I'm leaving because of you. And that's a truth you'll never be able to gaslight away."

"No. You want to know why you're really going on this cruise?" Ethan said, his words dripping with accusation. "It's because you want to meet someone. That's what this is really about."

Grace paused, her hands resting on the suitcase. She didn't look at him right away. Instead, she took a steadying breath, letting his words hang in the air like a foul odor. Finally, she turned to face him, her expression calm but unyielding.

"I want to meet someone?" she repeated softly, her voice carrying an edge of disbelief. "Ethan, I don't need someone else to escape this. I'm leaving because I can't breathe in this house. I'm suffocating under the impact of your lies and the endless excuses you think I should be grateful to accept."

Ethan's face flushed with anger, but Grace didn't give him the chance to interrupt. She stepped closer, her piercing eyes locked onto his. "You're the one who invited someone else into our marriage, not me. You made your choices. Choices that shattered every ounce of trust I had in you. And now you want to twist it around and make it about me?"

Ethan took a step back as if her words had physically struck him. For once, he was silent.

With that, she grabbed her suitcase and walked past him, her head held high, leaving him small and utterly defeated in the doorway.

"Wait," he said, almost casually. "When will you be back?"

Grace froze for a moment, then met his gaze. "Why does it matter?"

He shrugged, feigning indifference. "Just wondering how long you plan on 'finding yourself.' Don't want the neighbors thinking you've abandoned ship entirely."

She held his gaze for a beat longer than he expected, then turned and walked out without answering. She didn't owe him that.

Grace slid into the driver's seat of her car, shutting the door with a satisfying thud. The tension in her chest loosened as she finally left the house behind. She gripped the steering wheel, letting out a shaky breath. After a moment, she pulled into a parking lot, retrieved her phone, and tapped Zoe's number.

Zoe answered on the second ring, her voice laced with concern. "Grace?"

"I left," Grace whispered, her voice wavering. "I did it. I left him."

"Oh my God, Gracie." Zoe's voice filled with relief. Then, firmer: "Good for you."

Grace closed her eyes, the argument with Ethan replaying in her mind. "He saw me packing for the trip and accused me of running away from our problems."

Zoe's sharp intake of breath crackled through the line. "Typical. Like it's your fault he's been having an affair for three years."

"Exactly." Grace's voice broke. "When I told him I needed time to think, he had the audacity to act like he cared. And then his phone rang. Guess who?"

"No," Zoe groaned, disbelief and anger in her tone. "How ironic."

"Yeah." Grace's laugh was bitter. "He whispered into the phone like I wouldn't know. He said, 'I'll call you later.' He's making plans to see her right in my face."

"That's disgusting," Zoe spat. "You should've thrown something at him."

"Believe me, I wanted to." Grace's voice quivered. "But I'm done fighting for someone who clearly doesn't want me. I grabbed my suitcase and walked out."

"I'm so proud of you," Zoe said softly, "You're stronger than you think."

Tears stung Grace's eyes, but they weren't from sadness this time. "You keep saying I'm strong. I don't feel strong. I feel... numb."

"That's okay," Zoe reassured her. "You just took the first step. The feelings will come."

Grace wiped her eyes. "I can't go back to that house."

"You don't have to. My place is yours for as long as you need."

"Thank you," Grace whispered. "I don't know what I'd do without you."

"You'd figure it out," Zoe said firmly. "Like I said, you're stronger than you think. But I'm here every step of the way."

Grace put the car in drive, a flicker of relief easing the ache in her chest. "I'll be there soon."

The drive to Zoe's was quiet, giving Grace time to process her decision. A wave of relief washed over her when she pulled into the driveway. Zoe stood at the door, arms crossed, with a determined look.

As Grace exited the car, Zoe rushed to meet her and hugged her tightly. "You're safe now," she whispered.

Grace exhaled, exhaustion settling into her bones. "I didn't realize how much I needed to get out of there."

"You've got this," Zoe said, guiding her inside. She handed Grace a hot cup of coffee and led her to the back patio. "Sit. Talk to me. I know there's more to this, Gracie. Spill it."

Grace stared into her mug, watching the steam curl and fade. Her voice was brittle. "It's worse than I thought. He's been lying... to everyone."

Zoe's brow furrowed. "What do you mean?"

Grace's voice trembled. "I'm sure Olivia thinks he'll leave me for her. But he won't. He's been stringing her along. "

"If he doesn't want you, why doesn't he just go?"

"Because he wants to have his cake and eat it, too." Grace's tears shimmered. "He wants her, but he wants my money more." Grace nodded. "The house, the cars, the vacations—it's all me. He's promised her he'll leave, but deep down, Ethan knows he won't."

Zoe's face darkened. "So, you're the one footin' the bill for his 'luxury life'? I knew it. He's a parasite, Grace. You deserve so much better."

Grace swallowed hard, her voice steadier. "I know. I've been fooling myself for a long time. But now that I see it, I can't unsee it. He doesn't love me, Zoe. He never did."

Zoe gripped Grace's hand tightly. "You've got to think about yourself for once, Gracie."

A spark of certainty lit in Grace's eyes. "I'm done being his safety net. I'm done paying for his lies."

Zoe smiled fiercely. "Good."

Grace took a deep breath, clarity washing over her. "I need to take control of my life and stop making excuses for him."

Zoe squeezed her hand. "Exactly. Come on. Let's get you settled. You've got a big adventure ahead."

Grace could finally breathe and take the time to reclaim herself.

CHAPTER THREE

THURSDAY MORNING. THE DAY OF THE
CRUISE.

GRACE SAT AT ZOE'S kitchen table, hands cradling a steaming
cup of coffee. The house was still, the silence soothing but
fragile. Her phone buzzed against the wood, breaking the calm.
Ethan. His name flashed on the screen like a warning light.

She sighed, pushing the phone away. It was the seventh call in
an hour. He'd barely spoken to her all week, but now that she was
leaving, he couldn't stop harassing her.

The phone buzzed again, vibrating insistently. Her patience
snapped. She grabbed the phone and typed a sharp message:

Grace: *Stop calling me Ethan. If you don't, I'm blocking your
number.*

She hit send and dropped the phone onto the table as though
it burned her fingers. A wave of exhaustion washed over her. She
closed her eyes and took a deep breath, willing herself to stay calm.

The sound of Zoe's heels clicking against the floor snapped her back to reality. Zoe swept into the kitchen, suitcase in tow.

"Morning!" Zoe called, her voice clipped but warm. She paused, eyeing Grace. "You look like you've just seen a ghost. What's going on?"

Grace gestured to her still-vibrating phone. "It's Ethan. He won't stop calling."

Zoe frowned, dropping her purse on the counter and folding her arms. "Haven't you blocked him yet?"

"I told him I would if he didn't stop," Grace said. "I just don't want any trouble. If I block him, he might show up here. He can get... dramatic."

Zoe leaned in, her voice firm but gentle. "Gracie, he's already being dramatic. Bombarding you with calls isn't okay. He lost the right to your time and energy the moment he cheated. Block him."

Grace hesitated, her thumb hovering over the screen. "It's just... hard."

"I know," Zoe said, squeezing her hand. "But you need to protect your peace. Even if it's just for these three days. He doesn't get to keep taking pieces of you."

Grace swallowed hard and nodded, finally pressing the block button. Ethan's name vanished from the screen, and relief washed over her like a breath of fresh air.

"There. It's done."

"Good," Zoe said, smiling. "You'll thank me later."

Grace managed a small smile, but Zoe's tense posture caught her attention.

"Uh-oh. What's wrong?" Grace asked. "You look annoyed."

Zoe groaned, throwing her hands in the air. "My boss can't find a document I put on his desk yesterday. Instead of looking for it, he panicked and called me."

"On the day we're leaving for our cruise? Seriously?" Grace shook her head in disbelief.

"Yep." Zoe popped the "p" with irritation. "I have to go into the office, login, and print another copy. But I'll leave straight from there and meet you at the pier."

"Are you sure? I can get dressed and come with you."

"No way. No sense in both of us leaving early." Zoe waved her off. "Relax. Finish your coffee. Uber to the pier, so we only have one car to deal with when we get back."

Grace nodded. "Good idea."

"Perfect." Zoe's energy shifted, her movements quick and decisive. She paused at the door, suitcase in hand. "Seriously, Gracie. Are you okay?"

Grace smiled, a slight but genuine curve of her lips. "I'm okay. Better now. Thanks to you."

"Damn right," Zoe said, confidence breaking through her frustration. "Don't let that Uber make you late, or you're buying the first round of drinks."

Grace laughed, her spirits lifting. "Deal. Now go save your boss from himself."

Zoe blew a kiss, grabbed her suitcase, and disappeared through the door. "See you at the pier!"

"Drive carefully!" Grace called after her.

"Never!" Zoe's voice echoed faintly before the door clicked shut.

The house fell quiet again, but this silence felt different—lighter. Blocking Ethan was a small step, but it was a step forward.

Her gaze drifted to her packed suitcase by the door. This trip wasn't just about getting away. It was about rediscovering herself.

Her phone buzzed. A message from Zoe.

Zoe: *If I get to the pier before you, I'll have a pina colada waiting with your name on it.*

Grace laughed softly and typed back:

Grace: *See you there.*

She scheduled an Uber and leaned back in her chair. The coffee in her cup had grown cold, much like her house had become—just a house, no longer a home. She slid the mug into the microwave, its low hum filling the room as her thoughts churned.

When the microwave beeped, she removed it and slowly sipped the reheated brew. The minutes blurred together as she showered and dressed. The tension of the morning pressing down on her.

A honk outside. Her ride had arrived.

She slipped her phone into her purse, grabbed her suitcase, and hesitated at the door. This was it. One step forward—toward freedom or something close to it.

She squared her shoulders, walked out, and let the door click shut behind her.

CHAPTER FOUR

THURSDAY MORNING. THE PIER

G RACE LEANED AGAINST THE car window, her heart skipping a beat as the pier came into view. A flicker of excitement sparked in her chest, growing stronger with every passing mile. The salty tang of the ocean breeze drifted through the cracked window, mingling with her anticipation. For the first time in weeks, she felt something other than anger or despair—she felt alive.

The scenery unfolded like a living postcard: vibrant, bustling, and teeming with the energy of travelers ready for adventure. Towering cruise terminals shimmered on the horizon, sleek and modern against the backdrop of sparkling blue waters. Ships bobbed gently in the harbor, their hulls glinting under the Florida sun like scattered jewels.

Her Uber driver glanced at her in the rearview mirror. "First cruise?" he asked, friendly and curious.

Grace nodded, a soft smile curving her lips. "Yep. First one."

"Good for you," he said. "Nothing like the ocean to clear your head."

The car slowed to a stop at the terminal drop-off. Sunlight reflected off the glass and steel, casting shimmering patterns on the water. Grace stepped out, the warmth of the pavement grounding her. The scent of sunscreen and excitement filled the air. The pier symbolized a gateway to something she desperately needed: a chance to breathe, to think, and hopefully start over.

She lifted a hand to shade her eyes from the sun as the driver hefted her suitcase from the trunk, squinting at the gray clouds creeping in. The palm trees swayed, their fronds whispering of an uncertain forecast. Rain or shine, she thought, this is happening.

"Here you go, ma'am," the driver said, placing the suitcase gently at her feet. "Looks like we might be in for a little rain."

Grace smiled, brushing her hair from her face. "Fingers crossed that won't be the case. Thanks for the ride."

"Have a good time," he said, tipping his cap.

She wrapped her fingers around her suitcase handle, her gaze drawn to the massive ship. The name The Emerald Princess shimmered elegantly on its hull. The cries of seagulls blended with the laughter of children, the chatter of families, and the rumble of engines—a harmony reminding her that life moves on. She took a step forward, then hesitated. She turned and watched as the Uber driver disappeared in the distance. Then, her focus was reluctantly drawn back to the terminal. Just then, a familiar voice called out. "Gracie!"

She scanned the crowd until she spotted Zoe waving wildly on the ship's deck. "Don't just stand there!" Zoe shouted, cupping her hands around her mouth. "Move it!"

A laugh bubbled up from Grace, surprising her with its ease. She waved back, lifted her suitcase, and quickened her pace. "I'm coming!" she called, weaving through the throng of travelers, the pier's energy propelling her forward.

At the terminal, the flurry of activity intensified. Families hugged tightly in farewell, while others reunited with eager embraces. Porters expertly navigated mountains of luggage, and cruise staff in crisp uniforms directed passengers with practiced smiles.

Grace handed her ticket to an attendant, who efficiently scanned it and waved her through. Her pulse quickened. She was really doing this—stepping into the unknown, leaving the strain of her old life behind, if only for three days.

As she approached the gates, a brief moment of doubt crept into her mind. Could she truly leave everything behind, even temporarily? She shook her head as if to banish the thought. *I need this*, she reminded herself. *I deserve this.*

She spotted Zoe just beyond the gates, grinning with open arms. Grace rushed forward, their laughter mingling as they hugged.

"You made it!" Zoe exclaimed. "Told you I'd beat you here. How does it feel?"

Grace took a breath, the tension of the past week slipping away. "It feels... right."

"Good." Zoe's smile softened. "I'm proud of you, you know. Taking this step."

Grace blinked, her throat tightening. "Thanks, Zoe. That means a lot. Now, where's my Piña Colada?" Grace teased, her voice lightening.

Zoe grabbed her arm, eyes twinkling. "This way, my dear. Let's get this party started."

They weaved through the crowd, their excitement unmistakable. Grace's stateroom, 2B, was nestled midship, close to the central atrium and a short walk from the pool deck. Zoe's cabin, 2C, was just a door away.

As they rushed into Grace's cabin, she marveled at the chic, cream-and-navy decor, the king-sized bed with crisp linens, and the private balcony where sunlight danced on the water's surface. The air carried a faint trace of salt and new beginnings.

Zoe burst in through the connecting door, already shedding her shoes. "Come on, Gracie!" she urged, handing her a frosty Piña Colada. "We're wasting daylight!"

Grace laughed, kicking off her sandals. "I'm going as fast as I can!"

They clinked glasses, the quiet tink an echo of the freedom they were embracing.

Grace slipped into her sleek black one-piece swimsuit, the plunging neckline and twisted knot detail at the waist accentuating her curves. A sheer white cover-up billowed lightly as she moved, delicate embroidery adding a touch of elegance. Ever vibrant, Zoe chose a turquoise bikini with a playful bow and a tropical-print kimono that matched her personality perfectly.

"Why do I feel like you planned that outfit just to show me up?" Grace teased, tying her hair into a loose bun.

"Please," Zoe replied with a dramatic hair flip. "I'm just here to make the pool side prettier. Besides, you look like a Bond girl in that thing."

Grace rolled her eyes but smiled. "You're ridiculous."

"And you're gorgeous," Zoe shot back, grabbing her hand. "Now, let's go make some heads turn."

They grabbed their beach bags and towels, slipping from the staterooms into the cool hallway air.

Grace smiled with a certainty that warmed her from the inside out. This was precisely where she belonged.

CHAPTER FIVE

THURSDAY AFTERNOON. ABOARD THE
EMERALD PRINCESS.

T HE SHIP BUZZED WITH energy as Grace and Zoe wandered
through its endless corridors and open decks, marveling
at the grandeur of their floating vacation home. Although the
gray clouds hovered over them, the atmosphere was electric—filled with laughter, music, and the chatter of eager passengers ready to embrace their adventure.

"Can you believe this place?" Zoe asked, spinning slowly in
the massive central hall. The space soared several stories high,
with glass elevators gliding silently along mirrored walls. A live
band played jazzy tunes near the bar, where bartenders flipped
cocktail shakers theatrically, earning applause from the crowd.
"This is way better than the motel my mother took me to when
I was ten. Broken pool pump, no Wi-Fi—it was tragic."

Grace chuckled, her shoulders relaxing for the first time in days. "I didn't think cruise ships could be this extravagant. It's like a floating city."

They passed a café where the aroma of freshly baked pastries mingled with the sea air. At Zoe's insistence, they stopped to sample flaky croissants, rich chocolate éclairs, and tiny fruit tarts. Later, they stumbled upon the buffet—a dazzling spread of international cuisines.

"Is that a sushi bar?" Zoe's eyes widened. "This might be my favorite spot."

Grace smiled, filling her plate with grilled salmon, roasted vegetables, and pasta salad. "I'm trying not to overdo it on the first day."

"Live a little!" Zoe piled her plate high with shrimp cocktail and cheesecake. "We're on vacation!"

As they explored further, they discovered a rooftop pool with an infinity edge overlooking the vast ocean, a mini-golf course, and a glass skywalk jutting out over the waves below. The breeze carried a distant roll of thunder, adding a dramatic edge to the lively scene.

Grace glanced at the sky, where dark clouds gathered ominously. "Looks like we might get rained out."

"Rain, schmain." Zoe waved it off. "We've got an indoor spa, live shows, and a million places to hide if it pours. Besides, a little rain is romantic—like something out of a movie."

Grace laughed. "Then I'll try to channel my inner leading lady."

That afternoon, they claimed a cozy spot at the outdoor bar, sipping colorful cocktails garnished with tiny umbrellas and fruit slices. Zoe twirled her straw, her playful expression shifting to something more serious.

"All right, spill it," Zoe said. "What's the plan for when we get back? Have you thought about it?"

Grace sighed, staring into her drink. "I don't know. Part of me wants to file for divorce the second I step off this ship. The other part feels... stuck. Like I owe it to the past five years to at least try to figure out what went wrong."

Zoe snorted. "What do you owe Ethan? A handshake for cheating? A pat on the back for gaslighting you all these years? No, ma'am. You owe yourself peace, Gracie. You don't owe Ethan one damn thing."

"It just feels so final," Grace said. "Walking away feels like admitting failure."

"Failure?" Zoe's voice rose. "He's been having an affair for three fuckin' years. The only failure would be staying in a situation that makes you miserable. You deserve a fresh start—whether with someone new, a new city, or just being by yourself."

Grace blinked back tears. "I'll think about it. I promise."

"Think fast," Zoe teased, raising her glass. "We only have three days."

That evening, the deck sparkled with string lights, and the sound of a steel drum band filled the air. Grace and Zoe leaned against the railing; their laughter carried on the breeze.

Suddenly, Zoe stilled, her eyes sliding past Grace's shoulder. "Don't look now, but I think you have an admirer."

Curiosity got the best of her. Grace turned slightly, following Zoe's gaze. Near the bar stood a man with striking features. His medium-brown skin glowed under the deck lights, and his golden-brown eyes seemed to hold a lifetime of stories. When he smiled, it reached his eyes, crinkling them at the corners.

He wore a simple gray button-down shirt, khaki shorts, and slip-on shoes. There was no flash, no flair—just an effortless presence.

As Grace's gaze lingered, he nodded, a subtle acknowledgment that sent a ripple of awareness through her. Then, as if not wanting to push the moment, he slid on a pair of sunglasses and turned to face the ocean, his profile etched against the twilight sky.

"See?" Zoe whispered. "He's been watching you for the past five minutes. Wave, and I bet he'll come over."

Grace's cheeks flushed. "You're imagining things."

"I'm not imagining that he looks like he stepped out of a romance novel," Zoe teased. "Go talk to him."

"I'm not just walking up to a stranger," Grace laughed nervously. "That's not me."

"Maybe it should be," Zoe grinned. "If you don't go, I will."

Grace grabbed Zoe's arm. "Don't you dare!"

"Fine," Zoe said, raising her hands in surrender. "But if he comes over, you'd better not scare him off. He looks like trouble in the best way."

Grace shook her head, trying to dismiss the flutter in her chest. She was here to figure out her own life, not get tangled in someone else's. She took a deep breath, focusing on the sound of the waves.

She glanced back. The man's gaze had returned to her. Her heart skipped a beat, and she quickly turned away.

Zoe's chuckle broke the quiet. "This is going to be interesting."

Grace shot her a look. "What's that supposed to mean?"

"Oh, nothing." Zoe leaned against the railing, eyes twinkling. "Guys like that don't blend into the background. Trust me."

"My life's complicated enough," Grace insisted. "I don't need anything—or anyone—else adding to the clutter."

"Sure, sure," Zoe said, her grin playful. "But if he wanders over, you're not allowed to run away."

"I'm not running away," Grace muttered. "I'm just... focusing on myself."

Zoe winked. "Keep telling yourself that. Meanwhile, I'll be enjoying the show."

Grace groaned, turning back to the ocean. Just then, the breeze carried the sound of the man's low laughter. She shook her head, a faint smile tugging at her lips as she massaged the back of her neck.

CHAPTER SIX

G RACE LEANED BACK AGAINST the bar stool, sipping her drink as she watched Zoe animatedly argue with the bartender about the perfect ratio of lime to tequila. The bartender gave a bemused nod, mixing the drink precisely to her specifications.

Zoe turned back, eyes sparkling. "You know what they say—never trust a bartender who skimps on the lime."

Grace chuckled. "Some things never change. Thank God for that."

Zoe smirked, raising an eyebrow. "You're welcome, by the way."

"For what?" Grace teased.

"Never changing. Remember when we first met?" Zoe laughed. "You should thank me for saving you from a lifetime of wandering aimlessly through high school hallways." She grinned. "I Remember the lost girl with the crumpled campus map?"

Grace laughed. "Yeah, I was this close to giving up and heading straight for the exit."

"And then I swooped in like a superhero," Zoe declared, striking a dramatic pose. "Grace Richardson, saved by Zoe King, freshman guide extraordinaire."

Grace rolled her eyes affectionately. "'Extraordinaire' might be overselling it. You were more like... a whirlwind."

Zoe waved a hand dismissively. "Same thing. You looked like you needed rescuing."

"I definitely did." Grace's smile softened. "I was so nervous that day."

Zoe leaned in, eyes gleaming with nostalgia. "And yet you trusted me immediately. Didn't even question my so-called 'expert' navigation skills."

"Well, you did get us to homeroom without a hitch."

"See?" Zoe winked. "You were in good hands."

Grace's eyes twinkled. "And you've been bossing me around ever since."

"Hey, someone's gotta keep you in line," Zoe teased, her voice softening. "Hard to believe that was so long ago."

"Feels like yesterday," Grace admitted. "And yet, here we are."

"Guess some friendships are just built to last." Zoe clinked her glass against Grace's.

"To us, then," Grace said, warmth spreading through her chest.

"To us," Zoe echoed, her smile unwavering.

Grace closed her eyes, her thoughts drifting down memory lane. She remembered how they had lost touch after high school. It wasn't intentional—life had simply taken them to different colleges, different cities, and down different paths. But fate, ever the orchestrator of surprises, had other plans.

She could still vividly picture it: the buzz of the breakroom, the scent of burnt coffee, and her exhaustion weighing heavily on her shoulders. She was mid-pour, watching the dark liquid stream into her cup, when a voice broke through the haze.

"Gracie?"

The disbelief in that familiar tone froze her in place. The coffee pot trembled slightly in her hand.

She turned slowly.

In the doorway stood a woman with bright eyes and a confident smile that time hadn't dimmed.

"Zoe?" Grace's voice wavered, her eyes wide with shock.

Zoe's laugh rang out, clear and joyful. "Yeah! It's me—Zoe King!"

The coffee pot clinked back onto the counter as Grace's face broke into a wide grin. "Are you serious right now?"

Zoe strode over, pulling her into a tight hug. When she pulled back, she held Grace at arm's length, her eyes gleaming excitedly. "You're here? Working in this building?"

Grace nodded, still grinning. "Apparently, you are too! Right?"

"Just started last week!" Zoe gestured dramatically at the room. "Moved to Richmond two weeks ago. And here you are, drinking this sludge they call coffee. What are the odds?"

"This is insane!" Grace laughed. "How have you been? What's new?"

"Oh, you know—the usual crap." Zoe's eyes sparkled mischievously. "But we've got so much to catch up on."

"We really do." Grace felt warmth bubbling up inside her. "You busy after work?"

"For you? Never." Zoe grinned. "Drinks. Tonight. No excuses."

"Deal." Grace's shoulders relaxed.

They exchanged a knowing smile—one that spanned years of laughter, challenges, and the quiet understanding that some friendships don't fade. They simply pause, waiting for the right moment to shine again.

CHAPTER SEVEN

T HE DOOR TO GRACE'S cabin clicked shut with a quiet finality. The day's excitement lingered in the air, but the silence inside was thick—less a comfort and more a suffocating weight. Grace pulled her bag off the bed and placed it in the closet, her fingers unsteady as she slid off her sandals. Her feet ached, not from walking but from the strain of holding herself together.

Zoe followed her in, dropping onto the edge of the bed with a dramatic sigh. "Man, I am exhausted. Who knew having fun could be so much work?" She stretched her arms over her head, her eyes sparkling. "But that pool? Totally worth it."

Grace tried to smile, but her lips wouldn't cooperate. Her hands twisting together, her gaze fixed on the floor. The room seemed to shrink around her, walls inching closer and air growing heavier.

Zoe's laughter faded. She sat up, studying Grace's tense posture. Her voice softened. "Hey... you okay?"

Grace's jaw tightened. Her heart thudded painfully, the words she'd buried for so long clawing their way to the surface. She couldn't keep them down any longer.

"Zoe," she whispered, barely trusting her voice. "There's something I haven't told you."

Zoe's forehead creased. "What is it?" She scooted closer, her eyes sharp with concern. "Gracie, talk to me."

Grace swallowed hard, the lump in her throat nearly choking her. She felt like she was teetering on the edge of a cliff, the truth, a gust of wind threatening to push her over.

She took a shaky breath. "It's not just the affair."

The words hung between them, heavy and cold.

Zoe's eyes narrowed. "What do you mean?"

Grace's fingers dug into her palms, her voice wavering. "Olivia... is pregnant."

The room froze. For a long moment, all Grace could hear was the distant roar of the ship and the rush of blood in her ears.

Zoe's mouth opened slightly, then closed. Her expression shifted—shock, then anger, then something more profound. Grief. "She's... pregnant?"

Grace nodded, her eyes shimmering with unshed tears. "Yeah."

Zoe's hands clenched into fists on her lap. She inhaled sharply, her voice low and controlled. "That bastard."

Grace let out a bitter laugh that sounded hollow. "It's like some kind of twisted joke. As if the cheating wasn't enough, he had to give me this... this extra slap in the face."

Zoe shot to her feet, pacing the small cabin, her movements sharp and agitated. "I knew there was more to it. I could feel it. But this? God, Grace, this is... this is unforgivable."

"I know." Grace's voice cracked. "I've been carrying this around, trying to act like I'm fine. But I'm not. I'm humiliated, Zoe. I feel like a complete idiot."

Zoe stopped pacing and turned to face her. "No. Don't you dare blame yourself for this." Her eyes blazed with fury. "This isn't on you. This is on him. His choices. His lies. His complete lack of respect for you."

Grace wiped at her eyes, but the tears kept coming. "I didn't want to tell you. I didn't want to say it out loud. Because if I said it, it became real. And if it's real, then... then my marriage has been one big farce for five years. And there's a chance that it's really over."

Zoe knelt in front of her, gripping her hands tightly. "It is real, Gracie. She's having his fucking baby. That's as real as it gets. But that doesn't mean you're over. You're not finished. This isn't the end of your story."

Grace's shoulders shook, the tears finally breaking free. "I feel so... lost. Everything I thought I knew about my life was a lie."

Zoe's voice softened, a thread of steel beneath it. "You're not lost. You're finding your way. And you're not alone. I'm here. I've got you. You're not in this alone."

Grace's breath caught in her throat. She squeezed Zoe's hands, her fingers desperate for something solid, something real. "Thank you."

Zoe's eyes filled with tears, but her smile was steady and sincere. "You don't have to thank me. That's what friends are for."

They stayed like that for a while, the silence between them no longer heavy but filled with something stronger—a shared understanding, a bond that nothing could shatter.

Eventually, Grace's tears slowed. She pulled in a shaky breath and looked at Zoe. "I think... I think I'm almost ready to let go."

Zoe nodded, her smile softening. "Almost? Well, good." She fanned her hand dramatically. "You've got to start somewhere. And trust me, Gracie, you've got much more life ahead of you."

Grace wiped her eyes, a tentative smile breaking through. "Yeah. Maybe I do."

Zoe stood, pulling Grace to her feet. "No 'maybe' about it. You've got so much more ahead. Like the saying goes: 'Your future's so bright, you're gonna have to wear sunglasses… at night.'"

Grace managed a small, tired smile. "Let's bank on that."

Zoe squeezed her hand. "It is. But right now, we both need some sleep."

"Yeah, I'm exhausted."

"Me too." Zoe stretched, stifling a yawn. "Tomorrow, we wake up early, grab coffee, and claim the best spot by the pool. Deal?"

"Deal," Grace agreed, her smile a little more composed.

Zoe walked to the connecting door that led to her room and then turned back to Grace. "You've got this, Gracie Hargrove. One step at a time."

"I know," Grace nodded.

As the door clicked shut, Grace exhaled slowly. The cabin was quiet, but the silence no longer felt oppressive.

She slipped off her swimsuit, slid into a satin nightgown, and climbed into bed. Closing her eyes, she allowed the gentle sway of the ship to lull her to sleep.

CHAPTER EIGHT

THE RHYTHMIC POUNDING OF rain against the balcony glass pulled Grace from her sleep the following day. She blinked at the muted light filtering through the curtains and sighed. The storm clouds that had lingered yesterday had finally delivered. Sliding out of bed, she padded to the balcony doors and peeked outside. Sheets of rain blurred the endless ocean view, and the deck below glistened with water.

"Oh no," she murmured, disappointment tugging at her heart. She grabbed her phone and dialed Zoe's number.

After a few rings, a groggy voice answered. "Gracie, it's too early. Why are you awake?"

"We said we were going to get up early, remember? Claim the best spot at the pool? We may be unable to do that, but I want coffee."

"Wait till the rain stops."

"I don't want to wait. Come with me?"

Zoe groaned audibly. "No thanks. I'm still sleeping, Gracie."

"Fine. I'm on my own, then. I need coffee."

"Wake me when the rain clears," Zoe mumbled before the line went dead.

Grace sighed, staring at her phone. The quiet tick of the clock felt louder in the room's stillness. She wouldn't let a little rain ruin her morning.

Determined, she got dressed, pulling on a light sweater and jeans. The hallway outside bustled with early risers and crew members, the ship alive with its usual hum. The scent of fresh coffee drifted through the air, guiding her like a beacon.

The rain splattered softly against the ship's massive windows as Grace made her way through the atrium. Passengers milled about—some wrapped in raincoats, others content to stay undercover. The morning announcements invited guests to breakfast or the Java Lounge Café.

The café was her destination, but a small sign caught her eye as she turned a corner near the Observation Deck: The Reading Room.

Curiosity nudged her. She peeked inside.

The room was a haven of calm. Bookshelves lined the walls, stocked with books, magazines, and newspapers. Plush armchairs and small tables were scattered throughout, inviting passengers to sink in and lose themselves in their choice of reading material. A few early risers were already there, curled up with books and steaming cups of coffee.

Grace smiled. I'll come back, she promised herself. *But first, coffee.*

The Java Lounge Café was everything she wanted it to be—cozy seating, warm lighting, and a panoramic view of the rain-speckled ocean. She ordered a cappuccino and an almond croissant, and the barista's warm smile was a small comfort.

Armed with breakfast, she returned to the Reading Room and claimed a seat by the window. She had chosen a book with a bright cover and opened it, hoping to lose herself in the pages. But the words blurred, her thoughts drifting to places she didn't want to go. The irony of her choice—a self-help book on relationships—resembled a harsh truth more than a comfort.

The rain whispered against the glass, a gentle patter that soothed rather than disappointed. Grace took a sip of her cappuccino. The rich bitterness centered her. The croissant flaked apart, buttery and sweet.

She sighed and closed the book, her fingers tracing the embossed letters on the cover.

A warm voice broke the silence. "Careful with that one. I think they put all the answers in the appendix."

Startled, Grace looked up. Her eyes met the golden-brown gaze of the man from the deck yesterday. The spark of humor in his eyes softened her mood, his easy smile a balm she didn't know she needed.

"Oh," she said, a small smile tugging at her lips. "Good to know. Though I doubt the appendix has what I'm looking for."

His smile faded slightly, replaced by something gentler. He gestured to the shelves. "Maybe you just need a different book. Sometimes, the best answers show up where we least expect them."

Her laugh was soft, brittle at the edges. "That sounds about right."

He nodded toward the shelves, his eyes thoughtful. "Allow me the pleasure of choosing one for you?"

Grace hesitated, then handed him the book. "All right. Surprise me."

Ross raised an eyebrow, intrigued by her challenge. He purposely scanned the shelves, eventually pulling out a novel with a striking cover. Handing it to her, he grinned. "Try this one. It may not be an answer book, but it might give you a new perspective. Plus, I believe it's a great read."

She glanced at the title, 'What We Leave Behind: The Hidden Legacy of Choices.' "Sounds interesting." She said, lifting her eyes to meet his. "Thank you. Maybe a different story is exactly what I need."

He extended his hand, his voice warm. "Ross Henderson."

"Grace Hargrove," she replied, shaking his hand.

His fingers were warm. "It's nice to meet you, Grace."

"Likewise," she said softly.

He smiled, lingering for just a moment before he turned to leave. "Enjoy the book."

"Thanks again," she called as he stepped through the door.

The door closed behind him. Grace looked down at the book in her hands, the smile still on her lips. She didn't know why, but something about Ross—his kindness and humor—had slipped through her defenses. She shook her head, trying to brush it off, but as she opened the novel, her thoughts kept drifting back to him. Little did she know, this fleeting encounter would stay with her, planting a seed of trust she would come to rely on when their paths crossed again.

CHAPTER NINE

G RACE SAT CURLED UP in the cozy corner of the ship's reading room, the novel Ross had recommended resting in her lap. Her cappuccino had gone cold, and the last crumbs of an almond croissant clung stubbornly to the plate. Outside, the rain continued its relentless dance against the tall glass windows, the patter blending with the low buzz of quiet conversations.

She turned a page, the story pulling her in. The narrative flowed effortlessly. The protagonist's journey of rediscovery was inspiring, unsettling, and familiar. By the time she finished chapter eight, her determination had solidified. The protagonist, a woman named Celia, navigated a life of doubt, betrayal, and renewal. Grace paused, her fingers brushing the paper. One line lingered:

"Sometimes strength isn't about never falling—it's about standing back up every time you do."

A shaky breath escaped her lips. It's *about standing back up.* The words felt personal, like a whisper of encouragement. She carefully closed the book and pressed it to her chest for a moment as if holding onto its wisdom. The decision was made, and she admitted to herself as she stood to her feet, "I'm standing back up."

She gathered her things, slid the novel under her arm, and left the room. As she walked back to her stateroom, the ship's halls felt less like a maze and more like a path forward. The book offered something unexpected—an escape and a mirror. And Grace wasn't ready to turn away from the reflection.

Back in her cabin, Grace found Zoe perched on the edge of the bed, scrolling through her phone. Zoe's head snapped up, her eyes bright with curiosity. "There you are! Took you long enough. So, how was it?"

Grace smiled, setting the book on the nightstand. "It was nice. I found the coffee shop—cozy place, great cappuccino, and even better pastries."

Zoe's eyebrow lifted. "Pastries? If they're as good as yesterday's, I'm in."

Grace chuckled. "I had an almond croissant. Devoured it in thirty seconds flat. You would've loved it."

"See, this is why you're my best friend—you know how to prioritize food." Zoe's gaze landed on the book. "And what's this? Looks like you picked up more than just caffeine and a croissant."

Grace hesitated, her fingers brushing the cover. "It's a novel. The protagonist, Celia, is strong and independent, but sometimes she

41

forgets her own strength. She lets fear and doubt hold her back." Her voice softened. "It hit close to home."

Zoe's expression turned thoughtful. "Sounds like it's exactly what you need."

Grace's smile faltered. "It's... helping me see things more clearly." She paused. "The only difference is Celia's husband died. Mine cheated."

Zoe's jaw tightened, her eyes flashing with protective anger. "Death is death," she said sarcastically. "Either way, it's a loss. A betrayal. And you didn't deserve it."

Grace nodded, the gravity of her words settling between them. Before the silence could stretch too long, Zoe's tone lightened. "Okay, enough serious stuff. You want to go back to that coffee shop? I could use one of those magical cappuccinos."

Grace laughed. "Sure, let's go."

She paused, a glimmer of memory sparking—Ross's warm smile, his gentle humor. But she shoved it aside. If Zoe knew about the encounter, she'd turn it into a grand romantic sub-plot, and Grace wasn't ready for that. Not yet.

As they left the cabin, Zoe nudged her. "You sure you have room for another croissant?"

Grace grinned. "I think I can manage."

"Good. Lead the way, croissant queen."

The Java Lounge Café buzzed with quiet energy. The rich aroma of espresso and freshly baked pastries was like a comforting blanket settling around them. Although the rain tapped lightly against the windows, it was warm and bright inside.

They settled into a corner table, their cappuccinos steaming and plates holding flaky croissants. Zoe tore off a piece of pastry, sighing happily. "Okay, I have to admit, this makes up for missing the pool."

Grace smiled, her gaze distant. She stirred her cappuccino, the spoon clinking gently. "When we get home, I think I'm going to do something for myself."

Zoe looked up. "Like what?"

"I don't know... maybe take a class. Something that helps me figure out who I am outside of being Ethan's wife." Her voice wavered. "I've spent so much time worrying about my marriage I've forgotten about me. It's my turn now."

Zoe nodded, her eyes softening. "That's good, Gracie. You deserve it."

They sat in silence, the truth of Grace's words hanging in the air. After a moment, Zoe spoke. "You know, I get it. I was in a toxic relationship once."

Grace's eyes widened. "You never told me that."

Zoe gave a small, wry smile. "You were so happy after your wedding. I didn't want to ruin it."

"Zoe... you didn't have to go through that alone."

"I know. But I got out, and that's what matters." Zoe squeezed her hand. "Don't let someone else's poor decisions rob you of your happiness—life's too short for that. I don't want to see you lose yourself like I almost did."

Grace's eyes filled with gratitude, and she nodded. "I know. You're right. Thanks."

Zoe shrugged, her mischievous grin returning. "Okay, this has gone on long enough. No more talk about relationships. I'm getting another croissant. Want one?"

Grace laughed. "No, I'm good. If I keep eating like this, they'll have to roll me off this ship."

"Suit yourself." Zoe stood, stretching dramatically.

Just then, the ship gave a sudden, sharp lurch. Zoe stumbled, catching the edge of a table. Her eyes widened. "Whoa. What the hell was that?"

Grace's heart skipped a beat. "You okay?"

"Yeah," Zoe said, brushing her clothes like nothing had happened. "That was just... a mighty big bump." Her lips quirked into a smile. "For a second, I thought we were reenacting *Titanic*."

"Don't say that," Grace said sharply, her eyes narrowing.

Zoe laughed. "What? I'm just saying—if Leo DiCaprio shows up, let me know."

Grace shook her head, trying to hide her unease. "You're impossible."

"That's why you love me," Zoe shot back, making her way to the counter.

Grace exhaled, the humor not quite reaching her. The ship steadied, but the unease in her chest lingered. She glanced out the window at the churning waves, the clouds darkening again.

When Zoe returned, they chatted lightly, keeping the mood carefree. They wandered through the ship afterward, discovering an art gallery tucked away near the main staircase. Grace paused in front of a vibrant painting of a seaside village.

"Look at this painting," she said, pointing at the intricate details. "It's like you could step right into it."

Zoe squinted at the price tag. "For that price, it would be my home. Forever." She nudged Grace with a grin. "You should buy it. Start a collection for your new, single-woman apartment."

Grace rolled her eyes. "One thing at a time, Zoe."

The tranquil hum of the ship was abruptly disrupted by a deep, echoing groan. Without warning, the boat gave way to a powerful jolt. Both women instinctively grabbed each other and then claimed two of the available plush chairs.

"Geez," Zoe exclaimed, her voice a mix of surprise and annoyance. "What's going on? Must've hit a whale or something?"

Another slight lurch rippled through the ship, less dramatic this time. She glanced at Grace, whose face had gone totally pale but who was trying to maintain her composure.

"All right, tell me that was just some turbulence or whatever it is ships have," Zoe said, attempting a laugh to mask her unease.

"Probably just the waves. The storm this morning was rough—maybe we're hitting the tail end of it."

"Tail end or not, I'm telling you, I feel like I'm in a bad remake of *Titanic*," Zoe muttered, trying to inject humor into the moment but failing to convince even herself.

"Will you stop saying that," Grace said sharply, her tone half-serious. "We're on a modern ship, not some old liner. Everything's fine."

Zoe raised an eyebrow. "You don't sound convinced."

Before Grace could respond, an announcement crackled over the intercom. The captain's calm, authoritative voice filled the lounge:

"Ladies and gentlemen, this is your captain speaking. We've encountered some residual rough seas following the storm earlier today. Please remain seated and hold onto stable surfaces as we navigate through this area. Thank you for your patience."

"There, see?" Grace said, exhaling a shaky breath. "Just rough seas. Nothing to worry about."

Zoe snorted softly, releasing her grip on the table. "Yeah, sure. Tell that to my nerves. I'm one more jolt away from needing a drink stronger than cappuccino."

Grace chuckled, though her laugh was tight. "I'm with you on that."

The ship steadied, and the tension in the room began to ease as passengers returned to their conversations, though more subdued than before. Grace and Zoe exchanged glances, their usual banter softened by an unspoken agreement to keep things light.

"Well," Zoe said, forcing a grin. "That was fun. Let's not do that again, okay?"

"I agree," Grace said, finally letting go of her armrest. But as she gazed out the rain-speckled window at the churning waves, a trace of unease lingered in her chest. For now, though, she tucked it away, determined to enjoy what was left of the day.

They left the art gallery and wandered into the Boutique District. The stretch of high-end shops gleamed under warm lighting, displaying everything from designer clothing to sparkling jewelry.

Zoe immediately gravitated toward a display of wide-brimmed sunhats. She plopped one onto her head and struck a dramatic pose. "What do you think? Poolside chic or trying too hard?"

"Definitely chic," Grace said, her eyes twinkling. "But you'll need a boatload of confidence to pull that off."

Zoe twirled, her laughter ringing out. "Confidence? Honey, I've got that in spades."

As they continued through the boutiques, the ship's intercom announced a Mixology Class in the Tides Lounge. Zoe's eyes lit up. "Drinks? Made by us? Let's go!"

Grace hesitated. "I'm not sure I trust myself with a cocktail shaker."

Zoe looped her arm through Grace's. "Oh, please. What's the worst that could happen? We'll call it 'creative bartending.'"

The Tides Lounge buzzed with excitement. Passengers gathered around a polished bar, eager to try their hand at crafting cocktails. The cheerful bartender, Ray, grinned as he handed out shakers and garnishes.

"All right," Zoe said, rolling up her sleeves. "Let's see if I'm as good at mixing drinks as I am at drinking them."

Grace laughed, selecting a lime. "Just don't spill anything, or we'll end up as the entertainment of the evening."

"I thrive under pressure," Zoe smirked.

She laughed, watching as Ray expertly mixed another drink with practiced ease. It was clear that he was more than just the guy behind the bar—he was the heart of it, keeping everything flowing smoothly with charm, skill, and a little bit of showmanship.

Zoe leaned over the bar, her smile playful and eyes twinkling with mischief. "You look like you know what you're doing."

Ray smiled back. "Yeah, I kinda do."

Zoe flashed him a smile. "I'm Zoe, by the way. And this is my best friend, Grace. What's your name?"

"Ray," he said, picking up a shaker and expertly tossing it in his hands.

"Is that it? Just Ray?"

"Ray Franklin," he said with a smile, his tone smooth and confident. "And you're Zoe—" He paused, raising an eyebrow and gesturing with his hands, signaling her to fill in the blank with her last name.

"King," she offered. "My name's Zoe King."

Ray nodded in greeting.

"This is my friend Grace Har—" but before Zoe could get it out of her mouth, a smooth voice behind Grace said, "So, we meet again, Ms. Grace Hargrove."

Grace froze. Her breath caught. She turned slowly, her eyes locking onto Ross Henderson. He leaned casually against the bar, his golden-brown eyes glinting under the warm lights. His smile was confident but not arrogant, sending a ripple of unexpected warmth through her.

"Ross," she said, recovering quickly. "We keep bumping into each other."

Zoe, who had been inspecting a bottle of triple sec, looked up sharply. Her eyes widened with curiosity. "Wait... you two know each other?"

Grace shot Zoe a look, silently pleading with her to hold off on the interrogation. "We met in the reading room this morning."

Ross's smile widened. "How's the book I recommended? Had a chance to dive in yet?"

Grace brushed a strand of hair behind her ear. "I did. Definitely better than the one I chose."

"Good to hear." His eyes sparkled. "I'm curious to know what you think."

"You've read it?" her tone was a mixture of surprise and intrigue.

His smile turned slightly mischievous. "I wrote it."

Grace's eyes widened, her mouth falling open. "You're... R.J. Hender..." Then, with a spark of realization, "Of course. Ross Henderson."

He nodded with a slight bow, his eyes twinkling with amusement.

Grace smiled, "What's the 'J' stand for?"

He laughed, "Jerome. Ross Jerome Henderson at your service."

Zoe nearly choked on her water. "Wait—hold on. You wrote the book?" She turned to Grace, lowering her voice to a whisper. "What is happening right now?"

Grace ignored her, trying to regain her composure. "Well," she said to Ross, "it's not every day you meet the author of the book you're reading."

Ross chuckled, his gaze lingering on her. "It's always nice to see someone enjoying it."

The rain tapped gently against the lounge windows. Ross glanced outside and shook his head. "Looks like the pool deck's out of the question today."

"At least I have a good book to keep me company," Grace said, smiling softly.

"I'd like to think it will continue to keep you engaged," Ross said, his tone sincere. "It's fascinating to hear what readers take away from it."

"I'll let you know."

Ross took a small step back. "Please do. It was good to see you again, Grace." As he turned to leave, he paused and looked back. "I don't believe I've been introduced to your friend."

"Oh!" Grace said, flustered. "Ross, this is Zoe. Zoe—Ross."

Ross extended a hand to her. "Nice to meet you, Zoe. You've got a very interesting friend here."

Zoe raised an eyebrow, her tone dry. "Yes, apparently I do."

Ross nodded politely before disappearing into the crowd.

Zoe stared after him, then whipped around to Grace. "Okay. Spill it. Now."

Grace sighed, gripping her cocktail shaker. "It's nothing. We just met this morning."

"Yeah, and now he's casually dropping that he wrote the book you're reading? Grace, this cruise just got a whole lot more interesting."

Grace rolled her eyes, fighting a smile. The warmth of Ross's presence lingered, making it hard to concentrate. Zoe's teasing would have to wait.

The chatter and the clinking of glasses filled the Tides Lounge, where Grace, Zoe, and a handful of other passengers sat around a polished wooden bar, engaged in a mixology class. Ray, the ship's bartender and instructor for the evening, spun a bottle in his hands with practiced ease before pouring a perfectly measured shot of rum into a shaker.

Grace had barely touched her cocktail. She stirred the ice with her straw, her mind drifting somewhere else—anywhere but here.

A voice crackled through the ship's announcement system, snapping her out of her haze.

"Ladies and gentlemen, due to weather conditions, tonight's deck party has been moved to the Sunset Club on Deck 5. The music's already going, and our bartenders are ready to serve you—come join the fun!"

Zoe immediately turned to Ray, her eyes lighting up.

"Can you come?"

Ray smirked, wiping his hands on a towel.

"I've got to stay at my station for another twenty minutes. But I'll catch up with you later."

Zoe grinned and nodded, then turned to Grace with a mischievous glint in her eye. She grabbed Grace's wrist. "Let's go, no excuses!"

"Zoe, come on," Grace said, groaning. "I'm not in the mood for dancing."

But Zoe had already started tugging her out of the lounge. "Not in the mood for fun? That's exactly why you need to go then."

Grace sighed, letting herself be pulled along. Maybe Zoe was right. Maybe she should try, just for tonight.

The Sunset Club was alive with music and laughter. Neon lights glowed overhead, pulsing with the rhythm of the song blasting from the speakers. The dance floor was packed, bodies swaying, spinning, hands thrown in the air. The atmosphere was intoxicating, a temporary escape from whatever real-life burdens passengers had left behind.

Grace took a slow breath, scanning the room. It was a different world here—one where she could pretend, even if just for a while, that everything was okay. Then she saw him.

Ross.

He was standing by the bar, a drink in his hand, watching the scene with a quiet detachment. His eyes scanned the dance floor, amused but distant, as if he were an observer rather than a participant. He wasn't looking for company or vying for attention—he was simply *there*, wrapped in his own thoughts.

Something about it made Grace smile. Before she could think better of it, her feet carried her toward him.

"Let me guess," she said teasingly, "you're the guy who comes to the party but refuses to dance."

Ross turned, startled at first, but then his lips curved into a slow, knowing grin.

"Guilty. But in my defense, I'd rather watch than make a fool of myself."

"That's a shame. Sometimes, you have to do something ridiculous just because you can."

A hint of something crossed his expression—curiosity? Amusement? Whatever it was, it made her bold.

Before she could second-guess herself, she reached for his hand and tugged him toward the dance floor.

Ross hesitated for half a second, but something in her energy, the lightness in her eyes, made him give in.

"All right," he murmured. He set his drink on the bar and let himself be led.

The beat of the music pulsed beneath their feet as Grace and Ross moved together, their steps unpracticed but effortless.

She laughed as he stumbled slightly, pretending to be worse than he was, making her roll her eyes. "Oh, come on. You're not that bad."

He grinned. "I'm trying to keep up."

Their hands brushed. Their smiles lingered. The space between them tightened.

Grace felt weightless. Like she wasn't tethered to the past. She could breathe.

Then the song ended.

She didn't let go of Ross's hand, suddenly aware of herself, of him, of how easily she'd let herself enjoy the moment.

"Well," she said, "that was unexpected."

Ross looked at her, something unreadable in his eyes

"It was," he said softly, "very nice."

Before she could respond, another song began. A slow, sultry melody.

Grace hesitated. This was different. This was close.

Ross saw it—the way her expression changed, how her body tensed ever so slightly. He didn't let go. Instead, he tilted his head, studying her. Then, with a slight smirk, he murmured.

"This is more my speed."

His hands shifted, one settling gently at the small of her back, the other keeping a loose but steady grip on her hand. It wasn't demanding. Just a silent invitation."

Something in his presence soothed her, even as her heart started beating faster.

At first, her body was stiff. Uncertain. But then—something happened.

Ross guided her effortlessly, and she melted into him, fitting into the curve of his embrace like she belonged there. Their bodies moved in sync, unhurried, like they'd danced a hundred times before.

She closed her eyes for a moment, allowing herself to feel the warmth of him. The quiet strength in his touch. The steady rhythm of his heartbeat.

She hadn't been held like this in a long time. Not just in the physical sense but in a way that made her feel...seen. Safe.

When she finally opened her eyes, she found Ross looking at her—not just watching, but seeing her. The music, the people, the world around them faded. She, for the first time in a long time, felt something she thought she'd lost.

And then, too soon, the song ended.

She didn't move right away. Neither did he.

The moment stretched thick with something unspoken.

Then, as if remembering where she was, *who* she was, Grace took a step back, breaking the connection.

She let out a soft, slightly breathless laugh.

Ross studied her, his lips curving into a smile. But there was something deeper in his eyes. Something *knowing*.

And there it was. That shift.

A silent hint of something profound but nameless.

As Grace steps back, clearing her throat and forcing herself to break eye contact with Ross, Zoe appears at her side, having observed the entire exchange from across the room. She takes one look at Grace's flushed cheeks, the way Ross is still watching her with that unreadable expression, and the knowing smirk. And with a perfectly timed sip of her cocktail, Zoe tilts her head and says, "Well, damn. If that dance got any hotter, the ship's fire alarms would've gone off."

Grace lets out an awkward laugh, shaking her head, "Oh, please. It was just a dance."

Zoe raised an eyebrow, her smirk deepening. "Mmmhmm. And I suppose the way you two were looking at each other was just an optical coincidence?"

Ross chuckled softly at that, rubbing the back of his neck but saying nothing and enjoying watching Grace squirm.

Grace glares playfully at Zoe, then turns back to Ross.

"Sorry about my friend," She says teasingly, "she has a habit of narrating things like she's in a romance novel."

Zoe shrugged, "Well, I do love a good slow burn," she said, unfazed.

Ross smirked but finally spoke, his voice low and amused. His eyes flicking to Grace, "Then let's hope you're in for a long read."

Grace's breath catches slightly, but before she can say anything, Zoe claps her hands together and grins mischievously, "Carry on. I'm headed to the bar." With a wink at Ross, she saunters off, leaving Grace staring after her in exasperation. She turns back to Ross, who is still watching her, a knowing look in his eyes.

She swallows hard and sighs, half-laughing, "I swear, she's impossible."

"She's funny."

Grace nodded, "she is that."

Extending her hand and swallowing hard again, Grace said, "Thanks for the dance, Ross. Enjoy the rest of your night."

Her voice was steady, but Ross caught the way she hesitated—just for a second—before offering her hand.

He accepted it, his grip warm and sure, his thumb briefly brushing against hers in a way that sent a quiet ripple through her. He held her gaze for just a moment longer than necessary.

"You too, Grace," he said, his voice low. Then, with another smirk, he added, "I'm sure we'll see each other again."

There was something in the way he said it that made her stomach tighten—like it wasn't just a casual farewell, but a certainty. A promise.

She didn't trust herself to respond. Instead, she just nodded, turning on her heels and slipping back into the crowd toward the bar.

She could still feel Ross's presence as she moved further away—like an invisible tether stretched between them.

She exhaled, pressing a hand to her chest, trying to steady the wild rhythm of her heartbeat.

It was just a dance.

But somehow, as she walked away, it felt like something...more.

Back in their stateroom, Zoe flopped onto Grace's bed with a dramatic sigh. "So, are you finally going to tell me what's up with you and Ross? Because, honestly, the chemistry is not subtle."

Grace folded her sweater neatly. "There's nothing to tell. My god, we met in the Reading Room this morning, and he recommended that I read the book he wrote."

"And, what about in the club?"

"Zoe, it was just a dance."

"You can say that all you want, but I'm telling you, this story isn't over yet."

Grace shook her head, trying to hide her smile. "You're reading too much into it. And what about you and the bartender, Ray?"

Zoe shrugged, standing up with a sly grin. "Maybe something, maybe nothing. We'll see." She headed for the connecting door, pausing with a wink. "Don't stay up all night reading."

"No promises."

Dressed in her nightclothes, Grace sank into bed, the book balanced in her lap. She opened it to the bookmarked page, the story pulling her in again. Each sentence resonated deeply within her.

Time slipped away unnoticed. When she glanced at the clock, it was nearly 5 a.m. She was on the final chapter, reluctant for it to end. As she read the last page, her heart tightened with bittersweet emotion.

She closed the book, holding it to her chest, her eyes shimmering with unshed tears.

"Wow," she whispered, the word barely audible but carrying the weight of everything she felt.

The story had found her at exactly the right moment. It was a reminder of resilience, starting over, and the quiet strength she still carried.

She opened the book quickly, her fingers trembling as she flipped through the pages, searching for the words that had unsettled something deep within her. When she finally found them, she traced the sentence with her fingertips before reading it out loud, her voice barely above a whisper.

"You don't lose yourself all at once; it happens in the small compromises, the quiet silences, the moments you choose someone else's comfort over your own truth."

The words hung in the air, pressing against her chest. She swallowed hard, wondering what had happened in Ross's life that made him write something so profound. What pain had carved those words into his soul? What loss, what love, what moment of reckoning had led him to such clarity? And why did it feel as if he had written them just for her?

Wisdom like that wasn't simply learned—it was earned, often through the kind of suffering that leaves a mark no one else can see.

She couldn't sleep. It's wisdom lingered, seeping into the quiet spaces of her mind. It didn't demand her attention—it simply settled in, profound and unshakable.

CHAPTER TEN

T HE RAIN PAUSED BRIEFLY, leaving the air crisp and fresh. Grace rose from her bed, draping herself in one of the elegant loungers she had brought. Wrapping a warm shawl around herself, she stepped onto the deck and inhaled deeply. The cool air caught her off guard, sending a slight shiver down her spine. The distant hum of the ship blended effortlessly with the lull of the waves lapping against its side, creating a soothing melody that settled deep in her chest.

She spotted Ross leaning against the rail, his silhouette illuminated by the faint glow of deck lights. His posture was relaxed, but he had an air of thoughtfulness about him. Taking a deep breath, she walked over. "Couldn't sleep either?" she asked softly, stopping beside him.

Ross turned his head, a smile tugging at the corners of his mouth. "I'm an early riser. And you?"

She shrugged, resting her hands on the railing. "I was awake, and when I heard the rain stop, I thought I'd take advantage of it."

He nodded, looking out at the dark sky, heavy with clouds that threatened another storm. "Doesn't look like the rain's done with us yet. We're lucky to have this break, but I don't think it's going to last."

Grace glanced up, her lips curving into a smile. "The calm before the next downpour."

Ross chuckled, his gaze shifting back to her. "You've got a way with words."

"I could say the same about you." She paused, turning to face him. "I finished your book."

"You did? You're a fast reader." Ross said.

Grace nodded, glancing up at him. "I stayed up all night finishing it."

Ross's eyebrows lifted in surprise. "Now, that's dedication."

"No, seriously. I couldn't put it down. There was so much I gleaned from it. Your story gave me a whole new perspective on my life. It was like... seeing myself through someone else's eyes."

Ross stopped leaning on the rail briefly. "Really? How so?"

Grace tucked a stray strand of hair behind her ear. "The main character—she's strong, determined, but she doesn't always see it. She spends so much time doubting herself, letting others dictate her happiness. I've... I've done that. For years. The story was about you, wasn't it?"

Ross studied her closely, sensing the vulnerability in her words. He nodded. "How could you tell?"

"Only someone who's felt that kind of pain could've written about it in such detail," Grace said, her voice barely above a whisper. She glanced at Ross, her eyes searching his face for a reaction. "It was raw—like pulling a bandage off a wound that hasn't fully healed. Every word felt exposed, vulnerable, but real at the same time. Like you weren't just telling a story but living it."

The heaviness of her words hung in the air between them. Ross exhaled, looking away for a moment before meeting her gaze. "That's because I was," he admitted, his tone low. "Every chapter came from something I lived through. Writing it... it wasn't just telling a story. It was how I made sense of the mess I'd been carrying for so long."

Grace's breath caught. "You mean... it's all true?"

Ross hesitated, then nodded. "Most of it. I changed details, names, and circumstances. But, the emotions? Those were mine. The doubt, the hope, the heartbreak... It wasn't fiction for me. It was everything I didn't know how to say out loud."

"That's why it hit me so hard," she said softly. "I felt it. Every page. Like it was pulling things out of me I'd been trying to bury."

Ross's expression softened, a faint smile tugging at his lips. "I was hoping the reader would feel that. Hearing you say it... means more than I can put into words."Grace tilted her head, studying him. "It's brave, you know. Putting your pain out there like that for the world to see."

Ross shrugged, his smile bittersweet. "It didn't feel brave at the time. It just felt necessary." He paused, his eyes locking on hers. "But if it helped someone like you, even a little... it was worth it."

She looked away, a small smile on her lips. "More than a little," she managed to say. The connection between them grew, a shared understanding forged in the raw truth of their pain and survival. "I hated to have it end," she admitted. "The story pulled me in so much that I wanted it to keep going, even though I knew it couldn't."

Ross studied her. A glint in his eyes, a teasing smile playing on his lips. "That's exactly how I've felt during this cruise. The best stories stay with you long after they're over."

She tilted her head, curious. "Are you talking about books or something else?"

"Maybe both," he said, his voice quiet, almost introspective.

Grace felt her pulse quicken but kept her expression neutral, her fingers gripping the rail tighter. "I suppose some things are better left vague. Keeps you guessing."

"Or keeps you intrigued," he countered, his gaze warm and inviting.

She laughed softly, looking down at her hands. "You're not making this any easier."

"Making what easier?" he asked, the corners of his mouth lifting in a wider grin.

She raised an eyebrow at him, her own smile teasing. "Figuring you out."

"Maybe I'm an open book," he said, leaning slightly closer. "You just have to decide if you want to keep reading."

A quiet gasp escaped her lips, but she recovered quickly. "And here I thought I'd finished my last book of the trip."

"With any luck, that won't happen," Ross said. "Let's just say some stories have sequels."

Grace let out a soft laugh, shaking her head. "You're impossible."

"And yet, you're still here," he chuckled.

She glanced out at the ocean, her heart thudding in her chest. The conversation was light, but the meaning beneath it was clear. There was something here—something unspoken but undeniably present.

"I guess I am," she said, her voice softer now.

For a moment, neither of them spoke. The silence between them filled with the sound of the waves and the faint whistle of the wind.

Ross leaned back slightly, glancing at the sky. "Looks like the clouds are moving in again. We'd better head inside before the rain catches us."

Grace nodded, but she didn't move right away. "Yeah, I guess we should."

As they walked back toward the door, their shoulders brushed slightly, a fleeting touch that neither acknowledged but both noticed.

At the door, Grace paused and turned to face him, a hint of uncertainty in her eyes before she spoke. "So, listen, Ross. A few of us are meeting in the lounge later this morning for mimosas before the cruise ends. Why don't you join us?"

Ross tilted his head, his expression softening as he met her gaze. "You sure you want me crashing the party?"

Grace smiled, her tone light but sincere. "It's not crashing if you're invited. Besides..." She hesitated, then added with a playful grin, "I think the group could use your... conversational flair."

Ross chuckled, the sound low and easy. "Well, how can I say no when you put it that way?"

"Great," Grace said, the tension in her shoulders easing. "We'll be in the main lounge around 9:30ish. Don't make me regret inviting you."

"I'll do my best to behave," Ross replied with a mock-serious expression, though the glint in his eye suggested otherwise.

Grace laughed softly, stepping through the door as the sound of rain picked up behind them.

"Right on cue," Ross said with a soft chuckle.

The warmth of the ship's interior enveloped them, starkly contrasting the cool, damp air outside. For a moment, they stood there, the hum of the ship beneath their feet and the distant sound of rain beginning to fall harder on the deck behind them.

Grace looked up at him. "See you tomorrow, then," she said softly.

"I'll be there," he promised.

They went their separate ways, the night air thick with words neither dared to say. Ross walked slowly, his chest heavy, a quiet regret settling in—he would have given anything to know the feel of her lips against his.

Grace, her steps light but her thoughts tangled, felt the strange pull of a feeling she couldn't quite put her finger on.

CHAPTER ELEVEN

T HE SOFT MORNING LIGHT filtered through the cabin's curtains as Grace and Zoe bustled around, preparing for their final day on the ship. The small space was a flurry of half-packed bags, clinking makeup cases, and the faint scent of perfume and sunscreen lingering in the air.

"I still can't believe it's already the last day," Zoe said, tying her hair into a loose ponytail. "Feels like we just got here."

"Tell me about it," Grace replied, smoothing out a wrinkle in her palazzo jumpsuit. "These three days flew by."

Zoe grinned at her reflection in the mirror. "Well, at least we're going out in style—mimosas and good company. Can't ask for a better send-off."

Grace smiled, tucking a stray strand of hair behind her ear. "True. It'll be good to see everyone again."

"Especially Ross?" Zoe teased, her tone light but mischievous as she raised an eyebrow at Grace.

Grace's cheeks warmed, but she rolled her eyes, feigning indifference. "Don't be ridiculous. I'm going for the mimosas."

Zoe laughed, slipping on a pair of sandals. "Yeah, sure. You've been unusually chipper this morning, though. Just sayin'."

Grace shook her head, ignoring the flutter in her chest. She wasn't about to give Zoe the satisfaction of knowing that she was looking forward to seeing Ross again—his quiet smile and the way his eyes seemed to hold a little more depth than most.

Zoe, meanwhile, adjusted her earrings and let out a satisfied sigh. "I told Ray I'd keep in touch," she said, a sly smile touched her lips. "I like him. He's easy to talk to and has that charming, goofy thing going for him."

Grace smiled softly. "I'm glad. He seems like a good guy."

Zoe turned, her eyes sparkling. "He is. But enough about me. Let's go. The sooner we get there, the sooner you can accidentally-on-purpose run into Ross."

That's when the first jolt struck.

The floor shuddered violently. A glass on the nightstand trembled, then toppled, shattering into pieces. Zoe's water bottle hit the floor with a dull thud and rolled across the room. Grace grabbed the edge of the bed as the room swayed.

"Grace!" Zoe yelled, her eyes wide, fear creeping into her usually confident tone. "What the hell is going on?"

Before Grace could answer, a second, more violent jolt threw them both against the wall. The ship groaned—a deep, haunting sound that seemed to come from its very core. The overhead lights flickered. Somewhere down the hallway, screams erupted, echoing through the corridors.

Grace's pulse pounded. "We need to find out what's happening!" she said, her voice urgent. She reached for Zoe's hand, pulling her toward the door. They stumbled into the hallway, now filled with panicked passengers.

The ship's intercom crackled to life. The captain's voice boomed overhead, rushed and shaky. "Attention, passengers. This is the captain speaking. We are in an emergency situation. Please proceed to the deck immediately. This is *not* a drill. I repeat, this is *not* a drill. Locate the nearest life jackets and put them on. Do not delay."

The fear in his voice sent a chill down Grace's spine.

"We need to move. *Now,*" Zoe said, gripping Grace's arm tightly.

They pushed through the crowd, clutching railings as the ship lurched violently from side to side. People screamed and cried, their faces pale with terror. When they finally reached the deck, turmoil reigned. Rain lashed against the passengers, stinging their skin. Waves crashed over the railings, soaking the deck. The storm's fury roared around them, the wind shrieking like a living thing.

Crew members shouted instructions; their voices nearly drowned by the storm. Life jackets were thrust into trembling hands.

"Put these on!" he yelled, shoving bright orange life jackets toward them.

Grace's hands shook as she slipped hers over her head and adjusted the straps. She turned to Zoe, who fumbled with hers, her eyes wild. "This can't be happening," Zoe whispered, her voice unsteady.

The ship tilted sharply. Grace lunged, grabbing Zoe before she could lose her balance. Around them, people screamed and fell to the deck. Grace's heart clenched when she saw a man slip over the railing, his cry swallowed by the storm as he vanished into the churning water.

"Grace!" Zoe shouted, panic in her voice. "We have to move..."

A violent jolt cut her off. Someone slammed into Grace from behind, the impact knocking the breath from her lungs. Her fingers clawed at empty space as the deck vanished beneath her feet. She heard Zoe's sharp and desperate scream just before the icy water swallowed her whole.

The cold hit Grace like a sledgehammer, stealing the air from her lungs. The weight of the ocean dragged her down, disorienting her as she sank deeper into the darkness. Panic surged through her veins. Her arms flailed, reaching for something—anything—to hold onto. Her chest burned, her body screaming for air.

Just as the darkness threatened to swallow her for good, her life jacket jerked her upward. She broke the surface, gasping desperately, the sharp intake of air burning her lungs. Rain pelted her face, and waves crashed over her, but the life jacket kept her afloat, bouncing her like a cork on the heaving sea.

The storm's fury was deafening. Passengers' screams and the sound of the wind blurred into a nightmarish uproar. Grace's head spun as she watched the calamity around her.

"Zoe!" she screamed, but her voice was lost to the storm. Fear tore at her chest. She felt utterly alone, the vast ocean pressing in on her, indifferent and merciless.

It can't end like this!

A wave slammed into her, forcing her under. Saltwater filled her mouth and nose. She kicked frantically, breaking the surface again, coughing and gasping for air. Her strength was fading. Panic clawed at her mind.

Then, a voice cut through all the mayhem.

"Grace! Give me your hand!"

Her head snapped around. There, clinging to a jagged piece of debris, was Ross. His dark hair was plastered to his forehead, his eyes wild but focused. His arm stretched out toward her.

"Give me your hand!" he shouted again.

A rush of desperation flooded her heart. She kicked against the waves, her arms shaking as she reached out. Their fingers brushed, then locked. His grip was firm.

"Hold on!" Ross said, pulling her closer, his strength anchoring her against the wild waves. The debris shifted beneath them, but he held on, his muscles straining.

Grace coughed, tears mixing with rain. "Thank you, thank you, thank you!" she exclaimed over and over again. "Have you seen my friend?" she sobbed, panic thick in her voice.

Ross's eyes locked onto hers, steady and strong. "I think I saw her get into a lifeboat. She's strong, Grace. She'll be okay. Right now, *we* need to survive."

She clung to his words like a lifeline, fighting to steady her breath. The storm raged around them, but Ross's presence was a solid, unbreakable anchor. He pointed toward a lifeboat, its orange shape barely visible through the mist and waves.

"They're coming for us. Just hold on a little longer," Ross said, his voice calm.

Grace nodded, her fingers aching from gripping the debris. She focused on Ross's eyes—the calm within the storm—and let it steady her heart.

"We're going to make it," he promised, his voice fierce. "I've got you."

CHAPTER TWELVE

G RACE AND ROSS WERE hauled into the lifeboat amidst the pouring rain, waves, and frigid winds. The boat pitched violently
with each swell, its passengers clutching at each other and their
life jackets in desperation. Fear hung thick in the air, as cold and
biting as the sea spray that drenched them.

The captain stood near the bow, his stance wide to maintain
balance against the storm's relentless assault. His face was drawn,
eyes scanning the horizon with an intensity born of responsibility
and determination. He raised his voice above the howling wind.
"I believe that's an island ahead," he said, pointing toward a dark,
jagged silhouette barely distinguishable through the sheets of rain.
"It looks small, but it'll offer shelter. That's where we're headed."

A murmur rippled through the lifeboat, equal parts relief and
dread. The island represented safety, but between it and them lay
an unforgiving sea.

Ross leaned closer to Grace, his voice steady despite the storm's fury. "We're going to make it. You hear me?"

Grace nodded, her teeth chattering too hard to speak. She clung to his presence like a beacon, her body trembling not just from the cold but from the aftershock of survival.

The captain's voice broke through again. "I sent a distress call before we abandoned ship. I can't guarantee it got through, but a search party will be dispatched once we miss port. For now, we hold on and make for land."

"Captain," Ross called, his tone sharp but respectful, "what happened out there? Was it a tropical storm?"

The captain's gaze flicked to Ross, his expression grim. "Not tropical," he said, gripping the lifeboat's edge as another wave slammed against it. "We encountered a maritime wind event."

Grace creased her brow, looking at him. Her voice was barely audible over the storm. "What's that?"

The captain's tone dropped, heavy with explanation. "A tropical storm builds over time—it's massive, structured, and trackable. We'd have had days of warning. Maritime wind, on the other hand, is the opposite. It's sudden and localized. A shift in atmospheric pressure over open water creates winds that intensify in minutes. No way to predict it, no time to prepare. It's every sailor's nightmare."

The words hung in the air, a chilling reminder of how close they'd come to death.

Grace shivered, wrapping her arms tightly around herself. "So, we were just... unlucky."

The captain nodded solemnly. "Unlucky, yes. But also, still alive." He cast a glance at the distant island. "Focus on that. We'll make it."

Ross turned his attention to the horizon, his expression stern. "How far is the island?"

"It doesn't look like it's too far," the captain replied, his voice firm, although there was uncertainty in his eyes. "But in these conditions, it's going to feel like forever."

The boat lurched again, a rogue wave crashing over its side. Passengers cried out, clinging to each other as water sloshed around their feet. Grace's heart raced, her breaths shallow as she fought to stay composed.

She squinted her eyes, searching desperately. *Zoe. Where are you? Did you make it to another lifeboat? Or did we lose you to the storm?* Each unanswered question gnawed at her, threatening to drag her into despair.

A smaller wave rocked the boat, splashing cold water onto Grace's face. She coughed, blinking against the stinging salt. Beside her, Ross shifted closer, his body acting as a barrier against the worst of the wind.

He noticed her trembling hands clutching the edge of the lifeboat, her knuckles stark white. Without a word, he reached down, his hand covering hers in a gentle gesture that cut through the madness.

Grace flinched at first, startled by the warmth of his touch. Then, slowly, her grip relaxed. Her fingers unfurled, intertwining with his.

Their eyes met, and at that moment, the storm receded—at least in their minds. Ross's gaze was steady, a quiet reassurance amidst the turmoil. Neither spoke, but in that moment, words weren't necessary. The unspoken understanding between them was enough: *You're not alone.*

Grace drew a deep, shuddering breath, her focus sharpening on the faint outline of the island ahead. It wasn't just the promise of land that steadied her—it was the quiet strength in Ross's presence.

The captain's voice cut through the wind once more. "Keep your heads low and your grips firm! We'll reach the island soon. Don't lose faith!"

The lifeboat pressed onward, the storm's fury unabated. Grace clung tightly to the lifeline of Ross's hand, her resolve hardening with every passing second. They were battered, soaked, and terrified—but like the captain said, they were alive.

CHAPTER THIRTEEN

THE LIFEBOAT INCHED PAINFULLY toward the shore, each relentless wave stretching time into an eternity. Grace continued to grip Ross's hand, her body tense as exhaustion warred with the urgent need to hold herself together. Every time the boat pitched, her stomach twisted, and her mind raced with worry.

When they finally reached the beach, the sudden scrape of the lifeboat against the sand brought tears of relief to Grace's eyes. Her legs trembled as she tried to stand, the adrenaline still coursing through her.

Ross, steady, in spite of his own fatigue, reached out a hand. "Come on," he said gently, his voice cutting through the storm's noise. "Let's get you out of here."

Grace took his hand, the strength of his grip anchoring her. As her feet sank into the wet sand, the sensation of solid ground felt almost foreign. Survivors staggered ashore around them, their faces pale and drawn. Debris littered the beach, and the jungle beyond loomed dark and unwelcoming under the gray, rain-soaked sky.

"You all right?" Ross asked. "You don't look good." His eyes searched her face.

Grace nodded, her fingers still clutching his. "I think I am, but I need to find Zoe. I need to know she's safe."

Her voice was shaky, but as soon as the words left her mouth, she hesitated, realizing she hadn't asked Ross how he was. Guilt washed across her face as she glanced up at him. "Wait," she said softly, releasing his hand. "What about you? Are you okay?"

Ross exhaled, a weary smile curving his lips. "I'm still here. "Don't think this didn't shake me up, too. The last thing I expected from this cruise was to find myself floating in the middle of nowhere, clinging onto a piece of our ship." He let out a breath that was half-laugh, half-sigh.

Grace managed a small smile, appreciating his honesty. Before she could respond, a voice pierced the air.

"Gracie!"

Grace turned, her heart leaping. "Zoe?" she called back, breaking into a run.

Over a small rise, Zoe stumbled toward her, rain plastering her hair to her face, her life jacket hanging loose. When they collided, the force of their embrace sent them both stumbling, but they didn't break their hold on each other.

"You're okay," Grace whispered, tears mixing with the rain on her face.

"Of course I am," Zoe replied, her voice cracking with emotion. "You think I'd let a little thing like a shipwreck take me out?"

Grace laughed weakly, the sound a mixture of relief and disbelief.

Zoe reached out and brushed Grace's hair out of her face, "Are you okay, Gracie?"

Grace just nodded.

Ross watched the reunion from a distance, a faint smile softening his face. But the moment didn't last. Survivors were still emerging from the waves, and the beach was a hive of activity and fear.

The rain continued to drizzle as survivors gathered on the beach, their faces pale and exhausted. Crew members passed through the crowd, counting heads. The air was thick with tension, every second stretching like an eternity.

Grace and Zoe stood side by side, arms crossed tightly against the chill. Grace's eyes scanned the group, her stomach knotting with each face she didn't recognize. She glanced at Zoe, who was chewing her lip nervously, a rare crack in her usual bravado.

Finally, the captain's voice rang out over the rain. "We've accounted for most passengers and crew," he announced, his voice steady but heavy with sorrow. "Eleven people are still unaccounted for."

Gasps rippled through the group. A woman's anguished cry cut through the air as she collapsed into someone's arms, realizing one of those missing was her husband. Around her, others began to sob, the heaviness of grief on their shoulders.

Grace clutched Zoe's arm. "Eleven," she repeated, her voice barely audible. "It could've been..."

"I know," Zoe interrupted, her usual display of courage slipping. "But it wasn't. We're here, Grace. Focus on that."

The captain raised his hands, trying to calm the crowd. "I understand your concerns," he said firmly. "Right now, our priority is survival. We need to assess the situation and take stock of what we have."

"So, we're just stuck here, waiting?" someone yelled.

"For now, yes," the captain said, meeting their eyes. "Give 'em no more than a couple of days to find us."

"I don't understand why we can't use the lifeboats to get back to the pier?" Yelled another.

The captain straightened, his expression grave, but he spoke with authority. "Because the currents between here and the mainland are treacherous," he explained, his voice firm but forcing himself to stay calm. "Without proper navigation equipment, we could be swept further out to sea. It's too dangerous to risk it. If we try to leave without a solid plan, we're gambling with everyone's lives."

Ross stepped forward to add to the explanation. His voice was steady, with an edge of authority as well. "Even if we could navigate the currents, we don't have the food supply or water to sustain a trip like that. It's too risky. We've already lost some. We don't want to lose anyone else."

The waves crashed violently against the shore, the salty spray mixing with the taste of fear lingering in the air. The survivors stumbled onto the beach, their bodies battered, their clothes torn, and their minds barely processing the brutal reality that lay before them.

Zoe moved through the crowd, her eyes scanning frantically. *Where was Grace?*

Then—she saw her.

Grace stood a few feet away from the others, facing the ocean, unmoving. Her arms hung limply at her sides, her wet clothes clinging to her shivering frame. Her breathing was shallow, her eyes vacant.

Zoe's stomach twisted.

Something was wrong. She stepped closer, reaching out. "Grace?"

No response.

Grace's lips parted slightly, but no sound came out. She stared at the endless sea as if expecting someone to emerge.

Zoe followed her gaze—then realization hit her like a punch to the gut. They had done a head count.

Eleven people were missing.

Dead.

Lost to the storm.

Zoe's throat tightened. "Grace?" she tried again, this time shaking her gently.

Then—Grace's knees buckled. Her body went limp in Zoe's arms.

Panic surged through her. "Hey, there's something wrong with Grace!" she screamed, her voice breaking.

Ross was there in seconds, shoving past the others. His heart stopped when he saw Grace slumped against Zoe, her face pale, her lips trembling as if she were trying to speak but couldn't.

"Shit—she's going into shock." Ross scooped her up effortlessly, his grip desperate. Her body felt unnaturally cold against his. "What do we do?"

Ray rushed over, "Find somewhere to lay her down. Elevate her legs. We need to get her warm."

The captain didn't hesitate. His voice boomed over the sound of the crashing waves.

"Get her inland! Under the trees—there's better cover there!"

Ross barely registered the order—he was already moving. Holding her close, he rushed toward the tree line.

"Ray, help me clear a space!" Zoe called, running ahead to where the dense foliage offered some protection from the cool wind.

Ross followed, his grip tightening around Grace as she shivered against him.

Behind them, the captain was still barking orders.

"I want life rafts brought up immediately! Some overhead for shelter, the others on the ground—keep her off the cold sand!" His voice was sharp, urgent. "Now, everyone! move!"

Crew members scrambled into action, wading back into the shallows to drag the remaining life rafts ashore.

The captain shouted, "The material of the rafts is durable and waterproof. They'll serve as barriers against the rain and wind. We can drape them over branches to create canopies for shelter. We'll also use some as ground covers to keep us off the wet earth and prevent heat loss."

Ross knelt, gently lowering Grace onto one of the rafts. Her skin was pale, and her breathing still too shallow.

"Get her wrapped in blankets—anything dry! Zoe, get those wet clothes off of her." the captain ordered.

The damp fabric clung stubbornly to Grace's body, but Zoe worked fast, tossing the wet layers aside.

Ross turned away, giving Zoe space while keeping his ears tuned to Grace's breathing. His jaw clenched as he heard the faintest of whimpers from her lips.

"I know, I know," Zoe whispered. "But you'll warm up soon."

She grabbed two survival blankets—thin, crinkling sheets of reflective material designed to trap body heat. One wasn't enough. She wrapped Grace in both, cocooning her tightly, tucking the edges around her to keep any warmth from escaping.

Ray crouched beside them while Ross wrapped two more blankets around Grace's body. He shook his head. "She's too cold. It'll get worse if she doesn't start warming up soon."

Ross turned back, his gaze locking onto Grace's pale face. Her lips turning blue. It scared him. "Give me two of those other blankets," he yelled.

Zoe ran to get them and returned, wrapping them around Grace and covering her feet. She didn't speak, didn't tease—just worked. Minute by minute. Hour by hour.

With the rain letting up, they were able to start a small fire close by.

Ross pulled Grace gently but firmly against his chest. The survival blankets were allowing the warmth to seep through, surrounding her.

"Stay with me, Grace," he whispered against her hair. "I've got you."

The others worked around them, setting up makeshift shelters, securing the rafts, preparing for nightfall. But Ross barely noticed.

All he could focus on was the slow, uneven rise and fall of Grace's chest.

Ray pressed two fingers to Grace's wrist, his expression tight with focus. For a long, agonizing moment, Ross held his breath, his arms still wrapped around her.

Then—Ray's eyes flicked up, relief softening the hard edges of his face.

"It's getting stronger," he murmured. "Her color is coming back, too."

Ross exhaled sharply, his grip instinctively tightening around Grace for a moment before forcing himself to relax.

Zoe let out a breath she didn't realize she'd been holding. "Thank God." She rubbed her hands over her face, exhaustion crashing down now that the panic was ebbing.

But Ross wasn't letting go yet.

He brushed a damp strand of hair away from Grace's cheek, his fingers lingering. Her breathing was steadier now, her lips not as pale.

Ray sat back, nodding. "She's stabilizing, but she's going to be weak for a while. She needs rest. Water. Something warm when we can manage it."

Zoe sighed, looking around. "Well, we're fresh out of luxury accommodations." She patted the survival blanket wrapped around Grace. "This is the best we've got."

Ross didn't move. Didn't say anything.

His fingers grazed over Grace's hand, and he felt it—the slightest twitch.

His heart jumped.

"Grace?" His voice was low, cautious, hopeful.

A tiny sound. A barely-there whimper, like someone struggling to surface from deep water.

Ross leaned closer, his lips near her ear. "Grace, We're here. You're safe."

Her eyelashes fluttered. A small crease formed between her brows. She was coming back.

Zoe's hand landed on Ross's shoulder. "She's waking up."

Ross nodded, swallowing hard. "Thank God."

She stirred slightly in his arms, her body still weak, her skin still too cool despite the layers wrapped around her. The night was cool, but Grace felt the warmth returning under the layers of survival blankets.

She took in a sharp breath. A slight twitch of her fingers. Then, with a soft flutter of her eyelashes, she opened her eyes. And met Ross's gaze.

For a moment, neither of them spoke.

His chest clenched, relief crashing over him like a second wave. He had been waiting, watching, hoping—and now, she was here.

Ross let out a slow, shaky exhale. Then, softly, reverently—

"Hey, you..." His voice was a whisper, rough with exhaustion, thick with emotion. A quiet, unbreakable thread that pulled her back into the world.

He looked around until he found Zoe, and with a smile of relief, he said, "She's awake."

Grace's lips parted, her voice a fragile whisper, as if it took everything in her to form the words.

"You found me."

Ross's throat tightened, and he nodded, "Yeah, I found you," he said.

. The captain's voice cut through the air, firm and commanding.

"Let her rest, but keep checking on her. The rain let up. Let's keep these fires going to keep us warm," His gaze swept across the group, pausing on Zoe. "Make sure her clothes are laid out to dry. We'll need everyone as strong as possible if we're going to make it through this."

Ross nodded stiffly, still kneeling beside Grace, her breathing now steady.

The captain waved Ross over, gesturing to a group struggling to prop up a life raft as a makeshift shelter.

"We need this secured in case the wind picks up again," the captain barked.

Ross nodded, stepping into action. He grabbed the edge of the raft and helped brace it against a tree. The others worked beside him, tying ropes and anchoring them with rocks.

The flames from the fires flickered wildly as the wind blew through the camp. Someone called out about the fire running low on wood.

"I'll grab more," Ross said, his voice steady despite the weariness settling deep in his bones.

He picked his way through the dense trees, trying to find dry branches and debris. His mind, however, kept drifting back to Grace.

He could still feel the cold weight of her hand in his, the faint movement when she stirred. The image of her pale face, barely clinging to consciousness, was seared into his memory.

"Hey, Ross!" Ray's voice broke through his thoughts. "You okay?"

Ross shrugged, his jaw tight. "Yeah, I'm good. Just focused."

Ray gave him a knowing look. "She's strong, you know. She'll pull through. You did your part, man."

Zoe worked quickly, spreading Grace's wet clothes on a flat piece of driftwood, placing them close enough to the fire to dry but far enough to avoid burning. The heat from the flames sent a light steam curling into the cool night air.

Ross draped another blanket over Zoe's shoulders. She raised an eyebrow, trying to summon her usual sass. "No umbrella service, Ross? You're slipping."

He smirked, a hint of humor breaking through. "Next time, I promise."

"We'll get through this," Zoe muttered, though her tone lacked its usual confidence.

"I know we will," Ross answered with a nod.

Under the canopy of trees, the survivors worked together to transform the rafts into makeshift shelters. The captain coordinated the efforts while Ross and Ray led a group to secure the canopies in case the rain started again.

Zoe glanced at Ross, her expression a mix of exhaustion and admiration. "You're pretty good in a crisis," she said, her laugh soft but uneasy.

It was the kind of laugh that tried to lighten the mood but couldn't fully mask the weight of the situation.

His smile faded slightly, his eyes serious. "Let's just get through this one."

Zoe nodded, clutching the blanket tightly. Her only choice now was to believe that rescue would come—and soon.

The captain addressed the group again. "If you don't have a blanket, you can wrap this around you." He held up a piece of the raft. "It will act as windbreakers and provide some warmth. And," he added, pointing to the skies where the rain was starting to drizzle again, "their surfaces are perfect for collecting rainwater, which we'll need until rescue arrives." The crowd nodded, murmuring their agreement, as the captain continued. "You can use two, one for drinking water and the other for hygiene."

They moved quickly, forming small groups to execute the captain's instructions. Crew members demonstrated how to unpack the rafts, inflate them, and repurpose the material. Zoe watched as they hauled the fully inflated rafts toward the tree line to set up temporary shelters.

"Captain!" one of the men called out, his voice cutting through the chatter. He held up an object that gleamed in the light, catching everyone's attention. "I found this on one of the lifeboats," he said, stepping closer. It was a sturdy tin slab. "It's not a pan, but it's durable enough to cook on if necessary."

"Good work," The captain nodded his approval and said, "If anyone finds something useful, no matter how small, bring it to me. We'll make the best of what we have.

"Ray," the captain yelled, "help Ross throw those rafts over the tree branches and tie them together."

Some members of the group set up private sleeping areas, creating small spaces for solitude. Others, preferring companionship, chose to share a communal sleeping area.

Ross paused mid-task, stepping away from the canopies they had been securing. His gaze dropped to the ground as he began scanning the area, his focus shifting entirely. Ray, who had been tying down a corner of one of the rafts, noticed Ross's change in behavior and straightened up.

"What's up?" Ray asked, brushing off his hands and watching Ross curiously.

"I'm looking for something," Ross replied, his tone distracted as he crouched near a pile of debris. "Something we could use to cut some of these rafts—it could be better for ground cover or to keep people warm."

Ray tilted his head, then reached into his pocket with a sly grin. "What about this?" he said, pulling out a large, well-worn pocket knife. Even through the drizzling rain, Ross could see the faint gleam of the blade, its edge catching what little light pierced the watery veil. The weapon's sharpness was unmistakable.

Ross stood, his eyebrows shooting up in surprise. "How'd you manage to get past security with that?" he asked, his voice mixed with disbelief and amusement.

Ray shrugged, his grin widening. "I've got my ways," he said, his tone light but smug. "Let's just say it pays to know which lines to stand in."

Ross shook his head and chuckled. "I don't know whether to be impressed or worried."

"Go with impressed," Ray quipped, handing the knife to Ross. "Now, let's see what we can make out of these rafts."

Ross took the knife, testing its weight in his hand before nodding. "This will work," he said simply. He glanced back at Ray with a small smile. "Looks like your 'ways' came in handy."

"I'll have you know that I'm a man of endless surprises. You'll see."

Together, they worked quickly, slicing rafts into smaller sections to use as ground covers and additional windbreakers. Zoe watched from a distance, her heart aching with gratitude.

CHAPTER FOURTEEN

T WO DAYS PASSED SINCE the storm forced them onto the island. The second morning on the island dawned with a calm breeze, the sun casting soft golden light over the camp. The survivors moved about, gathering supplies and tending to fires, their routines settling into a rhythm born of necessity. Each hour felt like a lifetime.

Grace sat on a flat rock, inside one of the private shelters, still wrapped in blankets but feeling more like herself again.

Her strength had returned, though her cheeks still burned with embarrassment every time she thought about how she'd collapsed in shock, forcing the others to rally around her.

"Morning," Zoe called out as she approached, carrying Grace's clothes. Her voice was light, but her smile was warm. "Thought you might want these."

Grace smiled back, taking the clothes gratefully. "Thanks, Zoe."

She ran her fingers over the dry fabric, still stiff and rough from the ocean water. The material crinkled slightly in her hands, rigid from the dried salt.

Zoe smirked, watching Grace's expression. "Listen," she said, hands on her hips, "I did my best, but the 'delicate' cycle wasn't an option, and we're fresh out of dryer sheets."

Grace let out a small laugh, shaking her head. "Yeah, I can tell. Feels like I'm about to wear a burlap sack."

Zoe tapped her chin thoughtfully. "Well, if nothing else, just think of it as a full-body salt scrub. People pay good money for that."

Grace chuckled as she hugged the clothes to her chest. It wasn't much, but the moment of normalcy—of laughter—was something she desperately needed.

Zoe plopped down beside her, her expression playful. "So... feeling human again?"

Grace chuckled softly. "Once I get out of these blankets. Almost. Still embarrassed, though." She glanced at Zoe. "I must've been a wreck."

Zoe leaned back on her elbows, smirking. "Oh, you were a wreck, all right. But in fairness, we've all been there—well, maybe not quite that dramatic."

Grace groaned, covering her face with her hands. "Great. Just what I wanted to hear."

Zoe nudged her shoulder. "Hey, don't sweat it. You went through a lot. And for what it's worth... Ross didn't leave your side."

Grace's hands lowered slowly; she creased her brow. "What?"

Zoe raised an eyebrow, her tone teasing but laced with sincerity. "Oh, yeah. That man was glued to you like sap on a tree. Wouldn't let anyone else take care of you." She leaned in conspiratorially. "I mean, I thought he was going to throw Ray into the ocean when he suggested giving you space."

Grace blinked, the memory rushing back—the faintest glimpse of Ross's face, his voice steady and soothing. The way he'd held her as if the world might shatter if he let go.

"He stayed?" she asked softly.

Zoe grinned. "The whole time. Barely slept. When you opened your eyes that first time, I swear he looked like he'd just won the lottery."

Grace's cheeks flushed, a warmth spreading through her that had nothing to do with the fire. "I don't know what to say."

Zoe shrugged, her tone turning more thoughtful. "You don't have to say anything. Just... you know, maybe think about why he did that."

Grace's gaze dropped to the clothes in her lap, her mind swirling. She had always prided herself on trying to stay strong and on not wanting to need anyone. But when she had looked into Ross's eyes—when she had felt the safety of his arms—something had shifted, and for some reason, she felt guilty about it.

The fire provided comfort as the group sat in uneasy silence, their faces still etched with fatigue and worry. The flames spit embers into the air while flickering light danced across the sand, making their haggard expressions seem even more haunted.

"Captain," a man yelled over the crackling fire. "It's been two fuckin' days. I thought you said we'd be rescued by now!"

"That's not what I said," the captain snapped, his exhaustion evident. "I said they'd send a search team once they realized the cruise ship didn't return. We need to be patient. They're doing their jobs."

The group's attention shifted to the captain. His presence, usually steadying, now seemed strained. His jaw tightened as he studied their weary faces. "That was an estimate based on our last known coordinates and the search grid. But estimates are not guarantees."

"Estimates?" the man snapped, stepping closer, his hands gesturing wildly. "We're out here with barely enough food to last the week, and you're talkin' estimates?"

The captain stood slowly, his presence commanding. "I understand you're scared. We all are. But I need you to keep it together. Panicking won't help anyone."

The man scoffed, his frustration boiling over. "You don't get it, do you? Some of us have families waiting for us to return! You might be fine sitting here playing hero, but I..."

"Enough!" The captain shouted. His voice cut through the low muttering of the group and silenced the man. "I have a family too. Every single one of us here probably has someone waiting for us at home. That's why I need you to focus and not waste your energy blaming me or anyone else. Hell, we're not in control of the weather or the search parties either."

The man mumbled under his breath but backed down, slumping onto a rock with a frustrated huff. The tension in the group eased slightly.

Ross stood, brushing sand from his hands. "We can't afford to lose it now," he said, his voice steady but firm. "Ray and I are heading out tomorrow to look for more food. We're doing our part. I suggest you do yours by keeping it together."

A whisper of reluctant agreement rippled through the group, and although they tried to be hopeful, their eyes betrayed them. Some stared into the fire, while others shifted uncomfortably under makeshift shelters.

Grace smoothed down the dry clothes Zoe had brought her. She took a steadying breath, her fingers brushing her hair back as she glanced at Zoe.

"Ready?" Zoe asked, her tone light but her eyes watchful.

Grace nodded. "Yeah. Let's go."

They stepped out from the sheltered area, the sunlight filtering through the trees, painting golden streaks across the sand. The camp was alive with activity—survivors working together to build shelters, stoke fires, and sort through supplies.

But it was Ross who caught Grace's attention.

He stood near the main fire, his sleeves rolled up, his hands brushing off ash from a log he'd just added to the flames. As if sensing her presence, he turned.

Their eyes met across the camp.

For a moment, the world seemed to still. The hardship of survival, the weight of their circumstances—all of it faded into the background.

Ross's lips curved into a small, satisfied smile, and he gave her a subtle nod, a quiet acknowledgment of her presence.

A tightness clenched Grace's heart. There was something in his gaze—relief, pride, maybe even a flicker of something deeper.

She returned the nod, a faint smile tugging at her lips.

Zoe's voice broke the moment. "Should I give you two a moment, or...?"

Grace blinked, a flush creeping up her neck. "What? No." She cleared her throat and turned to Zoe, trying to keep her tone casual. "Come on, let's help with the fire."

But as they moved across the camp, Grace could feel Ross's gaze lingering just a second longer before he turned back to his work.

Ross walked toward the edge of the camp where Ray stood. The usual lightness in Ray's demeanor was replaced by a seriousness. "Hey," Ray said, lowering his voice. "Got a second?"

Ross frowned but followed him to a secluded spot behind the shelters. Ray crouched under a tarp and pulled out a carefully wrapped bundle. Peeling back the layers, he revealed a smartphone.

Ross blinked while disbelief flashed across his face. "You have a phone? Are you serious?"

Ray grinned sheepishly. "Kept it dry as best I could. Charged it with a battery pack. It got wet during the storm, but I dried it out. The screen lit up earlier—for a second. Thought it might come in handy. Only one problem."

Ross grabbed the phone, his hands steady, even with the rush of excitement coursing through him. He pressed the power button, and the screen flickered to life. A dim glow lit their faces as they stared at the device.

"No service!" Ray spat out, "No goddamn service! Can you believe that?"

Ross quickly swiped to the settings, his chest tightening as the dreaded words appeared: **No service.**

Ray groaned, running a hand through his hair. ""It's like we're on the edge of something, so close, but still... just out of reach. Feels like a cruel joke, doesn't it?"

Ross exhaled, his jaw clenching. "But, still, it's something. At least the phone works, and we've got power. Maybe we can boost the signal—rig an antenna."

"With what?"

"Don't know, but there's got to be something we can do."

Ray shook his head, his frustration barely contained. "We'd better think fast. That battery pack won't last forever."

"I know," Ross said, his voice firm. "For now, we keep this between us. No sense in getting everyone worked up until we have a plan."

Reluctantly, Ray nodded and rewrapped the phone, tucking it back under the tarp. They returned to the fire, the group still huddled in uneasy silence. Ross's eyes scanned around at the faces, his heart heavy. They needed reassurance, but it was becoming harder to provide.

Grace looked up as he approached. Her eyes, heavy with exhaustion, still held a hint of determination. "Everything okay?" she asked softly.

"Yeah," Ross replied, managing a faint smile. He picked up an extra blanket and laid it across her shoulders. "You need to stay warm and rested. Tomorrow's another long day."

Grace nodded, pulling her blanket tighter. Zoe leaned against her, trying to mask her fear with a half-hearted joke. "You think you can catch something other than fish tomorrow?" she asked, her voice laced with irritation. "If I have to eat one more goddamn fish, I swear I'll start flappin' around like one!" She exaggerated the motion, flapping her arms wildly for emphasis.

Ross chuckled quietly, the sound barely audible over the crackle of the fire. "You'll be the first to know."

Zoe smirked, wiggling her eyebrows as she stood and dusted off her hands. "All right, you two lovebirds," she gasped dramatically, placing a hand over her chest, "I mean, totally platonic, definitely-not-in-denial-about-each-other survival buddies."

Ross rolled his eyes, and Grace groaned. "Zoe..."

She held up a finger, cutting them off. "Don't 'Zoe' me. I'm just saying—keep it PG. Or don't. Whatever." She shrugged exaggeratedly. "Anyway, I'm out. Peace!"

She threw up two fingers in a dramatic deuces pose, twirled on her heel, and overdid a full-body stretch, groaning like an old woman. "Whew, these jungle nights really take it outta me. I need my beauty sleep."

She sauntered toward the shelters with an over-the-top yawn, tossing one last teasing glance over her shoulder. "Try not to stare into each other's souls too hard while I'm gone."

Ross shook his head, half-amused, half-exasperated. "Is she always like this?"

Grace sighed. "Oh, you have no idea."

The camp grew quiet, the others asleep in makeshift shelters, their soft snores and the crackle of the fire the only sounds that remained. Above, the stars spread across the sky, their brilliance undiminished by the storm, the waves whispering secrets to the shore.

Grace hugged her knees to her chest, her gaze fixed on the dancing flames as if they might hold the answers she desperately sought. The fire's warmth chased away the evening chill, but it couldn't still the restlessness inside her.

"Not sleepy, huh?" Ross's voice was low and gentle, as if he already knew the answer.

She shook her head. "I've slept for two days. Plus, I've got too much on my mind."

He nodded, watching the flames with her. "I'm a great sounding board if that's what you need."

For a while, neither of them spoke. The silence wasn't uncomfortable—it was the kind of quiet that felt intentional, like an unspoken agreement to let thoughts settle before turning them into words. She tucked her hair behind her ear.

Finally, Grace exhaled, measuring what she wanted to say. "There was a reason I came on this cruise," she admitted. "And now, being out here like this... I've started questioning it. Maybe it wasn't the best reason after all."

Ross's expression remained unreadable, but she could sense his curiosity. He didn't press, though. Instead, he simply nodded, waiting.

A moment later, she turned to him. "Do you have someone waiting for you at home, Ross?"

He lifted his gaze to hers, searching her face. "What do you mean?"

She tried for nonchalance, but even she could hear the slight edge in her voice. "A girlfriend? A wife?"

Ross held her gaze a beat too long as if weighing his answer—or maybe her reason for asking. Then, finally, he shook his head. "No."

The single syllable felt heavier than it should.

A beat of silence passed before he spoke again. "You?"

Grace hesitated, her fingers curling into the fabric of her pants. "Someone I'm... confused about."

Ross didn't react at first, but something flickered in his expression—understanding, maybe even disappointment. He didn't push, just let her words settle between them.

"Why confused?" he asked after a moment.

Grace exhaled, staring into the fire. "Sometimes life doesn't hand you the easiest circumstances to work with."

"Or to work through," Ross said. He glanced at her then, his gaze steady, warm. "Sometimes, we need to realize the past is the past... and move on."

Her lips parted slightly at his words, but no response came.

Instead, she watched as he leaned back, stretching his legs and tilting his head toward the sky. "You know, I've never seen stars like this before."

Grace followed his gaze, the tension in her chest easing just a little. "It's almost like they're trying to remind us of how small we are," Ross continued. "How temporary."

She tilted her head. "Or maybe they're trying to remind us of how much bigger life can be if we let it."

Ross turned to her then, and for a second, the fire wasn't the only warmth between them. "Maybe you're right."

She smiled faintly, her fingers relaxing. "I'll hold onto that. For now."

Ross didn't reply, but his expression said enough. The way his lips curved slightly, the way his eyes lingered on hers—it was undeniable.

Grace turned to study him. Talking to Ross was easy—too easy. Thought-provoking and effortless at the same time. He challenged her in ways she wasn't sure she was ready for. Each conversation revealed layers of him she hadn't expected, but the real problem?

She liked it.

And worse—she knew he did too.

"I like talking to you, Ross." The words left her lips before she could overthink them.

He glanced at her, his gaze unreadable but soft. "Likewise."

Then, after a pause, he added, "You know, I had my own reasons for coming on this cruise too." He exhaled, rubbing his hands together, warming them against the fire. "But none of that really matters now, does it? Everything's changed for all of us. We take things as they come and make the best of it until help arrives."

Grace studied him, watching the quiet certainty in his posture, in his words. "You sound so sure of that."

His lips lifted slightly, but there was something deeper in his expression—something unwavering. "I have to be."

Then, his voice lowered just slightly. "Now, here's my advice to you, Grace... don't let the past keep you from seeing what's right in front of you."

Their eyes met, and this time, neither of them looked away.

The fire crackled between them, but the real warmth—the one neither of them wanted to admit—had already taken root.

That night, Ross stood watch, his gaze fixed on the dark horizon. Somewhere out there, help was coming. It had to be. But for now, they were on their own. The days blurred into nights, and the nights bled into a restless repetition of time.

CHAPTER FIFTEEN

E THAN STARED AT THE phone, his fingers twitching but refusing to tap the number. He wasn't in a rush to make this call. In fact, he'd been dragging his feet for nearly a week. The thought of facing Grace's mother with the news of her daughter's disappearance. A chore. In fact, every interaction with her felt more like a formality, an obligation.

He phoned the cruise office every day, hoping they found them so he wouldn't have to deal with her at all, but now, with it going on a week, he couldn't put it off any longer. He closed his eyes for a moment, summoning the energy to dial.

His fingers hovered over the screen. Then his eyes flickered to the cruise office number. He let out a long breath, feeling the pressure of the situation closing in. One more time, he thought. This call would be the thin thread he'd cling to, the last chance before everything came crashing down. He dialed the number for what seemed to be the hundredth time.

When his call connected this time, he didn't bother with pleasantries. "This is Ethan Hargrove—again," he snapped, his voice strained with panic and irritation. "My wife, Grace, was on the cruise ship that's gone missing. It's been almost a week. She was only supposed to be gone for three days! Are there any updates?"

The voice on the other end was calm, professional, and infuriatingly detached. "Sir, I understand your concern. We are working closely with the authorities to locate the ship. At this time, we ask for patience."

"Patience?" Ethan barked, his voice cracking. "You want me to be patient when my wife is missing? Do you have any idea what it feels like not knowing if someone you care about is alive or dead?"

"Sir..."

"No," Ethan interrupted, slamming his palm on the table. "Don't give me another empty apology or 'we're working on it.' I need real answers, and I need them now."

The representative tried to respond, but Ethan, satisfied with his performance, ended the call abruptly, tossing his phone onto the counter. He was sure if asked, they would tell Mrs. Davis how distraught he was when he called. His chest heaved with shallow, uneven breaths. After a moment, he picked up the phone again and dialed another number. This was it. The dreaded call. The one he couldn't put off any longer.

Grace's mother was mid-chop on a cutting board when her phone buzzed. Seeing Ethan's name on the screen sent a jolt of unease through her. It was rare for him to call.

She wiped her hands on a towel and answered cautiously. "Ethan?"

"Mrs. Davis," Ethan began, his voice unsteady, "I... I don't know how else to tell you this, but Grace—she's missing."

The knife slipped from Mrs. Davis's hand, clattering onto the counter. "Missing? Ethan, what do you mean she's missing? Where is she?"

"She's on that cruise ship," Ethan explained hurriedly, "with Zoe."

"What cruise ship?"

"Haven't you been watching the news, Ma'am?"

"Wait. She's on that ship? The one that's been missing?"

"They were only supposed to be gone for three days. The ship hasn't returned to port."

Ethan, that ship has been missing for a week. Are you telling me that my daughter has been missing for a week, and you're just now calling me?"

He rushed on with an explanation, "They said they were coordinating with the authorities. I thought they'd have found them by now, and there would have been no need to worry you at all." His voice was raw with tension. "But since they haven't, I thought you needed to know."

She asked again, this time harsher. "Are you saying Grace has been missing for a week, and you're just now calling me? Are you at the cruise office?"

"Not yet, but I'm going."

"What did they say yesterday when you were there?"

"I wasn't there yesterday, but I called."

"You're not there today. You weren't there yesterday. Have you been there at all?"

"No, but I've been calling every day," Ethan said quickly--defensively.

"I'm on my way." Mrs. Davis said, ending the call. Her heart was pounding in her chest. The sound in Ethan's voice echoed in her mind. She couldn't quite put her finger on it. Was it a worry or a defensive tone she was hearing? She fumbled with her phone, scrolling through with shaky hands until she found Grace's number.

She didn't know why she was calling. If Grace were near her phone, she would've called by now, telling her not to worry. She would be saying, 'Mom, I'm fine. Don't worry about me. I'll be home soon.' But that didn't happen. So, for her own sanity, she tapped the number anyway.

The phone rang three times. "Come on, Grace, pick up," she pleaded. The ringing stopped, and the familiar tone of Grace's voice came on as a greeting:

"Hi, you've reached Grace Hargrove. I'm sorry I'm not available to answer your call, but please leave a detailed message after the beep, and I'll call you back."

The beep sounded, and her mother rushed to speak, her voice urgent.

"Hello, dear. I just got off the phone with Ethan. He says something's going on with the cruise ship you're on." Her breath stalled as she fought to steady herself. "I'm on my way to the cruise office to get some answers, Grace. If you get this message, please call me back immediately. I'm worried about you."

She ended the call but didn't feel any relief. The silence in the room hung over her.

Her thumb hovered over her phone again before quickly scrolling through her contacts and finding Zoe's name. She tapped the call button, biting her lip as the phone rang.

"Come on, come on," she whispered, her free hand gripping the counter's edge.

Zoe's voicemail greeting simply said, "*You know what to do.*" Mrs. Davis's heart clenched as she hung up without a word, the sting of tears in her eyes. She leaned against the counter again, gripping the phone tightly as if willing it to bring a connection, a voice, anything.

Taking a deep breath, she grabbed her purse and her keys, and with determination outweighing her fear, she headed for the door.

CHAPTER SIXTEEN

WORD OF THE MISSING ship rippled through homes, offices, and hearts, carrying an unshakable weight with every retelling. At the cruise line headquarters, the atmosphere was thick with tension. The air charged with a mixture of fear and frustration. Phones rang incessantly, a cacophony of desperate inquiries and pleas for updates.

At the heart of it all was Karen Fletcher, the operations manager, a sharp, no-nonsense woman whose efficiency bordered on ruthless most days. Today was no different. The staff watched Karen paced her office, a printout of the ship's last known coordinates clenched tightly in her hand. She stared at the marked spot on the map as if sheer willpower could illuminate the ship's location.

"It's not like them to be this late without any communication," she told her colleagues. Her tone was sharp, but worry flashed in her eyes. "The weather in that area is rough sometimes, but the ship is equipped to handle it. They should've contacted us by now."

A reporter rushed into her office, thrusting his microphone into Karen's face, his voice urgent. "Do you think... they came in contact with a major storm?"

Karen didn't answer. Her silence spoke volumes.

The cameras fired in rapid succession, their relentless click-click-click echoing off the walls. Flashes exploded in the tense air, illuminating the strained faces of Karen and her colleagues, capturing every flicker of their frustration. The room felt charged with anxiety as the reporters unleashed their barrage of questions, their voices overlapping.

"How soon do you expect to have answers about the missing passengers?" one reporter demanded, his microphone thrust forward as if to pry open the silence.

"Can you explain how communication was lost with the ship?" another asked, his eyes sharp, focused on any crack in the story.

"Is there any hope that the missing passengers might still be alive?" a third questioned, the urgency in their tone piercing the already heavy atmosphere.

The families shifted uncomfortably, their eyes darting from the reporter to Karen and then to the staff, but no answers came. The questions hung in the air.

When Karen nor her staff provided information the reporters were hoping for, the cameras quickly shifted to the anxious relatives, desperate for any content they could get.

"How are you holding up?" one reporter asked, his microphone shoved toward a woman clutching a photo of her missing family member.

Another reporter leaned in, voice heavy with urgency, "What are you hoping to hear right now? What's the latest update you've received?"

Families shifted uncomfortably, eyes darting to the walls, the floor, anywhere to avoid the spotlight. A father, his hands trembling, stepped forward, clearly weighed down by the mounting pressure. "We just want to know they're safe, that's all," he said, his voice thick with emotion.

As the questions continued, it became evident that the reporters were as desperate for answers as the families themselves. The air in the room seemed to grow heavier with each question, the tension rising as the clock ticked on. The families, already torn with fear and uncertainty, were forced to relive the torment of waiting—hoping, praying—that their loved ones would be found soon. They shifted nervously under the barrage of attention, some shielding their faces, others gripping the arms of their chairs as though the pressure might crack them open.

Karen pushed through the mob, her jaw clenched, her eyes flashing with rage. Her raised voice sliced through the chaotic scene.

"That's enough!" she snapped. "This is not the time or the place."

A reporter, holding a mic like a weapon, lunged forward. "But people have the right to know..."

"They'll know when there's something to tell!" Karen shot back, her tone steely. "Right now, you're not helping anyone. You're making things worse. These families are going through enough."

A low mutter of dissent rippled through the crowd, but Karen squared her shoulders, unwavering.

"Out. Now." She pointed to the door. "I want all reporters out of this office. If you can't respect the people waiting for answers about their families, you don't get answers either. Go."

A few grumbles rose up, cameras hesitating mid-air, but the force behind her words left no room for argument. Slowly, the reporters began to back off, some muttering under their breath, others retreating with reluctant glares.

As the last reporter shuffled out, Karen slammed the door shut, her chest rising and falling with the effort to keep her composure. The silence that followed was heavy but merciful. She turned to the people left inside, her expression softening.

"We'll get through this," she promised, her voice quieter now but no less determined. "We just need time."

The tension remained thick in the office. Occasionally, low, anxious voices erupted into heated demands for answers. Reporters hovered outside now, their cameras capturing each tear-streaked face and angry outburst they could.

Karen's gaze didn't waver. "I understand your frustration," she said evenly. "But search and rescue operations take time. The ship is equipped with emergency systems, and we are confident they are managing the situation on board."

"Confident?" a man scoffed. "That's supposed to comfort us?"

Mrs. Davis stepped forward, her voice shaking with emotion. "What about the passengers? I just found out that my daughter is on that ship. Do you have any idea how afraid they must be?"

Karen met her eyes, her own exhaustion visible. "I promise you, ma'am, we are doing everything possible to bring them home safely."

A man near the back scoffed loudly, "You should've had a damn rescue team out there 4 days ago. This isn't some little fishing boat—it's a cruise ship. How does a ship that big just disappear?" He said, his voice dripping with disbelief.

The hushed whispers in the room surged again, voices overlapping in a rising tide of fear and anger.

"When will we hear something?" a woman called out. "It's been too long!"

Karen held her ground, though the pressure of so many desperate eyes on her was almost unbearable. "We're prioritizing the safety of everyone on board," she said, her tone even but strained. "We'll share updates with you as soon as we have them."

"Updates?" Mrs. Davis's voice rose sharply from the crowd. She pushed forward, her eyes blazing with fear and frustration. "We don't only want vague updates. We need results!"

Karen met Mrs. Davis's fierce gaze with a steady one of her own, nodding slightly as if to acknowledge her pain. "A coordinated search effort is in place right now," she explained. "Helicopters and rescue vessels are combing the area of the ship's last known location. We have every reason to believe we will locate them soon."

"How soon is 'soon'?" Mrs. Davis asked, her voice cracking slightly.

Karen hesitated, choosing her words carefully. "As quickly as possible," she said finally. Her tone softened just enough to convey empathy. "Let me reiterate, the safety of our passengers is our top priority. She knew her words weren't enough to calm the situation entirely. Still, the room quieted slightly as people absorbed what she was saying. For a brief moment, the emotional turmoil that had been building up seemed to lessen.

Mrs. Davis sat anxiously in the corner of the cruise office, her hands trembling as she tried to compose herself. Her eyes darted to the doorway every time it opened, hoping, praying that Grace would burst through the door with the wildest story of a crazy survival adventure.

A frail woman reached over and covered her hand. She forced a smile of assurance. "Wherever they are," she said, "They're with my Lloyd; he's the captain. They're in good hands."

Mrs. Davis's lips quivered, the weight of her words almost too much to bear. Her eyes flickered with an ache that the other woman understood all too well. "Grace is all I have left," Mrs. Davis whispered, her voice barely audible over the buzz of the office. "I buried my husband during the pandemic. I can't lose her too."

The pain in Mrs. Davis's words struck the woman with an unbelievable force. She swallowed hard, trying to hold back a flood of emotion. Reaching out with her other hand, she gave Mrs. Davis a pat on her arm, the only thing she could offer in that moment of shared despair.

"You won't lose her. We can't think that way," her voice steadier now. "He's going to bring them home."

Mrs. Davis gave her a small, grateful smile, but the fear still lingered in her eyes. They continued to sit in silence, waiting for answers. Barely holding on to something as unstable as shifting sand.

Mrs. Davis's posture was stiff, and her face was pale when Ethan spotted her sitting in the corner. He hesitated before approaching, his guilt and frustration warring within him.

"Mrs. Davis," he said cautiously.

She turned sharply, her eyes narrowing. "Where have you been, Ethan? I've been here for hours."

"I had to make a stop," he said defensively. "Any updates?"

"No, I still can't believe you waited almost a week to tell me about this. I should've been your first call."

Ethan groaned, running a hand through his hair. "I didn't want to worry you unnecessarily."

Mrs. Davis's expression hardened. "My daughter is out there, Ethan. She's missing. You didn't have the right to keep this from me. Do you ever think of anyone other than yourself?"

Ethan didn't reply. He looked away, his jaw tight, as he tried to ignore her accusations.

"I'll tell you this, Ethan, if anything happens to her, I'll never forgive you."

Ethan clenched his fists but said nothing. He turned and found a seat at the far end of the room, muttering, "Like mother, like daughter."

Karen walked through the lobby, and Ethan stood abruptly, asking, "What if..." He faltered, his voice cracking under the weight of his thoughts. "What happens if you don't find them? What if they're all d..."

"Stop!" Mrs. Davis snapped, glaring at him, her eyes brimming with unshed tears. Her voice, though quivering, carried undeniable strength. "Don't even say that. Don't you dare!"

Ethan blinked, startled by the force of her interruption.

She drew in a shaky breath, her fists clenched. "We have to believe they'll find them," she said, her tone softer. "Grace is strong. She's out there, and she's okay. I have to believe that."

The room fell silent, her words hanging in the air. Karen's expression softened, and she nodded slightly, a glint of understanding passing between them.

"We'll find them," Karen said, her voice quieter now but still firm. "I promise you; we're doing everything we can."

Mrs. Davis didn't reply. Instead, she turned toward the crowd, her posture straight and unyielding even with the weight of her fear. Ethan chastened, lowered his head, his lips pressed into a thin line as he slumped into a chair at the edge of the room.

The silence stretched, punctuated only by the faint rustling and the quiet sniffles of those who couldn't hold back their tears.

Closing time for the office was its usual 5:00 pm. At 4:45, Karen reentered the lobby, her face a mask of professionalism, though the weight of the situation hung heavily on her shoulders. She took a deep breath, scanning the room full of anxious faces, their eyes still filled with desperation. She cleared her throat and spoke, her voice steady but laced with the tension she couldn't hide.

"There are no new updates at the moment," she said. "I know this is hard. Believe me, if it were my family out there, I'd be right alongside you. But with the office closing soon, I strongly recommend you all go home and get some proper rest. You'll be better positioned to handle things when you're well-rested, and some of you have been here every day."

A collective sigh filled the room, but no one moved. They were reluctant to leave as if leaving would mean giving up on the possibility of new information. Karen continued, her voice gentle.

"I will stay on top of this for the rest of the night," she said. "If there are any updates, the Coast Guard will contact me, and I will reach out to each of you personally. I promise you; I won't rest until we know what's happened."

The crowd remained still, some nodding slowly, but the weight of the uncertainty still hung in the air. Karen softened her gaze as she gave them a moment, her heart aching for the families. They needed answers just as much as she did.

She reiterated, "Please, go home. Get some sleep. I'll make sure you're the first to know when there's something new. We'll get through this together," she added, her voice barely above a whisper. Still, it was enough to reassure them that she was in this fight with them.

With a final, lingering look at the families, she turned and walked back to her desk, the burden of the night stretching before her.

The families began to stir, one by one, toward the exit. The low murmur of voices, the shuffle of feet, and the faint sound of crumpling paper bags filled the air. Coffee cups, empty wrappers, and discarded napkins littered the floor as they trickled out, leaving behind the remnants of a long, emotionally charged evening. The last person to leave gave Karen a weary glance before exiting, and with that, the office fell silent.

For the first time in what felt like hours, Karen allowed her shoulders to relax, the tension in her body easing as she took in the now-empty lobby. She exhaled deeply, releasing the pent-up stress that had been building. Her gaze flicked to Carla, quietly working in the corner, and she gestured to the scattered mess.

"Do me a favor before you go?" Karen asked, her voice soft but still tinged with exhaustion.

Carla raised an eyebrow as she stood up, stretching her stiff limbs. "Aren't you going home too?" she asked.

Karen shook her head, her eyes fixed on the debris scattered across the room. "We'll just continue what we've been doing," she said. "When you come in tomorrow, you can relieve me while I go home, get showered, and changed. I'm not leaving this office unattended until we find out what happened to that ship."

Carla paused for a moment, looking at her boss with a mixture of concern and understanding, before nodding. "Got it. Let's get this cleaned up, then."

Karen gave her a tired but grateful smile. Together, they tidied the room, picked up the trash, and straightened the chairs. Although there was a heaviness present, there was also a sense of shared determination between them. Both knew they couldn't afford to rest—not yet.

As the last piece of trash was tossed into the bin, Karen took another deep breath, her shoulders finally sagging in relief. Tomorrow would be another long day, but for now, she could take solace in the fact that she was doing everything she could to get the answers they all desperately needed.

CHAPTER
SEVENTEEN

T HE MOON'S SOFT GLOW stretched long patterns across the rough camp the survivors had assembled on the beach. Five nights had passed since the ship capsized, and the once pristine beach now bore the marks of survival. Footprints criss-crossed the sand, leading from the lifeboats to makeshift shelters and the dim glow of a dwindling fire. The fire's faint embers mirrored the traces of belief still lingering among them.

Ross stood at the edge of the tree line, arms crossed, his face etched with exhaustion. Beside him, the captain's expression was equally grim as they stared out over the dark water.

"I thought they'd have found us by now," Ross said quietly.

The captain exhaled heavily. "Me too. I keep looking out there, expecting to see something—a plane, a ship, anything. But there's nothing." He paused, his jaw tightening. "Still, we can't stop believing that they'll come."

Ross ran a hand through his hair, frustration deepening the lines on his face. "What are they waiting for? They have to know we're lost by now."

"They do," the captain replied. "But rescue missions take time. Weather, coordination, resources—it's not as simple as sending out a search party. Still, the longer this goes on..." His voice trailed off, and Ross didn't press him. Instead, he turned to look at the campfire, where survivors huddled together. Grace and Zoe sat side by side, Zoe's animated chatter contrasting with Grace's quiet demeanor. Ray joined them, earning Zoe's smile as she turned her attention to him.

Ross shifted his gaze back to the captain. "Ray showed me how to carve traps and spears for hunting. We caught three rabbits and two fish today. It's something, but it's not enough."

The captain nodded, scanning the surrounding trees. "We'll make it work. I saw a coconut tree inland. It'll give us water and food. It's not much, but, like you said, it's something."

"We'll set up a system," Ross agreed. "Rotate foraging, keep the stronger ones gathering wood, maybe send a few people deeper into the island to find more."

"Good thinking," the captain said. "Survival is about adapting, not just waiting."

Ross glanced back at the fire, watching Grace give a piece of rabbit meat to a younger survivor. "They're holding up better than I expected."

The captain's eyes softened. "Hope is just as important as food out here."

Ross nodded. "Then we have to keep hoping."

The captain clapped his shoulder. "In the morning, we'll figure out how to get those coconuts down without breaking our necks."

Ross managed a faint smile. "I'm with you, Captain."

The fire's warmth cut through the cool ocean breeze the next morning. A group of survivors rotated through gathering wood; their movements quick, although exhaustion continued to weigh on them. It wasn't home—nowhere close—but it was enough to keep them going.

Ross returned to camp, a bundle of coconuts over his shoulder. His shirt clung damp with sweat, and his arms ached, but a small smile touched his lips. Grace knelt nearby, tending to a younger passenger with a twisted ankle.

"You're becoming quite the medic," Ross teased, crouching beside her.

Grace smirked, brushing dirt from her hands. "I'm just trying to stay busy."

Before Ross could reply, a shout rang out, sharp against the quiet. "Hey! Something's floating in the water!"

Curiosity momentarily pushed aside exhaustion. Survivors rushed toward the shoreline. Ross and Grace exchanged a glance and followed.

A dark object bobbed on the waves, drifting closer.

"It's a suitcase!" someone called.

Two stronger passengers waded in, dragging the heavy suitcase ashore. The captain inspected it briefly, then unzipped it. Clothes—damp but wearable—spilled out.

Relief rippled through the group.

"We'll lay these out to dry," the captain announced. "Take what you need. They have to feel better than what you're wearing now."

Their clothes clung to their bodies like second skin, stiff and gritty. Each movement was a reminder of the week spent in damp misery. A sour, briny odor hung in the air, the scent of sweat, seawater, and survival. The thought of slipping into clean, dry clothes felt almost too good to be true—a simple luxury turned into a long-awaited salvation.

The suitcase was a precious lifeline. As clothes were spread out on a raft material, laughter erupted. Zoe held up a pair of oversized pants. "Not exactly fashion week, but it's better than nothing."

Grace found a cotton shirt and loose shorts that fit surprisingly well. She held up a pair of flip-flops. "Shoes," she said, smiling.

Ross grinned, holding a Hawaiian shirt against his chest. "I think I'm starting a new island trend."

"You'd look good in that," Grace teased, her smile softening.

As people found what they needed, the atmosphere in the camp began to shift. Laughter rippled through the air as survivors joked about their chosen clothes, sharing lighthearted stories that momentarily eased their burdens. It wasn't much, but it sparked a sense of camaraderie.

The days blurred together as the survivors adapted to island life. They established a routine: hunting small game and fish, foraging for coconuts and edible plants, and rationing the supplies they'd salvaged from the lifeboats.

Not all the plants they found were edible—something Ray learned the hard way. After popping a handful of suspicious-looking berries into his mouth, it wasn't long before Zoe had to half-carry, half-drag him back to camp as he groaned in misery. The ill-fated snack took its toll, leaving him out of commission for an entire day, making frantic dashes into the forest in a desperate race against nature.

Zoe stood over him, arms crossed, watching as he lay sprawled near the fire, looking defeated. She crouched beside him, her smirk unmistakable. Leaning in, she whispered, "I told you not to eat them." Then, with a mischievous glint in her eye, she added, "On the bright side, at least now you know what a full-body cleanse feels like."

The clothes from the suitcase became a small comfort, giving people something dry and clean to wear while they worked. Zoe often caught herself marveling at how resourceful everyone had become.

"We're like some kind of survival reality show," Zoe said one evening, poking at the fire with a stick. "Except there's no million-dollar prize at the end."

Grace laughed softly. "I'd settle for a warm shower and a piece of my mom's apple pie."

Ross joined them, carrying the crude weapon he'd carved from a sturdy tree branch. Its tip had been sharpened to a rough point—uneven but deadly, designed for fishing or defense against anything that might threaten their camp. He handed Grace another piece of discarded fish. "Did I hear someone mention apple pie? Pretend that's what this is. We caught even more today," he said, sitting beside her. "We're getting better."

"I don't want to get better. I want to go home," Grace said.

Ross glanced toward the horizon, where the sun was going down again. "They'll find us," he said quietly.

Grace nodded, her eyes fixed on the fading light. "I hope so."

Later that evening, as the sun dipped below the waves, Ross and Grace sat by the fire. He held up his makeshift spear, examining its roughly carved tip.

"This thing comes in handy. We're getting pretty good with it. Look how many fish we caught?"

"You're getting pretty good," Grace corrected, holding her ineffective spear. "I'm still figuring out which end is more dangerous." Her gaze drifted off, a wistful smile tugging at her lips. "I'd give anything for a plate of my mom's fried chicken, mashed potatoes smothered in gravy, and green beans right about now."

Ross chuckled, "Why are you torturing yourself?" He asked, glancing across the ocean sky. "Just like we found our way here, they will too."

Grace's eyes reflected the fading light. "I'm counting on that."

Ross's hand brushed hers. "Walk with me?"

She hesitated, glancing at Zoe, who smirked knowingly and waved her off. Curiosity tugged at Grace's lips, and she stood, following Ross toward the tree line.

The breeze rustled the leaves, the distant waves a constant rhythm. They walked in silence, the quiet between them oddly comforting.

Finally, Ross spoke. "Being out here... strips things down. Makes you see what really matters."

Grace nodded. "Right. That's because there's no noise, no distractions. Just... the truth you've been running from."

Ross glanced at her. "You've been running?"

She exhaled slowly, her gaze dropping to her hands. Slowly, she lifted her left hand, the thin gold band glinting faintly in the firelight.

"My marriage," she said softly. Her voice carried a weight that Ross didn't miss—an exhaustion.

Ross didn't interrupt, giving her the space to continue.

Grace exhaled shakily, "It hasn't been good for a long time. I thought if I tried harder and gave more, maybe things would change."

She paused, her lips pressing into a thin line. "But they didn't. And somewhere along the way... I lost myself."

A tightness clenched Ross's heart. He could see the pain etched into her face, the quiet battle she'd been fighting long before the storm had thrown them off course.

"I wasn't even me anymore," she continued, her voice barely above a whisper. "I was just... a version of myself that existed for him, not for me. You wrote something in your book..." Her brow furrowed as she tried to recall it. "You said, you don't lose yourself all at once; it happens in the small compromises." She turned to him. "That's what happened to me."

The rawness of her words hung between them, heavy and unyielding. "I don't even know who I am without him," she admitted, the words tumbling out before she could stop them.

Ross's jaw tightened. He nodded slowly, his voice low. "Then maybe it's time you find out."

They walked in silence, the distant crash of waves filling the spaces between their thoughts. The island air was warm but not stifling, carrying the scent of salt and earth.

Ross finally broke the quiet, his voice low but thoughtful. "I know the feeling, though. I stayed in a relationship much longer than I should've."

Grace glanced at him, curiosity flickering in her tired eyes.

"How long have you been married?" Ross asked.

"Five years."

He nodded, then tilted his head, his expression unreadable. "Well, that's impressive. How long hasn't it been good?"

She let out a small, humorless laugh, shaking her head. "Three of those five years."

Ross let out a slow breath. "That's a long time to feel trapped."

Grace nodded, her fingers instinctively brushing over her wedding band. "I kept thinking I could fix it. If I just did more and gave more, somehow, it would be enough. But I've been the only one trying."

Ross was quiet for a moment, then asked, "First marriage?"

Grace shook her head. "First and only. And you?"

Ross hesitated for a beat, his jaw slightly tightening before he answered. "I got close, but no."

Grace caught the shift in his tone, the barely perceptible change in his expression. "What happened?"

His gaze stayed forward, but his voice was quieter now. "My fiancée... died."

Grace stopped walking.

The words hung between them, heavy and unshakable.

She turned to him, her eyes searching his face. "Ross, I—I'm so sorry. That's tragic."

He nodded, but there was a tightness in his throat. "It was a long time ago, but yeah... It changed everything."

A sharp pang tugged at Grace's heart. She thought she knew pain, but losing someone like that? That was a different kind of heartbreak altogether.

She reached out without thinking, her hand grazing his arm—a silent acknowledgment of shared wounds, of under-standing that didn't need to be spoken.

Ross glanced at her, his expression softer now. "We all have our ghosts, don't we?"

Grace swallowed the lump in her throat, nodding. "Yeah. We do."

"I've heard that marriages sometimes go through rough patches." Ross said, his voice careful...measured. "Do you think it's fixable with counseling?"

Grace hesitated, the weight of the question settling between them like the shifting sand under their feet. "While on the ship, I had come to the conclusion that love—real love could not withstand betrayal. I mean, how could it be love if you have to fight to convince yourself that it existed?"

Their steps slowed, his words resonating. Grace's voice was soft. "I was so sure of what I wanted. I was healing, but now, I just want to go to my 'happy place.'"

"Which is where?"

"I'm not sure—to my mom—or back to my husband, Ethan? I don't know what I want anymore."

"What would make you choose Ethan over your mom?"

"Familiarity. He may have his flaws, but I'd accept them right now over being stranded out here."

Ross shrugged. "Being with Ethan must not have been so bad then. Huh?"

Grace let out a hollow laugh. "It was bad. He not only broke my heart, he shattered it."

The muscle in Ross's jaw flinched. "Is he the reason you came on the cruise? You needed to get away from him?"

"Uh-huh. I needed to clear my head. And look where that got me." She gestured broadly at the path ahead of them. "Marriage is supposed to be built on trust. It's supposed to be... sacred. A partnership where you can lean on each other, no matter what."

Ross nodded, sensing the pain behind her words. "It is," he agreed softly. "But not all partnerships are equal."

She gave a bitter laugh, her eyes glistening. "No, they're not. Sometimes, one person decides that promises don't mean as much as they once did. That loyalty is... optional."

Ross's jaw tightened again, but he said nothing, giving her the space to continue.

"I guess," she added, her voice faltering, "it's easy to ignore someone's sacrifices when you think you've found something—or someone—more exciting. But it leaves the other person feeling like... like they weren't enough. Like they never could be."

She turned to him then, her vulnerability laid bare. "Do you know what that feels like, Ross? To give everything you have and still not be enough?"

Ross's expression softened, his heart aching for her. "I do," he said gently. "And if that's how you felt, then you've been giving everything to someone who didn't deserve it."

He glanced at Grace as they strolled along the winding path, their footsteps filling the initial silence. He broke the quiet first.

"Do you ever think about how things would've turned out with Ethan if the storm hadn't happened?"

"As far as I was concerned, the first thing I was going to do when I got home was head straight for a divorce attorney."

"And now?"

"Now, I'm not sure. Being out here like this jumbled my thoughts. Maybe Ethan's had time to think too. I guess I'll find out when I get home—if I get home."

Ross smiled gently. "We'll get home, Grace."

She slowed her steps, tilting her head to glance up at him. "What made you choose a three-day cruise, Ross?"

He smirked, the corner of his mouth lifting with a hint of self-deprecation. "I needed inspiration for my next book. A friend swore a cruise was the perfect way to recharge—something about being surrounded by water and people without fully going off the grid."

Grace let out a laugh, light and warm. "That's rich. A creative escape that turns into the survival adventure of the year. How's that working out for you, Mr. Henderson?"

Ross chuckled, running a hand through his hair. "Oh, just splendidly. Nothing fuels inspiration like rationed coconuts and near-death experiences."

They laughed together and continued on their walk, their steps now synchronized.

She took a deep breath and pressed on. "I came on this cruise to figure out my life, Ross. My marriage, my future. Zoe practically dragged me here—she thought I needed an escape. And now, look at us." She gestured around at the wild landscape with a dry laugh. "Stranded in the middle of nowhere."

They walked on, their conversation trailing off into the sound of the waves. Neither of them pressed for more content in the connection that seemed to grow with every step.

CHAPTER EIGHTEEN

The shoreline had become their refuge. As a pastime, Ross and Grace had taken to walking here in the evenings, their conversations flowing as freely as the tide. They often spoke about life—testing the waters with philosophical questions, teasing out each other's perspectives. Tonight was no different.

"Do you think people ever really change?" Grace asked, her gaze fixed on where the ocean and sky blurred into a single, endless stretch.

Her words sank into the silence between them. Though she didn't mention Ethan's name, it was clear she was wrestling with the question of whether her future still included him.

Ross considered her question, his hands tucked into the pockets of his shorts. "I think people evolve," he said after a moment. "But change? Like flipping a switch? That's rare. It's more like... they grow into who they've always been meant to be."

Grace nodded thoughtfully, brushing a strand of hair from her face. "That makes sense. Growth feels more natural than trying to force change."

Ross smiled faintly. "Why do you ask?"

She hesitated, her pace faltering slightly. "I guess I'm trying to figure out what I'm meant to do next. I thought my decision was firm until this happened to us. Now, I'm starting to second-guess myself." Her voice softened as she added, almost as an afterthought, "Should I stay or go?"

Ross's gaze softened as he noticed the doubt in Grace's eyes. He stopped walking and turned slightly to face her. "Should you stay or leave?" he repeated gently, his voice steady.

Grace nodded, her arms wrapping around herself as if shielding against the breeze—or her uncertainty. "I've been asking myself that question over and over," she admitted, her voice barely above a whisper. "I just don't know if I'm holding onto something that's already gone or if I'm too scared to let it go."

Ross took a step closer. "I can't tell you what to do, Grace," he said softly. "But I do know this—you deserve to be where you feel loved, respected, and at peace. If staying feels like fighting a losing battle, maybe leaving isn't about giving up. Maybe it's about choosing yourself."

She glanced away, trying to process what he was saying—and to analyze what she already knew deep down.

"It's not just about me," she said, almost to herself. "It's about everything I thought my life would be. Everything I tried so hard to build."

Ross nodded, his voice sincere. "I believe sometimes the hardest part of growth is letting go of the picture you had in your head—so you can make room for something better. Only you can decide if staying means staying true to yourself."

Grace looked up at him, the vulnerability in her eyes meeting the quiet strength in his. Everything else fell into a blur, leaving only the truth they both felt but hadn't yet spoken.

Ross cleared his throat nervously and nodded, his tone lighter now. He glanced at her, a hint of a smile playing on his lips as they continued walking along the shoreline. His voice softened, carrying an undertone of something he'd been holding back.

"You know, when I saw you on deck that first day of the cruise..." He hesitated, his gaze shifting to the ocean momentarily before returning to her. "That wasn't actually the first time I saw you."

Grace tilted her head, curiosity glimmering in her eyes. "What do you mean?"

Ross slipped his hands into his pockets again, his pace slowing slightly. "I was standing at the ship's rail, watching people board. Just passing time, really. And then... I saw you."

Her brow furrowed. "On deck?"

"No," he said, his voice dropping just enough to draw her in, "before that. When you got out of the car. You weren't doing anything special—just grabbing your bag, looking around—but there was something about you. It was like you brought a piece of calm to all the noise."

Ross nodded again, a bigger smile tugging on his lips. "You were standing there, looking up at the ship like you were debating whether or not to board. I remember thinking, 'She's *not going to get on*.' And then I heard Zoe yell for you to hurry up, and it was like you came alive."

Grace tilted her head, her voice soft. "Really?"

"It's true. I saw you then, and something about you stood out. Like the universe had decided, I needed to notice you. What were you thinking that day?" Ross asked, glancing at the waves.

"I was wondering if I was doing the right thing by leaving when my life was in shambles."

"Because of your husband's affair?"

"Yep." She popped the "p," nodding as if confirming it to herself as much as to anyone else. "Because of his affair. My husband had an affair." Her voice faltered slightly as if the words were foreign, something she was saying aloud for the first time. She paused, her breath catching before she continued, her gaze fixed somewhere distant. "And that's not the worst of it." A bitter laugh escaped her lips. "His mistress—the one he's been seeing for three years—is pregnant. With his baby."

The muscle in Ross's jaw flinched, and he whistled softly through his teeth. "How'd you find out?"

She exhaled, her gaze dropping momentarily. "He told me—after I read the text messages on his phone."

Ross's brow furrowed. "Oh, so you already suspected he was messin' around?"

"I felt it," she admitted, her voice tight. "But he'd dismiss me whenever I brought it to his attention. Said I was imagining things—paranoid or jealous."

Ross nodded slowly. "So, you went through his phone to confirm it?"

She shook her head, her lips pressing into a thin line. "No. Actually, he left his phone on the counter one morning. It lit up with a text—a woman named Olivia. It was flirty, full of innuendos. I tapped on it, and... the whole thread of messages came up."

Ross wiped his hand across his face, his expression softening. "Whoa. I'm so sorry you had to go through that," he said, his voice laced with genuine concern.

Grace's shoulders lifted in a slight shrug as she let out a faint, bittersweet laugh. "Oh well," she said, her tone breezy but with a hint of resignation. "C'est la vie. Such is life."

Ross studied her for a moment, his brow still furrowed. "It doesn't have to be, you know. Life doesn't have to mean... accepting the hurt."

She met his gaze, a flicker of vulnerability flashing in her eyes before she quickly masked it with a small, forced smile. "Sometimes it does, Ross. Sometimes it's easier that way."

"Maybe," he replied softly. "But easier doesn't mean better."

He gently brushed a stray strand of hair from her face, lingering for a moment longer than necessary. The back of his hand grazed her cheek, warm and feather-light, sending a shiver down her spine. The world around them seemed to dissolve, leaving only the quiet intensity of the space they shared. Neither moved nor spoke as if doing so might shatter the beauty of the moment.

CHAPTER NINETEEN

T HE CAMPFIRE FLICKERED WARMLY, providing long silhouettes that danced across the makeshift shelters. The survivors huddled close, their conversations blending with the distant crash of waves. Grace sat on the edge of a log, staring into the dark forest beyond the firelight.

Her eyes narrowed as something moved in the trees—subtle but unmistakable. Then, in the blackness, two glowing orbs appeared. Her breath caught in her throat as she realized they were eyes. The eerie firelight reflected off them, giving them an otherworldly glow.

"Ross," she whispered, leaning slightly toward him. "There's something out there. Do you see it?"

Ross, seated beside her, glanced in the direction she indicated. His expression remained unchanged, but his hand instinctively rested on the spear he'd fashioned earlier that week.

"I've noticed it for a couple of nights now," he said, keeping his voice low to avoid alarming the others. "But tonight..." He paused, squinting toward the dense trees. "Looks like it brought friends."

Grace's stomach twisted as she followed his gaze. Sure enough, another pair of eyes emerged from the darkness, lower than the first but just as unsettling. The two sets of eyes stared at the camp, unblinking and unmoving—silently watching.

"What do you think it is?" Grace whispered, her voice wavering slightly.

"Don't know. Might be wild boar," Ross said, keeping his tone even. "Looks like quite a few of them. They're definitely watching us."

"Should we warn the others?" she asked, her voice rising slightly.

Ross shook his head, his gaze still fixed on the eyes. "No. Knowing the captain, he's already seen it. If he's not saying anything, there's a reason. No point in panicking everyone."

Grace nodded reluctantly, her grip tightening on the edge of the log. "What do we do?"

"Don't know. I'll go talk to the captain," Ross said, "I'll see what he knows and what he wants us to do about it. You stay here—and don't act scared. Predators pick up on fear." He rushed off.

Grace swallowed hard and nodded, though her heart pounded in her chest as she watched Ross slip away to find the captain.

Zoe had been watching Grace and Ross from the other side of the fire, where she sat with Ray. Something about their hushed conversation, their eyes darting toward the tree line, and Grace's tense posture set off alarm bells in her mind. When Ross walked into the darkness, Zoe got up, dusted off her hands, and made her way over to Grace, plopping beside her with an exaggerated sigh.

"Okay, Gracie," Zoe said in a low voice. "What's going on?"

Grace jumped slightly, her wide eyes meeting Zoe's. "What? Nothing's going on."

Zoe raised an eyebrow and crossed her arms. "Don't even try that with me. I've known you too long. You're doing that thing where you look like you've seen a ghost but pretend you didn't. And Ross? He practically bolted to the captain like the forest was on fire. What's going on?"

Grace hesitated, glancing nervously toward the tree line. The flickering firelight made her seem even more anxious, and Zoe noticed the way her hands fidgeted in her lap.

"Zoe, you can't say anything," Grace whispered, leaning closer. "There's... something out there."

Zoe stiffened, her voice dropping to a whisper. "Something? Like what? A bear? A boogeyman? Can you be a little more specific?"

Grace swallowed hard, glancing at the tree line again. "Ross thinks it's wild boar. Looks like quite a few. He's noticed them watching the camp for several nights now."

Zoe's mouth dropped open; her usual sass replaced with pure shock. "I'm sorry—did you just say boar? As in, big sow, sharp tusks, prowling in the night?"

Grace nodded, her voice shaky. "Yes. They're out there, watching us. Ross says the captain probably already knows. That's why he's gone to talk to him."

Zoe stared at Grace, her expression not just of disbelief but panic. "And you two weren't going to tell me? Oh, that's just perfect. Let's keep Zoe in the dark while fuckin' boars decide if we're dinner!"

Grace reached out, gripping Zoe's arm. "Zoe, please. Don't freak out. The captain might have a plan. As long as we stay here, by the fire, they won't come near us. I hope."

"Oh, the fire," Zoe said, gesturing dramatically toward the flames. "Great plan A. Because we all know animals are terrified of tiny campfires, right? That's foolproof. What's plan B?"

"Zoe," Grace hissed, her grip tightening. "I need you to calm down. The last thing we need is to panic everyone else."

Zoe took a deep breath, letting it out in a loud, exasperated huff. "Fine. But if one of those things decides to waltz into camp, I'm not staying quiet. I will scream bloody murder, Gracie. Just so we're clear."

Grace couldn't help but laugh softly, "I'd expect nothing less."

Zoe shook her head, glancing warily toward the tree line. "You're lucky I like you, Gracie," she teased, a playful smirk tugging at her lips. "Otherwise, everyone here would be wondering why I'm the one sleeping in a tree tonight."

Zoe's remark lightened the mood, and though it drew a nervous chuckle from Grace, Zoe edged a little closer, looping their arms together—a silent reminder that they weren't facing this craziness alone.

Ross found the captain near the edge of the camp, inspecting the dwindling firewood pile. He approached quietly, not wanting to startle the older man.

"Captain," Ross said in a low voice. The captain turned, his expression calm but alert. "We've got eyes on us."

The captain nodded slowly, his gaze shifting toward the tree line. "I know. They've been there a couple of nights now."

Ross crossed his arms, his voice dropping even lower. "What do you think it is?"

The captain's lips pressed into a thin line. "Probably a sounder of wild boar," he said finally. "Females with their young, since the males tend to be more solitary. That would explain all the other eyes."

Ross's stomach tightened. "Is it dangerous?"

"Extremely, if they feel cornered or think their young are in danger."

Ross glanced back toward the camp, his mind racing. "What's the plan? Do we warn people?"

The captain shook his head. "Not yet. We don't want to cause a panic, especially if they haven't made a move. I'm keeping an eye on them. We need to keep the fire going all night and stick together. That should keep them at bay for now."

Ross nodded, his jaw tightening. "And if it comes closer?"

The captain met his gaze, his voice hard. "Then we do whatever it takes to protect the group."

Ross returned to Grace, his expression composed, though the stiffness in his movements betrayed his unease. She and Zoe looked up at him, anticipation etched on their faces.

"What did he say?" Grace asked.

"They're wild boar," Ross said quietly. "Definitely more than one or two. He thinks they're curious, but we're not taking any chances. Keep the fire going, and don't wander off alone."

Grace's breath hitched. "Wild boar? I thought those were... somewhere else."

"They're here," Ross said firmly. "And they're watching. But the fire will keep them back."

Grace glanced toward the tree line, where the glowing eyes still lingered. They hadn't moved, but their presence was a constant strain on her nerves. "Do you think there's a chance they'll come closer?"

Ross placed a hand on her shoulder, his grip steady and reassuring. "Not if we keep the fire going. We'll be fine."

Regardless of what he said, Grace couldn't shake the feeling that the boars would come closer. As the night wore on, the fire burned brighter—but the watchers in the darkness remained, a silent reminder of the thin line between survival and danger.

The following morning, the sun hung heavy in the sky, beating down on them as they moved about the camp. The once-steady supply of rainwater had dwindled, leaving the group on edge. The captain walked over to Ray and Ross, a deep furrow in his brow.

"This is it," the captain said, gesturing toward the raft containing their drinking water. "We're down to the last of it. If we don't get rain soon, we're in trouble."

Grace glanced at the limited amount of water, her stomach knotting. "What do we do if it doesn't rain?"

"We'll figure something out," Ross said firmly, though his tone betrayed the worry lurking beneath his calm facade. "There are still a few coconuts on the trees, if we can figure out a way to get to them. We might need to go farther inland. It's risky, but we can't just sit here and do nothing."

Grace, still shaken, glanced up at Ross. "But... it's dangerous out there."

Ross gave a grim nod. "I know. Another reason to be careful—with our friends lurking around, but they're drinking water from somewhere. We need to find it."

The captain nodded grimly. "We'll have to consider it if it doesn't rain by tomorrow."

"We can move in pairs," Ross interrupted, his tone firm. "No one goes alone. And we'll stay alert."

The captain crossed his arms, his face thoughtful. "We'll need a plan. We can't send too many people out—we need to keep the camp secure and the fires going."

"I agree," Ross said. "Ray and I will go together. We'll keep it quick and stick to the edges of the forest. If we find a stream, we'll mark the path and come straight back."

"And what if you run into them?" Zoe asked, her voice tight as she hugged her knees to her chest.

Ross hesitated, his jaw tightening. "We don't run away. We stand our ground, make a loud noise, and use whatever we have," he held up his makeshift spear, "we also try to appear bigger, fiercer. Predators like them don't go after prey that fights back."

The group was scattered across the camp, some gathering firewood while others reinforced the canopies. The late afternoon sun cast long shadows on the sand, and the faint sound of waves mingled with quiet chatter.

A sharp, unmistakable hiss pierced the air, followed by a panicked yell.

"Ahhh! Damn it!" One of the survivors, Mark Baker's voice rang out, drawing everyone's attention. He stumbled back from the tree line, clutching his lower leg. "I think... I think it got me!"

Zoe spun around so quickly that she nearly tripped. Her eyes darted toward the sound, wide with fear.

"What the f..." she stammered, unable to finish her sentence as her voice caught in her throat.

The others rushed toward him as he collapsed to the ground. Grace and Ross were the first to reach him, their faces pale with fear.

"What happened?" Ross asked, crouching beside him.

Mark's breaths came in quick, shallow bursts. "A snake. It bit me... right here." He winced, pulling his hand away to reveal two puncture marks on his leg, already swelling and turning an angry shade of red. The skin around the bite began to discolor, stretching taut.

Ross glanced around frantically. "Did anyone see it? What kind of snake was it?"

"It sounded like a rattler," Ray said grimly. "I saw it slither off into the brush."

Grace's hand flew to her mouth. "Oh my God."

Mark groaned, his face slick with sweat. "It's burning. It's spreading. Do something."

"We need to slow the venom," Ross said urgently, his mind racing. "But we don't have a first aid kit... Damn it!" He stood abruptly, scanning the camp, hoping a solution would appear.

The captain rushed toward them. "What's going on?"

Ross pointed to Mark's leg. "Rattlesnake bite. We need to help him. Do we have anything?"

The captain shook his head slowly, the unspoken truth hanging heavily in the air. There was nothing anyone could do.

At first, they thought maybe it was just a graze. Maybe it wasn't a full envenomation. Maybe Mark would be one of the lucky ones.

But as the hours passed, the truth had become undeniable.

The swelling spread from his leg upward, creeping like an unstoppable force. His skin had turned a sickly shade, veins darkening beneath the surface. His breaths grew shallow—uneven. The pain—the agony—had been written across his face in a way that no words could capture.

"Am I gonna die?" Mark asked. His voice cracked as panic overtook him.

"No," Ross said firmly, gripping Mark's shoulder. "We're here for you. Just stay calm and keep talking."

"What do you want me to say?" Mark spat, tears brimming in his eyes. "How the hell am I supposed to stay calm when I know..." He broke off, his voice strangled by pain.

Grace knelt beside him, her hand trembling as she reached for his. "Mark, we're not giving up. Stay with us."

And then, the bleeding had started. From his nose. From his gums. From the wound itself.

Ray had tried to keep him still. Zoe had pressed a damp cloth to his forehead, whispering things that sounded like prayers. Ross had pressed down on his shoulders, trying to keep him grounded, as if sheer willpower could stop what was coming.

But none of them could stop it.

His body convulsed violently, a final desperate fight against the inevitable. Then, nothing.

The firelight cast flickering patterns over his face, but there was no life behind his half-lidded eyes.

Gone.

Ross let out a slow breath, the weight in his chest unbearable.

Zoe sat back, wrapping her arms around herself, staring at the sand. No jokes. No witty remarks. Just quiet.

Ray wiped a hand down his face, his voice raw. "We have to bury him."

Ross nodded but didn't move. His hands, still stained with the dirt and sweat of a fight they couldn't win, rested on his knees.

Finally, he exhaled, shaking his head. "He didn't deserve this."

No one did.

Grace watched from a few feet away, her face pale, her fingers digging into her arms as she hugged herself.

She had barely spoken since it happened.

Ross turned to her, his voice quieter. "You okay?"

Grace looked at him then, something hollow in her gaze. She didn't answer right away. Then, barely above a whisper—

"That could've been any of us."

Ross swallowed hard. She was right.

And the terrifying part? It still could be.

Ross's jaw tightened. He bowed his head. Grace sobbed quietly. The group stood in stunned silence. The strain of loss hung over them like a suffocating fog.

Ross placed a hand on Grace's shoulder, his touch anchoring her. "We can't just leave him like this. We need to bury him," she said softly. "But how?"

The camp was silent except for the crackling fire and the faint sound of waves lapping against the shore. The survivors stood in a somber circle, their faces reflecting the grief and exhaustion that had settled over them. The captain stood at the center, his expression grim but stern. He looked at the lifeless body of the man they couldn't save, the reality of their situation pressing down on him.

After a long moment of silence, the captain exhaled and addressed the group. "We don't have the means to bury him deep enough here," he said, his voice low but steady. "The ground's too rocky through the trees, and we can't risk drawing attention from predators. Our only choice is to lay him to rest in the water."

Gasps and hushed whispers rippled through the group. Grace clutched her arms tightly to her chest, Zoe reached for her hand, and Ross stood silently, his jaw tight.

One of the men stepped forward, his voice hesitant. "You're saying... we just let him drift out into the ocean?"

The captain nodded solemnly. "It's the only option. It's not what any of us want, but it's our most respectful choice. Without the right tools, we'd never be able to bury him deep enough."

Another man, older with a grizzled beard, frowned deeply. "Feels wrong. Feels like we're abandoning him."

"No," the captain said firmly, "We're not abandoning him. We're honoring him the best way we can in these circumstances. Out there," he gestured toward the water, "he'll be free. Not left to the elements or scavengers."

The survivors exchanged uneasy glances, the pressure of the moment heavy on all of them. Finally, Ross stepped forward, his voice steady. "I'll help carry him."

The captain nodded, gratitude flickering in his tired eyes. "Thank you. I'll need a few more hands."

Two other men stepped forward, their faces set with determination. Together, they gently lifted the body, draping a piece of the life raft over him like a shroud.

Grace turned to Ross as he moved past her. "Are you sure?" she asked quietly.

Ross glanced at her, his expression softening. "It's the least I can do."

"And from now on... we need to be more careful," the captain announced.

They exchanged solemn nods, the reality of their situation sinking in deeper than ever. They were not only fighting for survival; they were fighting against an environment that was as unforgiving as it was unpredictable. The cost of even a single mistake was devastating.

Grace felt the sadness of the loss settle deep in her bones, an ache spreading like a cold wave through her chest. Survival. The word echoed in her mind—hollow and relentless. Faces blurred together—one lost today, others long gone, swept away at sea. The thought of losing another was like standing on the edge of a cliff, staring into an endless void.

She turned to Ross, meeting his gaze. She saw something flicker in his eyes—a curiosity, a question. Then, he saw it too. The look in her eyes, the silent plea for something more—something she couldn't ask for, not now. Not while the remnants of Ethan's betrayal still tangled her thoughts.

In the blink of an eye, the moment slipped away. Grace turned her face, her eyes shifting back to the sky. But it didn't matter. He had seen it—the fragile flutter between them, something real, something they both longed for but felt they couldn't touch.

CHAPTER TWENTY

T HE WAVES LAPPED GENTLY at the shore, crashing against the sand, a soothing counterpoint to the heavy silence between them. Ross and Grace walked side by side, their footsteps leaving faint imprints in the damp sand, only to be washed away by the tide moments later. The evening sky, painted with streaks of purple and orange, seemed to stretch endlessly before them.

Grace could feel the stress of the day rest on her shoulders, the loss still fresh, the air thick with unsaid words. Every step felt like a small battle, her mind too full of confusion and guilt to focus on anything else.

She glanced at him from the corner of her eye. His expression was unreadable, but his presence was as solid as the ground beneath her feet. She could almost feel the pull of him—like the tide, steady and constant, a reminder that some things were just too complicated to name.

Ross finally spoke, his voice quiet but carrying the weight of something more.

"You ever feel like the universe is trying to tell you something?" he asked, glancing toward the horizon where the fading sun kissed the ocean's edge.

Grace turned to him, forehead creasing slightly, the question catching her off guard. "What do you mean?"

Ross paused for a moment as though considering the right words. "Like... everything that happens, all these little moments add up. And you don't always see it until after, but it's like there's this bigger picture you're not meant to see yet. You know?"

He looked at her then, his gaze intense, searching her face as if waiting for her to understand. He continued. "Like how we ended up here. This place, this mess we're in... feels like it was meant to happen."

A tightness coiled in Grace's chest as she processed his words. The idea of the universe guiding them felt too big, too grand for what they were enduring. Yet, in the quiet between them, it almost made sense. Maybe they were being led somewhere. Maybe all the pain, loss, and craziness happening around them wasn't random.

She didn't know how to respond, so she shrugged and said nothing.

"Do you believe in fate, Grace?"

She thought about the question, letting it hang in the air for a moment.

"I don't know if I believe in fate, exactly. I think life gives us moments—opportunities—and it's up to us what we do with them."

"That's interesting."

"Why so?"

Ross stopped walking suddenly, his expression shifting.

When Grace realized he was no longer beside her, she turned, her smile fading. "What's wrong?"

He closed the distance between them, his voice soft but steady, "You deserve so much more than you know." The air seemed to still. Grace's breath caught in her throat as Ross reached out, his hand brushing lightly against her cheek.

"Ross..." she began, her voice barely above a whisper.

Her hand against his chest meant to press a gentle restraint, but her fingers betrayed her intent. Instead, they slid up, finding the back of his neck, drawing him closer. Her lips parted slightly, a breathless invitation, and Ross leaned in, his mouth grazing hers in a soft, lingering kiss. What started as tender quickly deepened, their tongues meeting, moving in perfect rhythm with the pounding of their hearts. When Ross finally pulled back, his warm breath mingled with hers, the air heavy with unspoken words. He smiled, a quiet, knowing expression, his gaze searching her eyes for any sign—a flicker, a spark—anything that would tell him if this was a fleeting moment or something more.

She blinked, her chest tightened with the weight of the moment, her mind swirling with confusion and desire. "Ross," she whispered, "What are we doing?"

Ross didn't answer immediately. Instead, his hand slid gently along her jaw, his thumb brushing against her cheek. His touch was soft, almost reverent, and the tenderness in it made her heart swell as he said. "I'm Taking advantage of an opportunity," he murmured, his voice low and tender, teasing just slightly but with an undeniable sincerity beneath it.

Without hesitation, he leaned in again, kissing her slowly this time, savoring each second as though he were committing the moment to memory. When they finally pulled apart, his forehead rested against hers, and his words came out in a whisper, filled with emotion.

"Grace," he said, his voice heavy with a longing that matched her own, "If the universe is giving us this moment, let's not waste it."

Her eyes shimmered with unshed tears, and she started to look away, unable to fully meet his gaze, but Ross gently cupped her chin and guided her back, not letting her avoid him. "He doesn't deserve you," Ross said, his words firm and full of conviction. " Don't let him define what love looks like. You deserve so much better."

Grace swallowed, her chest tight with emotion, her heart aching under the gravity of his words. "But Ross, he's still my husband. I made a vow—for better or for worse. I feel the same intense pull between you and me, but I can't allow myself to become what I hated in him." she admitted, her voice barely above a whisper.

Ross's hand caressed her cheek, his gaze soft but intense. " It's clear to me that he can't give you the love and respect you truly deserve. You have the strength to move on and deserve someone who matches that strength. I see it, Grace. I see you. And if you let me, I'll show you what it means to be loved the way you deserve. No conditions, no half-measures—just all of me for all of you."

Tears slipped down her cheeks as she searched his face, her defenses crumbling under the weight of his words. "I don't know if I understand what that means," she whispered, her voice breaking. "I don't even know what love is supposed to look like anymore. I thought I knew once. Also, truth be told—I'm afraid."

He silenced her fears with a soft kiss on her forehead, his lips lingering just a moment longer. "I know you're scared," he said gently, his voice warm with understanding. "But I'm not Ethan. And I would never hurt you like he has. All I'm asking is for a chance—to prove what a real man can do for a woman like you."

Grace closed her eyes, her breath catching as his words draped over her. When she opened them again, she saw his gaze filled with quiet strength. It made her heart ache and hope, all at the same time.

"I don't know, Ross," she whispered, her lips curving into a faint smile, unsure but moved by the sincerity in his eyes. "What if I get home and Ethan and I are able to reconcile? Then I've hurt you."

Ross leaned in. His lips brushed the side of her cheek as he whispered, "That's a risk worth taking." His words struck a chord she wasn't ready to acknowledge. She looked away.

Ross smiled, brushing a strand of hair away from her face. "All I'm asking is for a chance," he said softly. Then, stepping back just enough to give her space, he added, "No pressure, Grace. I'll be here when you're ready."

With that, he gently took her hand, his touch grounding and warm. "Come on," he said. "We'd better get back before it gets too dark, or Zoe comes looking for us."

Grace nodded, the tension easing just a little as she allowed him to pull her along, knowing, in the face of everything, something profound had just happened between them.

Chapter Twenty-One

REPORTERS WERE ALLOWED BACK into the cruise office with a stern warning to respect the families. They lined the edges of the room like a living wall of spectators, their lenses aimed and hungry for a fresh angle to fuel the next headline.

Employees darted between desks, their movements hurried as the air thickened with desperation. Nearby, Mrs. Davis sat, her face pale and drawn. The tension in the room was suffocating. "How do they expect us to stay calm while our families are out there—somewhere—and these reporters have their cameras stuck in our faces?" Mrs. Davis muttered.

She rose abruptly, pressing a nervous hand to her forehead. "I need to step away for a minute," she whispered and hurried toward the bathroom.

Inside, she splashed cold water on her face, gripping the sink tightly as she stared at her reflection. "Pull yourself together," she whispered. But the reflection staring back at her was weary, helpless.

When she returned to the waiting room, she paused in the hallway. Ethan stood just a few feet away, his back to her, his head resting on his forearm against the wall. He spoke in hushed tones on the phone, but his voice carried, and she couldn't help but overhear.

"Baby, I know... I miss you too," Ethan muttered softly. "You know I love you, Olivia. But I have to be here right now."

Mrs. Davis froze, her heart sinking. She crept closer, careful not to make a sound.

A nearby reporter slowly turned his camera in their direction and whispered to his comrade, "Hey, this might be something."

"Yeah," Ethan continued, "I told her everything before she left. She knows about you and the baby. I want to see you too, but I can't leave right now. I need to be here. I'll come by later." He paused, listening to the person on the other end, and said, "Yeah, it's been over a week, and they still haven't heard anything. So, if she's dead... our lives are getting ready to change drastically. I trust you're ready for that."

Mrs. Davis's blood ran cold. She took a step closer, barely breathing, moving with a deliberate calm that silenced even the reporters. A camera zoomed in on her steely gaze, and tension hung in the air. Whispers rippled through the group of journalists. One reporter exchanged a glance with another. "Isn't he the 'grieving' husband of one of the missing passengers? What do you bet that's not his missing wife he's talking to."

Ethan hung up and turned. His face immediately drained of color when he saw her standing there, eyes narrowed, lips pressed into a tight line.

"Who's Olivia, Ethan?" Mrs. Davis asked, her voice full of suspicion.

Ethan stiffened, slipping his phone into his pocket. "Just a friend," he said briskly.

"A friend?" Mrs. Davis asked, sharpening her gaze. "Why are you telling your 'friend,' Olivia, that you love her while my daughter—your wife—is out there, somewhere?" She gestured wildly toward the office window, her fury rising with each word. "If you've got somewhere else you need to be, GO. Why are you here when you've got Olivia waiting for you?"

Ethan's face flushed, and his eyes darted nervously around the room. "Mrs. Davis, I think you're blowing this completely out of pro..."

"I don't think so." She said, cutting him off, "I know exactly what I heard. So that's why Grace suddenly decided to go on a trip. She was getting away from you."

His jaw clenched, but Mrs. Davis wasn't finished. She stepped even closer, her eyes blazing. "Let me ask you again. Why are you here?" She demanded, "If you don't love Grace and can't wait to see Olivia, why are you standing here pretending? For the cameras?"

Ethan's smirk faltered under her glare. "Look, I care about Grace, okay? Maybe I'm not ready to end the marriage yet."

"You're not ready?" Mrs. Davis's voice was thick with disbelief. "You have a mistress and a baby on the way, and you're not ready to end your marriage?" No. You're not ready to lose the wife who's been taking care of you for five years. The woman whose money supports your lifestyle. That's what this is really about, isn't it? You're not ready to fend for yourself. You're a lousy excuse for a man. You're waiting around, hoping Grace is... d—hoping they don't find her so you and Olivia can live off her money. You're nothing but a leech. A parasite."

Ethan bristled. "That's not true. Grace and I have a mutual understanding."

Mrs. Davis's laugh was sharp and bitter. "An understanding? Grace would never understand you sneaking around with another woman. She found out about you and Olivia. Ethan, you have stripped my daughter of everything she ever thought she loved.

The room fell silent as Mrs. Davis's words hung heavily in the air.

"Man, this is gold," one cameraman muttered.

"Yeah, get it all," another whispered urgently.

They exchanged knowing glances, their mics vibrating with excitement.

"Zoom in on her face. She's furious," another reporter said as her mic brushed her lips. "Get closer."

Ethan's face darkened, but Mrs. Davis wasn't finished. "You don't love her. And if you have even an ounce of decency left in your selfish heart, you'll get out of her life and let her find the happiness she deserves."

Ethan opened his mouth to respond, but Mrs. Davis raised a hand, silencing him. "Don't bother, Ethan. I've heard enough."

Mrs. Davis's voice softened, though her anger remained. She shook her head, tears pooling as her words cut through the air. "You've done more than hurt her. You've crushed her. The woman I saw the last time she visited me was barely holding herself together. And now I understand why." She took a deep breath, her voice lowering but gaining more weight. "Grace deserves better than you. And one day, she'll realize it. God help her. I'd like to think she's somewhere realizing it right now and comes back with the strength to get you out of her life for good."

Ethan opened his mouth to respond, but the disgust in Mrs. Davis's eyes stopped him cold.

Without another word, she turned sharply and left him standing there, his excuses and deflections hollow in the wake of her fury.

Ethan remained in the corner of the cruise office lobby, his face a mask of simmering anger. Mrs. Davis's public chastisement still echoed in his mind, and the curious, judgmental glances of everyone around him weighed heavily on his shoulders. He could feel their eyes on him—reporters, families, and staff —whispering among themselves, just low enough for their words to sting. Even Karen Fletcher stood in her doorway, shaking her head in disbelief.

He sat as far away from Mrs. Davis as possible, crossed his legs, and bounced his foot aggressively on his knee, the movement betraying his embarrassment. His fists clenched and unclenched on the armrests of the chair.

Reporters moved around him, capturing his expression from every angle.

Mrs. Davis's words repeated in his head, each one cutting deeper than he wanted to admit. She had stripped him of all his pretense, reducing him to a caricature of betrayal in front of strangers. Now, in their eyes, he was exactly that.

Unable to take it anymore, Ethan stood abruptly. A few heads turned, their expressions unreadable but heavy with judgment. His jaw tightened as he grabbed his jacket, muttering under his breath, "This is ridiculous."

Without another glance at Mrs. Davis or anyone else, he strode toward the door, his shoulders stiff with indignation.

As the door swung shut behind him, Mrs. Davis muttered, "Good riddance, jackass."

A faint ripple of conversation spread through the room, followed by suppressed chuckles and knowing glances exchanged among the reporters. Mrs. Davis didn't care who heard. She exhaled deeply, feeling a small weight lift from her chest. She returned to the task, praying they'd find her daughter and bring her home.

Someone in the crowd had pulled out their phone and recorded the entire confrontation, capturing every cutting word, every camera flash, and every flicker of Ethan's faltering confidence. The raw, unfiltered clip was uploaded, and within minutes, the video began circulating on social media, accompanied by hashtags like:

#MrsDavisSpeaks and #GraceDeservesBetter.

Comments flooded in:

"This is the kind of mother everyone needs."

"Ethan's face when she called him a leech and a parasite—priceless."

"Protect Mrs. Davis at all costs."

The flashes from the cameras slowed, but the damage was already done. Ethan's carefully constructed facade had crumbled—and the world was watching.

The camera caught the tears welling in Mrs. Davis's eyes as she watched Ethan's exit. Her final words were captured by every social media platform on the internet: "Good riddance, jackass."

The clip exploded on TikTok first, with captions like:

"The showdown of the century: Mom vs. Narcissist."

"Ethan's downfall, courtesy of Grace's mom."

"Mrs. Davis for President—this is how you defend your daughter!"

The comment sections flooded with reactions:

"This woman deserves an award for how she handled this!"

"Grace, I hope you know how amazing your mom is. She's a superhero. Dump him already!"

"Ethan's face when he knew he was caught—PRICELESS!"

The video spawned hashtags like #MrsDavisSpeaks, #StandUp-ForGrace, and #DumpEthan. Reaction videos flooded social media, with people reenacting Mrs. Davis's fiery takedown or offering commentary.

As for Ethan? His attempts to spin the situation only fueled the fire, as the world collectively decided that Mrs. Davis's words were a truth that couldn't be ignored.

Chapter
Twenty-Two

T HE RAIN STARTED SUDDENLY, a relentless downpour that soaked everyone within moments. They scrambled to their shelters, but Grace stood still, her hands frozen on the canopy she tried to tie down.

Ross appeared by her side, a quiet determination glimmering in his eyes. "Grace, you're getting drenched," he said, gently tugging her under a piece of tarp he held over both of them.

"I'm fine," she protested, but the tone of her voice suggested otherwise.

"You're shivering," he countered, pulling the tarp tighter around her shoulders. His fingers lingered for a moment as he adjusted the covering. "You've got to take care of yourself, you know."

She threw herself into gathering wood, helping tend to the injured, and finding anything—everything—that could distract her from the thoughts inside her mind. The camp was a constant flurry of activity, each task keeping her tethered to reality.

But Ross was always there no matter how hard she tried to distance herself. Never too close, never too far away.

She'd feel his gaze sometimes, unwavering, like a lighthouse cutting through her crazy thoughts. When she looked up from whatever she was doing, she'd spot him in the distance—talking quietly with the captain, helping someone tie down a shelter, or carving tools with Ray. His hands were always busy, his focus intent, but the way he kept her within his sightline rattled her the most.

One morning, her frustration boiled over as she struggled to split a stubborn coconut. She slammed the husk onto a rock, the impact jarring her hands. Her breath came in short, angry bursts.

"Need some help?" Ross's voice was gentle, the question loaded with quiet understanding.

She stiffened, refusing to look up. "I can handle it."

"I know you can," he said, his tone calm. He didn't step back, didn't push. He just waited.

Her hands shook as she tried again, but the husk refused to give. She felt her composure slipping. *Damn it.* She wouldn't break down. Not here. Not in front of him.

A warm hand covered hers, stilling her movements. His touch was light, his fingers barely pressing against her skin.

"Grace," he said softly, "it's okay to let me help you."

Her throat tightened, and she shook her head, her voice a strained whisper. "I don't need you to save me, Ross."

"I'm not trying to save you. Let me help."

She closed her eyes. Ross's hand lingered for a moment longer before he pulled away, giving her the space she thought she needed. But he didn't go far. He never did.

Ross settled a few feet away, picking up a piece of driftwood and quietly carving it with the knife. The distance between them was enough for her to breathe, but not so much that she felt abandoned. He seemed to have perfected a delicate balance—giving her freedom while tethering her with his steady presence.

One week blurred into another. The more Grace tried to wall herself off, the more Ross's quiet determination chipped away at her defenses. Grace found herself both comforted and unnerved by Ross's quiet steadiness. He never demanded answers, never pressed too hard. Yet, his presence was unmistakable, like the steady pull of the tide—gentle but impossible to ignore.

As the setting sun spilled streaks of gold and crimson across the water, Grace wandered along the shoreline, the cool waves licking at her ankles. The rhythmic ebb and flow of the ocean mirrored the war within her—a push and pull she couldn't escape.

She paused, the wind tangling her hair as she stared out at the ocean. The sound of approaching footsteps broke the stillness, and without turning, she knew it was Ross. He didn't speak, choosing instead to stand beside her, his gaze fixed on the fiery horizon.

As the group gathered around a modest fire, Ross handed Grace a piece of fish, slightly larger than the others.'

"This is too much, Ross," she protested, pushing it back toward him. "You need it."

"You didn't eat much yesterday," he said simply, sitting beside her. "You need it more than I do."

Her stomach growled, betraying her hunger, but she hesitated. "You'll go without," she said softly, her tone carrying a mix of concern and frustration.

Ross's gaze held hers. "I'll manage. Just eat."

The warmth of his gesture tugged at something deep inside her, even as the familiar weight of guilt followed. She took a small bite but couldn't ignore the unease rising in her chest.

After a moment, she set the food down and turned to him, her voice barely above a whisper. "You can't keep doing this."

Ross met her gaze. He gave her a reassuring smile and said softly, "Caring about you isn't something I can just turn off."

Grace shook her head. "But you're putting me before yourself, Ross. You can't keep doing that. It's not fair."

"Making sure you're okay doesn't take anything away from me. It's not a burden—it's a privilege."

Grace shook her head. "You are making this so difficult. I've got crazy shit going on inside my head –decisions that have to be made. And when you come to me with the last of your food, the warmth of a blanket, or even offering help for a task that you think might be too much for me, you cloud my thoughts. And I don't know what's right or wrong."

"Yes, you do, Grace. You've already given *him* a chance. He blew it. I'm only asking you to take a chance on us."

"I'm not free to make a decision like that."

"And I'm not stepping aside to make it easy for you to choose him when I know I'm the better choice. You matter to me—more than you realize."

"Ross, if I choose to pursue this thing between us, I hurt Ethan, and if I decide to go back to my husband, I hurt you. Either way, somebody gets hurt. I don't want you to get hurt because of me."

"You're not hurting me. If anything, you're healing parts of me I didn't know were broken. So, if it's okay with you, I'm going to keep showing up for you every chance I get."

Why, Ross?" she asked, her voice barely audible.

He leaned closer, his eyes searching hers. "Because you're worth it," he said. "Every moment, every effort—you're worth it."

She walked away, taking the food to a younger survivor who looked hungrier than she felt. As she moved briskly through the camp, her shoulders stiff with tension, Ross stayed where he was, watching her retreating figure.

The truth hit him hard: The truth struck him with brutal clarity: Grace wasn't simply running from him—she was fleeing from the bond they shared, a connection almost too overwhelming for her to face. But Ross wasn't the kind of man who would abandon someone he cared about, especially not now. Deep in his bones, he understood that she belonged to him, even if she couldn't bring herself to acknowledge it yet. A quiet certainty secured him, a determination that even her retreat couldn't shake.

"Grace!" he called and hurried after her.

She didn't slow down, her hands clenched at her sides, but he caught up, stepping in front of her path and forcing her to stop.

"Grace, wait," Ross said, his voice softer now. "Is this about the kiss? If so, I can't apologize for it. As a matter of fact, I crave more of it every day. But if it's bothering you that bad, I promise it won't happen again. Just—please—don't shut me out."

Her head snapped up, her eyes blazing with emotion. "That kiss..." her voice trembled. "That goddamn kiss keeps me awake at night, Ross. Your kiss burns in the depths of me, in a place I can't ignore no matter how hard I try."

Ross's heart pounded, his chest tightening as he took in her words. "Then why are you running from me? Why are you punishing yourself for something that feels so..."

"Right? This isn't right, Ross. It's wrong!" Grace said, cutting him off, anguish pouring out of her. "Don't you see that? It's all wrong. You and me, this... this thing between us. It shouldn't be happening."

Ross's jaw clenched, his eyes narrowing slightly. "You think about what Ethan did to you, Grace," he said, his tone hardened. "And then define wrong for me. Because I'll be damned if this is wrong..." he gestured between them, his voice breaking slightly.

Grace stared at him, her chest heaving, her glare sharp enough to cut. "It doesn't matter what Ethan did. What matters is what I'm doing. I can't be like him, Ross. I can't..." Her voice cracked, and she turned abruptly, walking away before he could see the tears threatening to spill over.

He stood frozen, his words caught in his throat, regret slamming into him. His eyes followed her retreating figure as she disappeared into the shelter area. This time, he didn't go after her. He stayed rooted in place, the weight of his own words hanging heavy in the air.

CHAPTER
TWENTY-THREE

THE FIRE BURNED SOFTLY. Grace sat staring into its glowing embers, her thoughts swirling in the quiet of the night. She barely noticed when Ray walked over, his footsteps crunching on the sand. He plopped down beside her, leaning forward with his elbows on his knees.

"Hey, Ray," Grace said, turning toward him with a faint smile. "What's up?"

Ray shrugged, his gaze fixed on the fire. "Nothing much. Just saw you sitting here by yourself and thought we could chat."

Grace chuckled lightly, her eyebrow quirking. "Mhmm. Chat, huh? Somehow, I don't think that's the only reason you came over here."

Ray looked at her, his mouth twitching into a sheepish grin. "All right, you got me," he admitted. "I know you and Zoe are good friends. Figured you might have some... insight."

Grace smirked knowingly. "Ah, so this is about Zoe. What's going on with you two? You've been spending a lot of time together."

Ray rubbed the back of his neck, a nervous habit she'd noticed before. "I like her, Grace. I really do."

Grace tilted her head, teasing him with a playful tone. "And let me guess—you want me to spill the details, don't you?"

"What do you mean?" Ray asked, his voice feigning innocence though his face betrayed him.

Grace laughed softly, leaning closer. "Ray, do you want me to tell you about Zoe or not? Just admit it."

Ray sighed and nodded, a grin tugging at the corner of his lips. "Fine. Yeah, okay. I want to know more about her. We've talked, and I think I'm starting to get her, but I want to hear it from her best friend. What's she really like?"

Grace's smile softened, and she leaned back, folding her arms as she considered how to answer. "Well," she began, her voice warm with affection, "Zoe's one of the most loyal people you'll ever meet. She'll go to the ends of the earth for the people she cares about."

Ray nodded, his expression serious. "Yeah, I've noticed that. She's got this... protective vibe."

"She does," Grace agreed, her tone more reflective now. "But she's also hilarious. I mean, she'll keep you laughing even when things are at their worst. She's the kind of person who makes you feel like everything's going to be okay just by being around."

Ray's lips curved into a small smile. "That's exactly how she makes me feel."

Grace's expression turned thoughtful. "But Zoe's been through a lot. She's strong, but a part of her is still healing. Her dad was never around. She doesn't even talk about him. And her mom... her mom passed away about six years ago."

Ray's face fell slightly. "That's tough. She's been through all that and still gives so much of herself?"

Grace nodded. "That's Zoe. But she's also careful. She needs a safe place to land, someone who will be patient and steady with her. She deserves that."

"I'd like to be that for her," Ray said quietly, his eyes meeting Grace's. "I really would."

Grace studied him for a moment, her gaze soft but assessing. "I believe you, Ray. And I'll tell you this—what you see with Zoe is what you get. She's real, through and through. She'll be good to you if you're good to her."

"That's what I'm figuring out," Ray said, his voice thoughtful. "So far, she's incredible."

"She is," Grace agreed, a small smile tugging at her lips. "Just don't screw it up. Or you'll have me to deal with."

"Message received loud and clear, Ma'am." Ray laughed, holding his hands up in surrender.

He gave a half-smile, looking down briefly before meeting her gaze again. "What about the other stuff. You know, the not-so-good stuff."

She crossed her arms. "The not-so-good stuff? You looking for reasons to back out already?"

Ray chuckled. "No, just trying to be realistic. Nobody's perfect, right?"

Grace turned her gaze toward Zoe, who was across the camp, animatedly talking to one of the survivors, likely telling some sarcastic joke to lighten the mood.

She looked back at Ray and gave a slight shrug. "Is there really a negative side of Zoe?"

Ray blinked at her as if waiting for a real answer.

Grace smiled, shaking her head. "Even if there was, what kind of friend would I be to spill her secrets when she's not standing here?"

Ray let out a short laugh, shaking his head. "Fair point."

She patted his arm. "That's something you're on your own with."

Ray sighed dramatically. "Great. Guess I'll have to do my own investigating."

"Sounds like a challenge. You up for it?" She asked with a grin.

Ray glanced back at Zoe, a thoughtful smile playing on his lips. "Yeah... I think I am."

The two sat in silence for a moment, the firelight flickering between them. Grace turned to him. "How exactly did you land a job on a cruise line?"

Ray chuckled, "Honestly, it's a bit of a story, really."

"Do tell," Grace laughed.

"It all started when I was just a young boy, polishing the finest whiskey glasses in a little pub on the corner of 5th and Main, dreaming of bigger...things"

Grace laughed and raised an eyebrow. "Are you seriously about to give me the 'I worked my way up from the bottom' speech?"

His laugh was easy, warm as he continued, "I saw a listing for *The Emerald Princess*, and I knew it was my moment. A little hustle, a little charm, and a whole lot of confidence. I tracked down the job through one of those hospitality boards. He held up a finger. "But here's the thing: It wasn't just my resume that got me in. It was the glowing recommendation I got from the last bar I worked at. Trust me, once they saw that, the rest was easy."

Grace nodded in approval, pretending to be impressed. "So, it was all about who you knew, huh?"

Ray grinned. "Well, that and my sparkling personality," he said, raising an eyebrow. "I mean, I did have to prove I could handle the high-volume craziness of a cruise ship bar. You've seen the kind of crowd we get." "But it's not just about shaking up drinks. It's about keeping people happy. You know, making them feel like they're the most important person in the room. And then... of course, there's my secret weapon."

She leaned in and laughed again, "Secret weapon?"

Ray's eyes sparkled with amusement. "Oh, yeah. The charm. The wit. I can make an entire bar full of people feel like they're in the best show in town. And trust me, that's half the battle."

Grace let out a mock gasp. "A showman! How could I have missed that?"

"Hey," Ray said, holding up his hands in mock defense, "I'm just there to entertain." He pretended to pick up a shaker and toss it back and forth in his hands. "But here's the real kicker—after all the training they put me through to learn the drink menu and safety protocols, it was my military background that sealed the deal."

Grace blinked in surprise. "Wait, seriously? You're a vet? Thank you for your service."

Ray nodded, his expression softening just slightly. "Yeah, a few years in the military gave me the mental toughness you need for the job. I've been trained to keep cool in emergencies—whether it's a spill at the bar or something a little more... serious. It's the calm in the storm kind of thing, you know?"

Grace looked at him for a moment, her expression shifting to one of respect. "Well, I didn't know that about you, Ray. You're more than just a face behind the bar."

Ray chuckled, shaking his head. "Anyway, that's how I landed the job. A little military discipline, a lot of charm, and a reputation for getting people their drinks with a side of entertainment." He pretended to pour a drink and handed it to Grace.

Grace smiled, playing along, lifted the drink in a mock toast, and took a playful sip. "Well, I think they're lucky to have you, Ray, and so is Zoe."

Grace finally nudged him with her elbow. "Go on then. If you like her so much, maybe stop sitting here chatting with me and go talk to her."

Ray grinned, standing up and dusting the sand off his pants. "Thanks, Grace. I owe you one."

"Yeah, yeah," Grace teased, waving him off. "Just make her happy."

Ray gave her a quick nod before heading off toward Zoe, his steps a little lighter, his confidence a little stronger. She watched him go, her smile lingering as she turned back to the fire.

Ray moved quietly through the camp, his eyes fixed on Zoe as she sat near a different fire area, the soft glow of the flames painting her face in warm hues. She didn't notice him at first, her attention lost in the dance of the firelight. But when he lowered himself onto the sand beside her, she turned to him, her lips curving into a gentle, surprised smile.

He leaned in, his movement slow and deliberate, brushing his lips softly against her cheek. She closed her eyes at the touch, her breath catching just slightly. He lingered there for a moment before letting his lips drift down to the side of her neck, the warmth of the gesture sending a quiet shiver through her. Her hand rose instinctively, her fingers grazing the side of his face in a tender caress.

Zoe tilted her head, welcoming the closeness, her face turning toward him as if drawn by gravity. Their lips met, the kiss unhurried and full of quiet promise. It wasn't rushed or frantic but deeply personal, a silent conversation between two hearts seeking connection amidst their unpredictable circumstances.

Grace watched them from her spot a few feet away, the firelight flickering in her eyes. A soft smile touched her lips as she observed the tenderness between them. It wasn't jealousy she felt, but a warm sense of approval. For a fleeting moment, the weight of survival lifted, replaced by the simple beauty of human connection.

Ray leaned closer, his lips brushing Zoe's ear as he whispered something only she could hear. She nodded, a quiet laugh escaping her, and then the two rose to their feet. His arm slipped around her shoulders naturally—protectively, as they turned and began to walk toward the small shelter area Ray had claimed for himself.

As they moved away, Zoe glanced back over her shoulder at Grace. Their eyes met, and Zoe smiled—a wordless acknowledgment of trust and gratitude. Grace nodded in return, her smile deepening as she silently urged her friend forward, giving her blessing without saying a word.

The campfire hissed softly. The night felt like an embrace wrapping around them. For a moment, all was calm, and love, even in the midst of hardship, found its place.

CHAPTER
TWENTY-FOUR

Ross continued to stay close, a quiet, steady presence that never strayed too far. Whether gathering supplies or sitting together on the beach, his watchful eyes followed her, not out of obligation but out of care. Every now and then, as the tide whispered against the shore, his hand would brush against hers as light as a breath yet charged with meaning.

Their eyes would meet, lingering for a fleeting moment before one of them looked away, the tension weaving between them like a thread. It was a silent promise, a connection neither dared to name, but both felt. Grace's heart raced in those moments, torn between the pull of his quiet devotion and the walls she tried to keep intact.

The sun hung low over the horizon, painting the beach in soft hues of gold and pink. They were sitting in comfortable silence near the shore, the sound of the crashing waves filling the space between them. Ross shifted slightly, allowing his arm to brush against hers. Each touch sent a jolt through Grace, her heart racing even as she tried to keep her face neutral.

Ross caught her gaze for a moment, his eyes warm and searching. She felt the tug again—the one that made her want to lean closer, to say something, anything, but the words stuck in her throat. She turned her face to the ocean, trying to compose herself.

"Oh, for crying out loud," Zoe's voice rang out, breaking the quiet moment. Grace looked up just as Zoe plopped onto the sand between them, cutting off their line of sight like a wall. "You two need to get a room or whatever the island equivalent is," she teased, grinning mischievously.

Ross raised an eyebrow, amused. "A room? Really?"

"Yes! Or at least try to be a little less obvious," Zoe said, dramatically fanning herself. "My God, the chemistry between you two is enough to set this whole island on fire. Watching you is like experiencing the push and pull of two lovers in a romance novel." She glanced from Grace to Ross, her grin widening. "Keep it up, and I swear, we're all going to have an emotional breakdown from secondhand longing."

Grace's cheeks turned crimson, and she immediately looked down at the sand. "Zoe," she muttered, her voice tinged with embarrassment. "You're imagining things."

"Imagining?" Zoe shot back, her voice laced with disbelief. She gestured between them. "Grace, honey, I could cut the tension with a butter knife. I've seen less smoldering in bonfires."

Grace's words slipped out in a harsh whisper, edged with urgency, and barely contained frustration, "Zoe!"

Ross chuckled, shaking his head. "Is that so?" he asked, his voice calm but his lips twitching with amusement.

"Oh, don't play coy, Ross," Zoe said, nudging him with her elbow. "You've been glued to her side since we got stranded. Protecting her, watching over her, and finding excuses to accidentally brush her hand. You're not fooling anyone."

Grace groaned, covering her face with her hands. "Zoe, please."

"What?" Zoe said, shrugging dramatically. "I'm just saying what everyone's already thinking. The kids have started calling you the island's lovebirds. Did you know that?"

Ross laughed softly, his eyes twinkling as he glanced at Grace. "Well, that's news to me."

Grace glared at Zoe, her mortification now mixed with exasperation. "You're not helping."

"Oh, I think I'm helping plenty," Zoe said with a smirk. "You've been stuck in your head for days, Grace. Maybe it's time to admit what's glaringly obvious to the rest of us."

Grace shook her head vehemently. "It's not like that. Ross and I are just... friends."

Zoe snorted, crossing her arms. "Friends? Yeah, sure. And I'm the Queen of England." She turned to Ross, arching an eyebrow. "What about you, Mr. Henderson? Do you buy this whole 'just friends' thing?"

Ross's smile faded slightly, and he looked down at the sand, choosing his words carefully. "I think Grace has been through a lot," he said quietly. "She doesn't need me—or anyone else—pushing her into something she's not ready for."

Grace glanced at him, her heart twisting at the tenderness in his voice. "Ross..."

Zoe leaned back, throwing her hands up. "Well, look at that. Even his restraint is romantic. Seriously, I can't take this anymore." She stood up dramatically, brushing the sand off her clothes. "I'll leave you two to your friendship, but don't think for a second you're fooling anyone."

As Zoe walked away, she called over her shoulder, "Just make sure you invite me to the wedding!"

Grace groaned again, her face buried in her hands. "I'm going to kill her."

Ross chuckled, leaning back on his elbows. "She's not wrong, you know."

Grace peeked at him through her fingers, her voice soft. "Not wrong about what?"

"There is something very special here," Ross said, his eyes meeting hers. "But I'll let you decide what to do with it."

"Really? You're going to let me decide?"

"Maybe." He smiled. With a little help from me because I know you so well."

She looked at him with disbelief. "You've only known me for a couple of weeks. How can you say you know me well?"

"If you treasure something, you take the time to read the fine print to know how to care for it."

Grace laughed, "What is that supposed to mean?"

He looked out at the ocean and smiled, "Sometimes, Grace Hargrove, I think I know you better than you know yourself."

"What do you think you know about me?"

"I know that you tuck your hair behind your ear when you're thinking like you're trying to make room for your thoughts. I've even done it for you a few times. I know that you hold on to things long after they've stopped serving you because you care so damn much. And I know you stay in the quiet moments just a little longer than most people. Like you don't want to rush through something that feels important."

Grace couldn't find the words to respond, so she simply looked away, the weight of Zoe's teasing and Ross's quiet admission settling heavily over her. The ocean seemed louder now as if the waves were echoing her conflicted emotions.

Most of the survivors had settled into their makeshift shelters for the night. Only she and Ross were left sitting together by the fire, watching it spit its embers into the night sky.

His mind was restless, swirling with thoughts he could no longer ignore. He turned to Grace and offered his hand as he stood. "Walk with me? He asked."

Grace looked up, surprised by the serious tone in his voice. "Sure," she said, standing up and brushing the sand off her hands. She followed him a short distance from the camp, the fire's soft glow shrinking behind them.

"What's up?" she asked, her voice light, though her heart sped up.

Ross hesitated, running a hand through his hair as he glanced at her. "I've been thinking about what to do with this—*friendship* of ours."

Grace opened her mouth to respond, but he held up a hand. "Let me get this out first," he said gently. "I know this island isn't the place for this, and the timing is completely off, but I have to say this. I care about you, Grace, more than I should, given our current situation. I don't think it's just because of what we've been through here. From the first moment I saw you, I felt something... a magnetic pull. I can't explain it," Ross said, his voice low, eyes locked onto hers. "I know you feel it, too. It's like," he shook his head slowly, "what we talked about before—the universe is trying to tell us something. I want to take the time to listen to it, Grace. I want to explore whatever this is between us. But I need you to want it, too."

Grace blinked, caught off guard by the raw honesty in his words. She felt a warmth rise in her chest, but it was quickly followed by the familiar shroud of guilt.

"Ross," she began, her voice barely a whisper.

He cut her off. "You're feeling guilty because you're obligated to Ethan, but you're in love with me."

Grace's heart sank. She looked away, her arms crossing in front of her as if to shield herself from his words. After a long pause, Grace said, "I won't lie to you—I have feelings for you."

He studied her. His expression softened, "You love me, Grace, plain and simple. Stop trying to act like you don't. It's not working for you."

"Ross, you're not making this easy."

"I don't intend to. I've watched you torment yourself over someone whose loyalty has been a lie. Are you really going to let his actions define what's right for you? You keep saying we met at the wrong time. But, Grace... what if the storm, the shipwreck, the chaos—what if all of it had to happen just so I could find you? "

"But you don't just walk away from years of a life together like it meant nothing. What he did hurt me to my core, but he's still my husband. I made vows, Ross. And as much as I want to ignore them for you, I can't."

Ross stepped closer, his voice low but steady. "You don't owe him anything, especially your loyalty. He broke those vows when he cheated on you. When are you going to see that you deserve so much better?"

Tears welled in Grace's eyes as she shook her head. "I don't know what I deserve anymore. And it's not just about him—it's about me. I can't make this kind of decision while we're stuck on an island. It's just not right. How can you ask me to do that?"

Ross sighed, the tension in his shoulders visible as he searched her face. "I'm not asking you to choose me or Ethan. I'm asking you to choose you."

The air between them was thick with a whirlwind of emotions. Grace's arms were still crossed tightly over her chest, her eyes fixed on the ground to avoid meeting his. On the other hand, Ross couldn't look away, his expression desperate and determined.

"Grace," He began, his voice steady but laced with raw emotion. "I'm not giving up on us. And you can't either."

She squeezed her eyes shut. Us. That word carved through her, shaking the walls she had built around herself.

"There is no 'us,' Ross," she said, her voice sharper than she intended. She forced herself to meet his gaze, her eyes brimming with an ache she refused to name. "You have to stop this."

Ross took a step closer, closing the space between them. "Stop what, Grace?" His voice was quiet, but the intensity behind it made her pulse race. "Stop loving you?" He shook his head, his jaw tight. "I can't do that. Not any more than you."

She took in a sharp breath. No, no, no...

"Am I wrong?" his voice dropped lower—rougher as if the words scraped his throat on the way out. "Can you look me in the eye and tell me you don't love me? That none of this means anything to you?"

Grace swallowed hard, her heart slamming against her ribs. Her lips parted, but no sound came out.

Because he wasn't wrong.

And they both knew it.

She pressed her nervous hands against her temples. "It doesn't matter what it means, Ross. It's still not right. None of it is. Regardless of how we feel."

"Right?" Ross repeated bitterly. "You're holding out for *right* in a situation where your husband betrayed you, lied to you, and broke every vow he made. And you're punishing yourself and me for... for what? Finally feeling—something real?"

"Don't do this," Grace whispered, shaking her head. "Please. Listen, I know I'm complicated."

"You're not complicated. You're human. You've been hurt, and you're careful with your heart. But loving you isn't hard, Grace. It's the easiest thing I've ever done."

The sound of waves crashing in the distance was a constant backdrop, but Grace barely registered it. Her footsteps faltered as she followed the path back to the camp. Her heart still pounding painfully in her chest, a war drum keeping time with the turmoil raging inside her.

Ross walked at her side, his strides longer, more urgent. The silence between them was heavy—thick with everything neither dared to say.

He reached out and pulled Grace back to face him. He took a deep breath, his shoulders rising and falling, his eyes searching hers with a mixture of frustration, hurt, and love.

"Grace," he started, his voice strained, "I would fight the world itself before I let Ethan have what I know belongs to me."

She closed her eyes. His words fell between them, thick and meaningful. She couldn't look at him. Not now. Not when every fiber of her being was pulling her toward him, begging her to give in.

Ross took a step closer, his presence a warm, steady force she wanted to collapse into. He gently reached for her hands, and she let him.

"Ethan will always be a cheater," Ross said, his voice low and careful, each word deliberate. "He broke your heart. He broke your trust. And he'll do it again."

He released her hands, dragging his own through his hair, his fingers digging in as if trying to tear away the frustration coiling inside him. He turned away and then spun back to face her. Through clenched teeth, he said, "I love you, Grace." His voice trembled with emotion, "I'm- in love- with you."

"Don't say that!" she snapped, her eyes flashing with anger, pain, and confusion all at the same time.

"Then you say it," Ross demanded. I'm willing to open myself up to you. To lay everything on the table. He stepped closer, the space between them shrinking. "Say you don't love me, and I'll walk away."

She tried to speak, but the words stuck in her throat, heavy and suffocating. Her lips trembled, her breath coming in sharp, shallow bursts. The truth clawed at her from the inside, desperate to be free, but she couldn't let it out.

"You can't, can you?" Ross whispered, his voice softening as he searched her eyes. "Because it's true. You love me. And it's tearing you apart."

He had been patient, given her space, and let her wrestle with her thoughts, but tonight, she had to hear the truth because it was tearing him apart, too.

"Grace," his voice was low but urgent, "I love you."

She opened her mouth, but he shook his head, stepping closer. His eyes searched hers for the truth she kept trying to bury.

"Ethan had five years compared to the short time I've known you, and I can tell you this, He will never love you the way I do. He will never know you like I do. You belong to me, and I refuse to let you slip through my fingers. This is what love is. It's precious...it's raw, unpredictable, and sometimes terrifying. But when it's real, you don't run from it—you fight for it."

"His hands curled into fists at his sides before he forced himself to relax, to reach for her instead—gently, as if afraid she might pull away. His fingers brushed her wrist, barely touching, yet sending a quiet, undeniable plea through the space between them.

A sob escaped her lips, raw and broken. "You don't understand."

"Help me then," he said, his voice rough now, "What are you holding onto? What is it that keeps you clinging to a man who treated your love like it was disposable when I'm standing right here, ready to love every part of you?"

"Because I have to!" she yelled. "I have to show Ethan it can be done. I can't do to him what he did to me just because it's convenient."

Ross's eyes widened, hurt and disbelief flickering across his face. "Convenient? This isn't about convenience, Grace. This is about love. Real, messy, complicated love. And you're throwing it away—to be what? A martyr for Ethan?"

Her eyes flared, and she took a step back. "A martyr? Is that what you think of me? I can't believe you're saying that."

Ross's tone softened, his frustration giving way to a quiet ache. "Why are you holding yourself to rules he's been breaking all along? Does everything need to be 'right' on paper for you to believe what's real between us?"

"It has to be right," she whispered, tears streaming down her cheeks. "Or it won't be real. Don't you see that?"

Ross's gaze held hers steady. "Here's what 'right' feels like to me, Grace."

Before she could resist, he pulled her gently into his arms, his eyes searching hers for permission. And then his lips, filled with hesitation and longing, pressed against hers and quickly deepened, igniting a fierce passion that neither of them could deny.

Her defenses crumbled. For a moment, she melted into him, her arms sliding around his neck. The warmth of his kiss and the strength of his embrace felt like everything she'd been yearning for.

But then reality struck her like a lightning bolt. The image of Ethan's betrayal, her shattered marriage, and the guilt she carried all crashed down upon her. She gasped, tearing her lips away, her hands shaking. She pushed Ross back.

His eyes widened, confusion and hurt etched into his face. "Grace..."

Her hand flew out, slapping his cheek with a sharp crack. The sound echoed in the night air, and the silence that followed was deafening.

Ross barely flinched. He stood there, his jaw tight, eyes locked onto hers, searching, pleading.

Her breath came in short, ragged bursts. "I can't do this," she choked out. "I can't."

"Grace, please..." he started, but she was already turning away.

She fled into the trees, branches whipping against her as she ran. Tears blurred her vision, but she didn't stop. She couldn't stop. The kiss still burned on her lips, a haunting reminder of everything she was running from and everything she was terrified to want.

"No, Grace!" Ross yelled, panic rising in his voice. "It's too dangerous!" But she disappeared into the darkened tree line.

Zoe rushed from the shelter in time to see Grace disappear. She sprinted over to Ross, her face pale with panic. "Ross! What the hell was that about? What just happened?"

Ross didn't respond immediately. He stood frozen, his gaze locked on where Grace had vanished. Zoe grabbed his arm, shaking him slightly. "Ross! Talk to me! What happened? What did you say to her?"

He put up a hand. "Zoe, please," he said. Without another frustrating word, he grabbed his spear and one of the waterproof blankets and rushed toward the same tree line.

Zoe stood stunned; her words caught in her throat as the forest swallowed him whole.

The captain emerged from his sheltered area, his expression stern. His eyes darted around the camp, "What is it? What's going on?"

Zoe yelled back. "It's Grace. She ran into the forest."

"What? Why?"

"We don't know, but Ross went after her. He'll find her." Then, to herself, she pleaded, *'Please find her.'*

CHAPTER
TWENTY-FIVE

H IS MIND RACED AS he pushed past branches and underbrush, calling her name. "Grace—Grace! Please! You can't be out here like this. Come back?"

Ross's heart pounded as he navigated the dense forest, the dim moonlight barely illuminating the path ahead. His mind raced with fear—fear that she was hurt, that she was lost, but mostly, fear that he had pushed her too far.

"Grace!" his voice echoed through the trees. "Please, stop running! I'm sorry!"

There was no response, only the sound of his breathing and the rustle of leaves around him. He stopped for a moment, hands on his knees, his chest heaving. He couldn't lose her—not like this. Not because of his own stupidity.

"Grace," he said, quieter this time, his voice cracking. "Stop."

Ross moved forward, pushing through more dense under-brush. Then he heard it. The faint sound of Grace's soft cry. It led him to her, but there was something else—something primal, something dangerous in the air.

"Grace?" he called out.

A rustle to his left drew his attention. There she was, standing frozen, her back against a tree. Her wide eyes glistened in the moonlight, but it wasn't him she was looking at. She was staring into the darkness.

"Ross," she whispered. "Stay back. D-Don't come any closer."

Ross followed her gaze, and his stomach dropped. A wild boar, its sinewy muscles coiled and ready to strike, stood half-ob-scured by the darkness, tusks glinting in the night. It snorted loudly, its breath visible in the cool air. The beast's eyes were wild, burning with primal frenzy.

The boar's focus was fixed entirely on Grace. It stomped its hooves into the earth, shaking the ground beneath him. With every stomp, a bone-rattling warning echoed through the silence.

Ross's heart hammered in his chest. His eyes fixed on the creature. Without thought, he moved slowly between Grace and the boar, his body a shield against danger. "Stay behind me," he barked, his voice sharp and urgent.

Ross lifted the spear high, his grip firm, his arm steady as he prepared for the strike.

The boar's eyes narrowed. It grunted in fury, its nostrils flaring as it lunged forward. Its body instantly became a blur of muscle and rage, charging toward Ross.

Grace screamed as Ross's arm shot out, the spear thrusting forward with terrifying precision. The spear's point pierced the boar's side, just behind the ribs. A loud grunt of pain escaped its throat as it staggered and momentarily faltered, its wild charge losing momentum. Enraged by the injury, it twisted, trying to rip itself free from the spear.

Grace, go!" Ross shouted, "Run!"

But Grace couldn't move. She was frozen, horrified by the sight of the beast thrashing around with the spear still lodged in its side.

Ross didn't hesitate. He pulled the spear free and raised it again, eyes fixed on the boar's bloodshot gaze. The creature wasn't done. It charged again, its roar of fury piercing the air as it barreled toward him.

Ross moved, his heart pounding, his instincts screaming for survival. He took one final, decisive step forward, positioning himself squarely in the boar's path. In that heartbeat, the world slowed. With a savage thrust, he drove the spear down, piercing the boar's chest with a sickening thud.

The forest seemed to hold its breath. The boar's final agonized grunt shattered the stillness, and its massive body crumpled to the ground with a resounding crash. For a moment, it twitched, its blood staining the earth beneath it, before lying still.

Ross stood over it, his chest heaving, his body shaking from the adrenaline rush. The spear, now slick with blood, buried deep in the boar's body. He watched the lifeless form of it at his feet, its violent thrashing finally silenced.

"Grace," he breathed, turning to her, his voice hoarse. "Are you okay?"

Grace nodded weakly, but her legs gave out beneath her. Ross caught her, pulling her into his arms. She buried her face in his chest, clutching at his shirt as her body trembled against his.

"I thought we were going to die," she whispered.

"Not if I can help it," Ross said softly, tightening his arms around her.

They stood like that for a moment, their breaths mingling, their hearts racing in unison. Then, as if pulled by an invisible force,

Grace tilted her head to look at him. Their eyes met, and without thinking, Ross leaned down.

Their lips met in a kiss that was a collision of urgency and relief, a desperate release of everything left unspoken. Fear, longing, and the ache of nearly losing each other tangled in their embrace, each touch a silent plea. Grace's hands moved to his shoulders, clutching him as if he were the only thing tethering her to the earth. Ross held her close, his fingers tangled in her hair, as the moment's intensity overwhelmed them both.

When they finally broke apart, they rested their foreheads together, their breaths mingling in the cool night air.

"You could've been killed. What were you thinking," Grace whispered.

Brushing a strand of hair from her face, Ross studied her. "I was thinking, I'm not letting anything or anyone take you away from me, Grace."

This was the first time in five years that Grace allowed herself to feel safe. Completely—safe.

The forest was quiet now. The echoes of danger faded into the night. Slowly, the adrenaline that charged through their veins gave way to a profound relief—a raw, overwhelming gratitude for life. Ross and Grace stood close together, their breaths still mingling in the air, although, in the distance, a familiar campfire waited for them.

Ross reached out, his fingers lingering against her cheek. "You scared me back there," he said softly. "When you ran off... I thought I'd lost you."

Grace looked up at him, her eyes shimmering with unshed tears. "I didn't mean to scare you. I just... I just needed a moment to rationalize what I was feeling."

"And now?" Ross asked, his voice barely above a whisper.

Grace's breath caught as she stared into his eyes, the intensity of his gaze pulling her closer. "Now, I know exactly what it is," she admitted.

Ross cupped her face in his hands, his thumbs gently brushing her cheeks. "Say it," his voice was raw with passion. "I need to hear you say it."

Her hands reached up and cupped his face, her eyes blazing with intensity. "I love you, Ross. I..." her words were silenced as his lips met hers again.

The kiss was slow, tentative, and searching, but it was quickly fueled by the emotions they'd been holding back. Ross's hands slid to her waist, pulling her closer as their bodies pressed together. Grace's fingers tangled in his hair, her heart racing and her body pleading for more.

When they broke apart, Ross rested his forehead against hers, his breath warm on her skin. He smiled, his lips brushing against hers in a tender kiss. "Life's too short, Grace. Too unpredictable. All we have is this moment."

She nodded, her hands sliding down to rest on his chest.

He spread the blanket across the forest floor and gently laid Grace upon it. His movements were as if he was handling the most precious gift. The earth cushioned them, the canopy of leaves above filtering the moonlight into a gentle glow. Ross leaned over her and placed his lips on her forehead. He kissed her so softly it felt like a whispered confession. He traced a path from her forehead to her cheeks, then her neck. Each second stretching out as if he could pour all his feelings into that one touch.

"I love you," he whispered. The words were like a prayer against her skin. His hands gently explored every inch of her. Each touch ignited a fire that burned away every fear and uncertainty.

Grace hooked her thumbs into the waistband of her shorts and eased the fabric down over her thighs, craving the closeness of his touch with nothing left between them. His eyes softened with affection, his excitement deepened as he watched her offering herself to him— unguarded in a way that spoke of trust and longing. His heart swelled, and in a slow, measured motion, he slid out of his shorts, his gaze locked onto hers, heavy with the desire to completely yield to her unspoken request. She arched against him, her hands roaming across his shoulders, down his back, and then around to the most intimate part of his body, exploring—caressing until she heard him moan of sheer pleasure. His body shuttered with intense eagerness. His arms tightened around her, pulling her closer, his breath hot against her ear. He covered her body and then slid slowly into the warmth within her—deeper. "Ross..." she called out. They moved together with shared urgency. Their kisses hungrier, more desperate as they offered themselves to each other in a pure, unfiltered surge of emotions.

Ross's whispered words of love blended with Grace's soft moans of pleasure and became like a symphony of ecstasy carried away by the gentle rustling of the trees. Once again, the world around them faded, leaving only the rhythmic sound of their lovemaking. And then Ross groaned as torrents of pleasure erupted from the inside, igniting a flood that surged through Grace in relentless waves. Each wave more intense, more consuming than the last, leaving her trembling and breathless. Ross held her close, his arms wrapped tightly around her as they lay breathless on the forest floor. Grace rested her head against his chest, listening to the steady beat of his heart. In that moment, it was just them. Nothing else mattered. Nothing else existed. Even the thought of Ethan lost all power.

"You undo me, Grace. I don't know how you do it, but I never want you to stop." Ross whispered, the words settling softly between them like a shared secret.

She nodded, knowing, at that moment, their bond was undeniable. "I feel safe here. Like nothing can hurt me as long as I'm with you."

Ross kissed the top of her head, his fingers threading gently through her hair. His voice was soft, a reassuring whisper against the quiet. "I love hearing you say that," he said, his words tender. "I know what love has cost you before, but that's not what this is. This isn't pain disguised as love. This is safe. This is real. And, if you let me, I will spend the rest of my life proving that to you. Everything seems to fade away being together like this. It's just us. No shipwreck, no unforeseen dangers... just us."

Suddenly, a wave of reality crashed over her. Her eyes widened as she pulled back, her voice rising with alarm. "Ross, what are we doing? What if there's a sn-sn-snake? Or another wild boar comes? Get up!" she pleaded.

Ross met her gaze and smiled, his eyes steady. He reached his arms out to her. "No! Come back to me." His voice low.

"Ross, please, get up. We're not safe here," she said. With trembling hands, she slipped her legs into her shorts and pulled them up. Ross reluctantly did the same. He quickly closed the distance between them and kissed her passionately, then whispered, "I'm not done with you, woman." He picked up the blanket, gave it a brisk shake, and wrapped it snugly around her shoulders. The warmth of the fabric and his sensuous whispers in her ear settle her nerves — but only for a moment.

A rustling sound shattered the calm.

Grace's breath caught in her throat, her eyes darting toward the sound. Ross's expression turned serious in an instant. He pressed a finger to his lips, "Shhhh," he whispered, his voice barely audible as he held out his other hand toward her in warning. His eyes scanned the darkness, every muscle in his body poised and alert, ready to defend her from whatever danger lurked before them.

Ross rushed over and wrestled the spear from the dead boar's chest. He lifted it high, his eyes narrowing, trying to focus through the trees. He prowled toward the sound of the rustling, moving carefully and holding the spear higher, ready to attack. He motioned for Grace to stay back, his gaze darting over to her for a split second.

Every muscle in his body coiled, ready to strike the moment the threat revealed itself. The night air was thick with tension, every heartbeat a drumbeat of anticipation. He reached out, his fingers closing around a cluster of tree limbs, snatching them back.

And then —

Ross froze his grip on the spear tightening, his mind struggling to process the sudden shift from predator to human. His blood still racing with adrenaline. "My God, I could've killed you, Captain. What are you doing out here?"

"Looking for you," he said, releasing a shaky breath. He shouted behind him, through the darkness, They're over here! They're all right!"

Within moments, the quiet of the forest filled with footsteps and concerned faces of some of the survivors. Their eyes etched with relief and exhaustion.

The captain's gaze settled on Ross. "I could ask you the same thing. We've been combing these woods for over an hour, searching for the two of you. We didn't know if you were alive or dead. We heard Grace scream, and when you didn't come back, we got a group together and came looking for you."

Zoe burst through the crowd, her face pale, eyes wide and glistening with unshed tears as she rushed to Grace, throwing her arms around her in a fierce embrace.

"Are you okay? My God, you had us so worried." Zoe whispered. She held Grace tighter as if afraid to let go. "You nearly gave me a heart attack. Do you have any idea what was going through my mind?"

Grace's eyes shimmered with emotion as she clung to her friend, fear and relief settling over her. "I'm okay, Zoe."

Ross gestured toward the dead boar, its powerful body sprawled lifeless on the forest floor. "This thing tried to kill us," he said, his voice tight with lingering adrenaline.

The captain stepped forward, his eyes widening as he took in the animal's size. He let out a low whistle. "That's one hell of a boar. You're damned lucky."

Ross wiped the sweat from his brow, his grip on the spear finally loosening. "Yeah, luck and desperation," he muttered. Then, a thought crossed his mind. "What about food? Can we use this? Is a boar good for eating?"

The captain crouched next to the animal, examining it thoughtfully. "It's uncommon, but you eat what you can in survival situations. The meat will be tough, but it'll keep us going."

Ross nodded, determination flickering in his eyes. "Then let's not waste it. We'll haul it back to camp."

The captain stood, clapping Ross on the shoulder. "Good thinking. This could keep us fed for days." He turned to the group behind him. "All right, let's get this thing back before the others decide to come looking for him. We need to move quickly."

Together, they worked to lift the boar, survival heavy on their shoulders, but the relief of finding each other gave them strength.

As they trudged back toward camp, Grace walked beside Ross, her hand brushing his arm. "Thank you," she whispered, her voice barely audible. She wasn't just thanking him for his protection—it was for everything—the safety of his arms, the way he made her feel seen, and the unbelievably intimate moment they shared. She hoped he understood what she couldn't put into words.

Ross glanced at her, his expression softening. The corners of his mouth lifted in a knowing smile, and he gave her a sensuous wink. "We're going to make it, Grace. I promise." It was his way of saying, I know. I loved it, too.

The subtle yet undeniable flirtatious exchange sent Zoe a spark of recognition.

She paused, her brows drawing together as her gaze swept over the two. The clues that had seemed insignificant before now snapped into focus — Grace's tousled hair, the dirt smudged on her clothes, the faint pink flush on her cheeks. Her eyes narrowed as she took in Ross, his protective stance, and the way his gaze lingered on Grace just a heartbeat too long.

Zoe's lips curled into a knowing smile. Oh, she thought, so that's what's going on.

She circled them slowly, her eyes sharp and perceptive, gathering the silent clues they thought were hidden. Her fingers reached out, brushing a twig tangled in Grace's hair. With deliberate care, she plucked it free, her movements slow and exaggerated, as if unveiling a hidden truth.

Zoe held the twig between two fingers, her brow lifting ever so slightly. She tilted her head, her eyes glinting with amusement and silent understanding. Without a word, she let the twig fall to the ground and stepped back, a sly smile tugging at her lips as she walked away, leaving the impact of her realization hanging in the air.

CHAPTER
TWENTY-SIX

T HE GROUP GATHERED AROUND. The events of the night—the boar attack, the sheer terror of survival—had left them shaken. Now, the lifeless body of the boar lay a few feet away, its sleek body catching the flickering firelight. It was a haunting reminder of both Ross and Grace's victory and their dire situation.

Ross sat on a log, sharpening his spear absentmindedly, while Grace stood nearby, arms crossed tightly over her chest. The captain's voice broke the heavy silence.

"We're running out of food," he said, his tone grim. "The fish have been scarce, and the rabbits aren't enough to feed everyone."

The group exchanged uneasy glances, some avoiding the sight of the boar altogether. Finally, someone spoke, his voice uncertain. "Are you saying... we eat that thing?"

The captain nodded slowly. "I'm saying we don't have a lot of options."

"That's insane," Zoe shouted. "It's a boar, for God's sake. We're not... supposed to eat something like that."

Ross looked up, his face calm but serious. "It's meat. And right now, meat is survival. I know it's not easy to think about, but we can't afford to let it go to waste."

"It's not just about thinking," one of the survivors interjected. "What if it's not safe? What if it makes us sick?"

The captain gestured toward the fire. "If we cook it thoroughly, it'll be safe enough. Wild game meat isn't ideal, but it'll keep us alive. And right now, staying alive is all that matters."

The group fell silent again, the pressure of the decision pressing down on them. Grace stepped forward hesitantly. "I don't like it," she admitted, her voice shaking. "But he's right. We don't have another choice."

Zoe shook her head, her eyes glistening with unshed tears. "I can't believe we're even talking about this."

"It's not a choice anyone wants to make," Ross said gently, standing and placing a hand on Zoe's shoulder. "But this is survival. And if we don't do this, people will start to starve. We don't know how much longer we'll have to be here."

Grace swallowed hard, her gaze fixed on the boar's body. "How... how do we even prepare it?"

The captain knelt by the boar, his face set with grim determination. "We butcher it like any other animal. Skin it, clean it, and cook it over the fire. It will have a richer, stronger flavor compared to domesticated pork, but, like I said, it'll keep us alive."

Ross nodded, stepping forward. "I'll help. No one has to watch if they can't handle it."

"I'll help too," Grace said quietly, surprising even herself. She felt Zoe's hand on her arm.

"Are you sure?" Zoe whispered.

"No," Grace admitted, her voice wavering. "But if we're going to survive, we all have to do our part."

Ray stepped up. "I'm in."

They all worked together, carefully skinning and butchering the boar under the fire's dim light. Grace stood nearby, assisting where she could but keeping her gaze averted from the grimmer details. The group sat in uneasy silence, some openly crying, others staring blankly into the flames.

As the meat sizzled over the fire, a bold, earthy aroma filled the air, thick and pungent. The fat dripped onto the flames, sending a cloud of oily, acrid smoke that made their noses wrinkle. There was a deep richness to the scent, almost like something metallic and wild, mixed with a strangely fishy undertone. It wasn't a pleasant odor—far from it—but it was food.

The fire crackled, its glow casting shifting patterns across Grace's face as she sat, poking at the embers with a stick. Her expression unreadable, distant.

Ross watched her for a moment before lowering himself beside her, close enough to feel the warmth radiating from both the fire and her body. He didn't say anything at first. Just let the night settle around them. The distant murmur of the others preparing the boar faded into the background.

"You okay?" He asked softly, his voice gentle, meant only for her.

She hesitated before turning to him, her eyes lifted, searching the storm of emotion in his gaze. "What we had out there. Is ours. No matter what happens next."

Ross exhaled slowly, nodding as he reached for a small rock near the fire and rolled it between his fingers. He turned and waited for her to look at him again, and when she did, he whispered, "I can still feel you, Grace. Even now."

She couldn't pull her eyes away. "I know. Me too."

Ross tilted his head, studying her. "Still think what we have is wrong?"

She drew in a breath. The firelight softened the sharp edges of his face, but his eyes—unwavering—held something deeper.

"I don't know... but if it is, I have no regrets," she murmured, her voice carrying a weight he didn't miss.

He hesitated, then reached out, brushing his fingers against hers where they rested on her knee. She didn't pull away. Instead, she let out a slow breath, her hand shifting just enough that their fingers intertwined.

For a long moment, neither of them spoke. The fire crackled between them, the world quiet but for the steady rhythm of their breathing.

Finally, Ross gave her hand a gentle squeeze. "We're going to get through this."

Grace blinked, her throat tight. She wasn't sure if he meant the island, Ethan, or the storm brewing inside her—but she wanted to believe him.

The heat of his palm seeped into hers. She traced her thumb lightly over his skin, memorizing the feel of him and centering herself in the moment.

The weight of everything—their journey, their survival, this—settled in her chest, pressing against her ribs like something urgent, something inevitable.

Slowly, she lifted his hand, her fingers brushing over the lines of his palm as if reading the map of his life. Her eyes met his, searching, holding, feeling.

Then, without thinking—without hesitation—she gently pressed her lips to the center of his palm.

Ross sucked in a sharp breath. His fingers curled slightly against hers, as if trying to hold onto the feeling.

Her lips lingered a moment longer before she pulled back.

"I love you," she said. The words drifted between them like a sacred secret.

Ross's eyes darkened with emotion. His jaw tensed as he exhaled slowly. Turning her hand in his, he brought it to his chest over his heart, then kissed the back of it.

His voice was rough when he finally spoke, raw with depth and certainty.

"I love you too, Grace. More than you know."

Grace felt it—the truth in his words, the way his heartbeat thundered beneath her palm, steady and strong.

No more running. No more fear. Just this.

Just them.

The captain nodded as he turned the meat. "It'll be ready soon. Small portions for everyone. We don't waste any of it."

When the meat was done, the captain distributed small pieces to each of them. The boar meat was dark and tough, the flavor intensely gamey. Grace hesitated as the small chunk sat in her hand. She looked up at Ross, who gave her a reassuring nod before taking his first bite. He chewed slowly, grimacing at the taste but swallowing without complaint.

Grace took a deep breath and did the same. The texture was strange, the flavor strong and unfamiliar, but it filled her empty stomach, and she felt a glimmer of strength returning.

Around the camp, the group ate in silence, their faces a mix of revulsion and relief. Zoe sat next to Grace, nibbling on her portion with tears streaming down her cheeks. "I hate this," she whispered. "I hate all of this."

Grace reached over and squeezed her friend's hand. "Me too," she said softly. "But we're alive. And we're going to stay that way."

Ross sat across from them, watching the group as they quietly ate. His gaze lingered on Grace for a moment, admiration shining in his eyes. Despite everything, she was strong. And right now, that strength was what they all needed to survive.

CHAPTER
TWENTY-SEVEN

THE CRUISE OFFICE WAS still bustling with tension and damage control. The overlapping voices of frazzled staff buzzed through the air. Reporters clamored for statements, families demanded updates, and corporate executives wanted answers. Karen sat at her desk, her fingers flying over the keyboard, stacks of incident reports, press releases, and half-empty coffee cups piling around her like fortifications.

"Carla," she barked without looking up, waving a sheet of paper. "Get this release out to the media now. I don't care if they want more details. This is all we're giving them for the next three hours."

"Yes, ma'am," Carla replied, practically running to her desk.

Karen didn't spare her a glance, already moving on to the next task. She picked up a ringing phone and barked, "Cruise Line Emergency Response, this is Karen. No, we don't have updates on individual passengers yet. We'll release the list when we've confirmed with the families. Yes, I said *when*. Goodbye."

She slammed the receiver down just as Ethan entered the office. Dressed sharply in a tailored suit, he exuded the polished confidence of someone used to getting his way. His expression was carefully crafted to look concerned. The staff barely glanced up, though a few exchanged knowing looks, their expressions wary. Ethan's reputation for self-serving theatrics preceded him.

Karen noticed him immediately, though she didn't acknowledge him until he stopped directly in front of her desk.

"May I have a word?" Ethan asked, his voice low and measured.

Karen didn't look up from her computer. "Make it quick. As you can see, we're a little busy dealing with an actual problem."

Ethan straightened, unfazed by her tone, and pulled a neatly prepared document from his folder. He placed it on her desk.

"I wanted to issue a personal statement to the press," he began, his voice taking on a rehearsed sincerity. "Expressing my heartfelt concern for Grace and all the passengers. It's important that people know how deeply I care about this tragedy."

Karen finally looked up, her piercing blue eyes locking onto his. She leaned back in her chair, crossing her arms as a smirk tugged at the corner of her mouth. She glanced down at the document and met his eyes again.

"Heartfelt concern? Really?" She said, her voice low but commanding. "You want to issue a statement? You? The same man who was caught on the phone cozying up to his mistress—his pregnant mistress—while his wife is lost at sea? Do you have any idea how ridiculous you sound?"

Ethan's jaw tightened, but he tried to maintain his composure. "Ms. Karen, that's not fair. I'm here because I care, and I want to share my heartfelt concern." He said again, sliding the document closer to her.

Karen let out a short, humorless laugh. "Your heartfelt concern? You don't have an ounce of concern in your whole body. Everyone in this office knows the only reason you're here is to save face. The same face that's been plastered on the front page of every newspaper in town and went viral on almost all social media platforms. Now you want to play the grieving husband for the cameras? Nobody's buying it."

The staff around them worked quietly, pretending not to listen, though their ears were clearly perked in the direction of their boss's office. Ethan shifted uncomfortably, his polished exterior starting to crack.

"I just thought..." he began, but Karen cut him off again. Her voice turned ice-cold.

"Don't think, Ethan. Leave that to the people who are actually trying to help. If you truly cared, you'd focus on Grace and your mess of a life instead of using this tragedy as damage control for your reputation." She motioned toward the door. "Now, unless you've got something useful to contribute—like a miracle to bring Grace home—I suggest you leave. We don't have time for your theatrics here."

She shifted in her chair. "Carla, see Mr. 'Heartfelt Concerned' out, please."

Ethan stepped back, clearly stung by her words, but he quickly masked it with a curt nod. "Fine. I'll leave you to your... madness. Hope you find 'em...alive."

Karen raised an eyebrow but didn't respond, already turning back to her computer. Carla gestured toward the door, and Ethan followed her out. He felt the eyes of the office staff on him, their judgment hanging heavy in the air.

Once the door closed behind him, the buzz of the office resumed as if he'd never been there. Karen glanced at the document he'd left on her desk and slid it into the shredder without a second thought.

The faint hum of the machine was the only acknowledgment she gave it.

"Heartfelt concern," she muttered under her breath with a scoff. "Yeah, right. And then she muttered the very words she heard come from Grace's mother the last time she was there. "Good riddance... jackass."

The staff exchanged smiles before returning to work, knowing their manager had said exactly what everyone else was thinking.

CHAPTER
TWENTY-EIGHT

T HE OCEAN STRETCHED ENDLESSLY before them, an expanse of rolling waves and indifferent silence. For days, the rescue team had searched—grid by grid, coordinate by coordinate—covering every possible drift pattern. And for days, they had found nothing.

But today felt different.

Commander Whitmore stood at the helm of the Horizon Sentinel, his knuckles whitening around the railing as he scanned the water ahead. The morning sun glared off the waves, its light rippling over the wreckage that bobbed lifelessly in the current. Pieces of the Emerald Princess—shattered wood, luggage, personal belongings—drifted like ghosts on the tide.

And yet, no bodies. No survivors.

It didn't make sense.

Ships sank, and people went somewhere. They didn't just disappear.

Behind him, Lieutenant Harris lifted his binoculars. "Sir, we've expanded our search area twice. If they're out here, we should've found something by now."

Whitmore exhaled, the weight of failure pressing into his chest. "Keep looking."

But even as he said it, the gnawing doubt in his gut whispered a different truth. Maybe there was nothing left to find.

Karen Fletcher was drowning in silence.

Her office, usually filled with the quiet hum of activity—phones ringing, voices murmuring updates—was now eerily still.

The families of the missing were gathering in the lobby, their weary faces marked with an exhaustion that ran deeper than sleepless nights. It was the kind of exhaustion that came from carrying too much hope for too long.

The crowds had thinned, and the once-swarming sea of reporters was now reduced to a handful of journalists who lingered nearby. The frenzy that had dominated the first few days was fading, replaced by a quiet, uneasy patience.

The cameras still rolled, but the urgency had dulled. No new updates. No dramatic rescues. Just waiting.

Those who remained were there for one reason—to keep the world informed of whatever came next. If there was anything left to report.

If there were any survivors left to bring home.

When her phone rang, Karen snatched it so quickly that her coffee spilled.

"Commander?"

The pause on the other end made her stomach drop.

Too long.

Then, Whitmore's voice came through—low, steady, but carrying something she didn't want to hear.

"Karen... we've found more wreckage."

She swallowed hard. "And the people?"

The words stretched like a blade against her throat, waiting to cut.

Another pause. Too long.

The kind that makes the air too thick to breathe.

Whitmore exhaled. "We haven't found them. Not a trace."

Karen's grip tightened on the phone. "That doesn't mean they're gone."

She could hear Whitmore exhale and practically feel the exhaustion in his voice.

"Karen, we've searched every probable location. If they were out here, we would have found them."

Her body went rigid. "So that's it? You're giving up?"

A beat of silence.

Then—

"We're staying out one more day."

Karen's eyes burned, but she held her ground. "And after that?"

Whitmore's voice was softer now but no less final. "After that... we have to accept the possibility that they won't be found."

She closed her eyes. "No."

"Karen..."

"No! They're out there. You hear me? They are out there."

She slammed the phone down before he could say anything else.

She refused to grieve.

Not yet.

Morning bled into the afternoon, the sun glaring harshly against the water. The crew of the Horizon Sentinel was restless—tired, frustrated, haunted by the silence.

Then, a voice cut through the radio.

"Sir! Over here!"

Whitmore's heart kicked against his ribs as he turned to see a rescue boat approaching. There was urgency in the crewman's voice that set his pulse racing.

For a split second, he thought they had found survivors.

Then he saw the bodies.

His stomach twisted.

Two figures lay at the bottom of the boat, partially covered with tarps. Even from a distance, he could see the telltale signs of death—the way the skin had lost its warmth and the sea had begun its slow reclamation.

Whitmore descended the ladder quickly, stepping onto the smaller vessel.

One of the crewmen pulled back the tarp.

A man. Mid-forties. No life vest. His body had been adrift for days, his clothes waterlogged and torn.

Whitmore exhaled through his nose. "And the other?"

The crewman hesitated, then peeled back the second tarp.

A woman. Late thirties. No life jacket.

Whitmore's jaw tightened. He forced himself to push past the emotion. "Any signs of others?"

"Not yet, sir, but..." The crewman hesitated. "We found some-thing else."

Whitmore's gaze snapped to him. "What?"

The crewman reached beneath the tarp and pulled out a tattered orange life jacket. The name Emerald Princess was barely visible on the back.

Karen's phone rang again.

This time, she hesitated before answering. She wasn't sure she could take any more bad news.

But when she lifted the receiver, Whitmore's voice was different.

"Karen... we found two bodies."

She drew in a sharp breath. "Bodies?"

"One man, maybe in his 40s, and a woman who looks to be in her 30s. We won't know anything else until an autopsy is done. And we think some lifeboats made it out."

Karen sat up straight. "Made it out?"

"We can't be certain. But Karen—if they did survive, you're right, they're out there. Somewhere."

A weight pressed against her chest. The grief was there, but so was something else—a pulse of hope so fierce it almost hurt.

"Then don't stop looking."

Whitmore's voice was resolute. "We won't."

And for the first time in days, Karen let herself believe it.

CHAPTER
TWENTY-NINE

THE DENSE FOLIAGE RUSTLED softly as Ross and Ray pushed through the undergrowth, their wooden spears held at the ready. The afternoon sun filtered through the trees above, dappling the forest floor with patches of light. They had been walking for what felt like hours, though it was just that they had wandered in different directions, searching for water. Finally, the faint sound of a stream reached their ears.

Then, through the thick trees, something unexpected came into view.

"Wait," Ross said, stopping abruptly. He pointed ahead. "What's that?"

Ray squinted, brushing a low-hanging branch out of his line of sight. "What the...?" His voice trailed off as his gaze locked on the structure ahead—faded metal walls streaked with rust, partially concealed by vines and moss. A large, weathered satellite dish jutted from the roof at an awkward angle.

The two men exchanged stunned glances before stepping cautiously closer.

"What do you think it is?" Ross asked, his voice low, almost reverent.

Ray shook his head, creasing his brow in disbelief. "It looks like... some kind of research station? Maybe a weather monitoring outpost?" He gestured to the crumbling dish. "That thing's been here a while."

They moved closer, their footsteps crunching on the gravelly earth as they approached the structure. They looked inside. The building was small, with one main room and what looked like an attached storage area. A faded government insignia was barely visible on the side, the lettering too worn to make out.

"Think anyone's been here recently?" Ross asked, scanning the area.

"No way," Ray replied. "Not with the shape this place is in. Looks like it's been abandoned for years, maybe decades."

Ross placed a hand on the cool, rusted wall, his mind racing. "If this was a research station, equipment might still be inside. Maybe even a radio."

Ray's eyes lit up. "We might be able to use it to call for help."

"Maybe," Ross said, his tone cautious. "If it still works—or if we can rig something together."

Ray stepped through the door that hung crookedly on its hinges. He squinted his eyes, adjusting to the dim light. "There's definitely stuff in here," he said, turning back to Ross. "A desk, file cabinet, some old machines... and something that looks like a control panel."

Ross followed, ducking through the doorway. The air inside was musty, the faint scent of mildew mingling with rust. The room was cluttered with debris—broken chairs, faded papers scattered across the floor, and dust-laden equipment. A narrow hallway led to a smaller room with more old chairs covered in dust and cobwebs.

"Looks like someone just walked away from it," Ross said, running a hand over an old radio transmitter. The knobs were rusted, and the wires dangled loose, but it was intact.

Ray knelt beside a stack of overturned crates, rummaging through their contents. "There are power cables in here," he said, pulling out a tangled bundle. "And look—this might be a battery pack. It's old, but maybe it's got some juice left in it."

Ross examined the cables with growing excitement. "If we can get this hooked up... we might be able to send a signal. Or at least boost the range on your phone."

He rubbed his hands together, his gaze sweeping over the rusting equipment scattered throughout. Dust clung to forgotten machinery, metal corroded with time and neglect, a silent testament to how long this place had been left to rot. "Well," he muttered, exhaling sharply. "This is either a goldmine... or a graveyard."

Ray stepped forward, squinting at a half-buried control panel. Without missing a beat, he grinned and clapped his hands together like a game show contestant.

"I'll take 'Goldmine' for $100." He shot Ross a smirk.

Ross chuckled, but the sound was short-lived. His eyes drifted over the wreckage again, his fingers brushing against a rusted console. "Let's hope you're right. You think you know what you're doing?"

Ray paused, squinting at the mess of circuits before them. "Somewhat."

"What the hell does 'somewhat' mean?"

Ray let out a humorless laugh, rubbing the back of his neck. "It means I have some partial knowledge... from a military survival course." He gestured at the equipment, his fingers tapping nervously on the radio's casing. "They taught us a few technical tricks to get by if we were ever stranded. MacGyver-level stuff. But that was a long time ago."

"So, basically, we're winging it."

Ray shrugged, "Pretty much. Let's hope I remember enough of that shit to pull this off."

They exchanged a look—a mixture of determination, resignation, and a touch of dark humor.

Ross took a breath. "Well, it's the best shot we've got. What do we do?"

Ray kneeled to examine the radio again. He grinned. "I say we come back in the morning with the phone, ready to get to work."

"We'll need to figure out what's usable," Ross said.

Ray nodded, then stood and brushed off his hands. "We will. This could be our way out."

Ross stared at the abandoned station, the faint hum of possibility thrumming in his chest.

That evening, they approached the captain.

"What's on your mind?" the captain asked, his voice edged with curiosity.

Ross glanced at Ray before speaking. "We found something out there. On the other side of the island," he said, his tone steady but low enough to keep their conversation private. "A stream. Fresh water."

The captain's eyes lit up briefly, relief breaking through his weary features. "That's good news," he said. "We'll need to set up a rotation to gather some and bring it into the camp."

"That's not all," Ray interjected, leaning forward slightly. "There's something else."

The captain's brow furrowed. "Go on."

Ross took a deep breath. "We found an old abandoned research station. It's in bad shape, but there's equipment inside—machines, wires, even an old radio."

The captain's lips parted slightly in surprise. "Research station?" he echoed, leaning in closer. "You think any of it's still usable?"

"That's what we're hoping," Ross said, his voice tight with the thought of their slim chance. "The radio looks like it's intact, but it needs power. We found some cables and what we think might be a battery pack. It's all a long shot, but it's a shot we need to take. It's just that it's been sitting for years. If we can get everything hooked up and working, we might have a chance to send a signal out. But we're running on nothing but hope here."

The captain nodded, his mind already racing. "That could be our way out," he said, then hesitated. "But we'd need a device to connect to—something like a phone." He looked at them both, his expression falling slightly. "No one here has one." Without a device to connect to the radio, we're stuck."

Ray glanced at Ross before reaching into his pocket and pulling out a small, carefully wrapped bundle. He unfolded the fabric, revealing his phone. "Actually... I do."

The captain stared at him, his jaw tightening slightly. "You've had a goddamn phone this entire time?"

"It's not what you think," Ray said quickly, holding up a hand. "It got soaked during the storm. I dried it out. But when it finally came on, there was no service. I didn't want to give anyone false expectations."

Ross chimed in, his tone calm but firm. "He's right. The phone works, but there's no signal. We think we might be able to use the equipment at the station to boost the range or send a signal to the mainland."

The captain's expression shifted, uncertainty battling belief. "And you're telling me this now because...?"

"Because we didn't want to say anything until there was something to say," Ross said. "What would've been the sense in stirring everyone up with no plan in place? Now we've got one. Let's see if it will work."

Ray nodded. "If we can rework the antenna and power it up, we might be able to piggyback the phone signal off the radio's transmission strength. It's a long shot, but it's the best one we've got. My battery pack died a few days ago. It's not going to be long before the phone dies too. We need to hurry."

The captain stared at the phone for a moment, his lips pressing into a thin line. Finally, he exhaled and nodded. "All right," he said. "Let's keep it quiet for now."

"We'll head back to the station in the morning and work on it," Ross said.

"Just keep me updated."

The captain gripped his spear tightly and watched the two men walk away. It wasn't much, but enough to keep the spark of possibility alive. For now, that was all they needed.

CHAPTER THIRTY

T HE SUNLIGHT BARELY PENETRATED the dense canopy, casting a muted glow over the forest floor. Ross's jaw set with determination. Ray stood beside him, staring at his phone, his face pale. The screen displayed a painfully clear 49% battery life.

Ray exhaled slowly, his voice tight and low. "We've got a problem, Man."

Ross's eyes narrowed, "What's up?"

Ray held up the phone, the percentage glaring back at them like a countdown to disaster. "The battery pack died. Remember? We're at 49% and dropping fast."

A chill settled in Ross's gut. The numbers on the screen might as well have been a ticking time bomb. He clenched his fists, his voice edged with frustration. "You're sure the pack's done?"

Ray nodded, his expression grim. "I tried everything. It's dead, and we don't have another power source. If we're going to make this work, we have to do it now, and there's no room for error."

Ross let out a slow breath, scanning the oppressive shadows of the forest. He could feel the weight of time pressing on them, each second slipping away like sand through their fingers. They were running out of time.

"Then we move," Ross said, his voice steely as he reached down and picked up his spear. "We get to that station and figure out a way to boost the signal."

Ray's jaw tightened. He gripped the phone. "We've got one shot at this, Ross. If the signal booster doesn't work ..." He didn't need to finish. The silence between them spoke louder than words.

Ross nodded, his eyes hard. "We're wasting time. Let's go," he said. They turned to leave the camp when a familiar voice called out.

"Hey, it's early. Where you off to?" Grace asked.

Ray stepped closer to Ross and whispered, "We need to have been gone, like, five minutes ago. Every second we waste, my phone gets closer to being a very expensive paperweight."

Ross nodded but paused, his eyes meeting Grace's. He hesitated, knowing the truth would only add to her anxiety. He took a breath, trying to keep his tone steady.

Ross reached out, his fingers brushing her arm. "Trying to figure out this water situation. Don't worry. We'll be careful."

She searched his face, her lips pressing into a thin line. The thought of them venturing back into the unknown made her chest tighten. She didn't want to let him go, not now, not after she finally said the words that had been buried inside for so long. She clung to his hand, her fingers tightening as if holding on a second longer would keep him with her. Her voice was barely above a whisper but carried the weight of everything in her heart

"Promise me you'll come back." Her eyes searched his, desperate for reassurance.

Ross's eyes softened. He gave her the assurance she needed through a smile that was meant only for her. "I will. I promise."

She nodded, though the knot in her stomach remained. And then she squeezed his hand tight before letting it go.

Ray cleared his throat gently, reminding Ross of the urgency pressing down on them. The phone's screen flickered, showing 45% battery. Time was slipping away, and they were nearly an hour from the research station.

He gave her one last look, a silent vow passing between them before he and Ray disappeared into the forest.

Grace watched until they were out of sight, a whisper of the breeze ruffling her hair. The world felt heavier without Ross beside her.

Ross and Ray crept through the crookedly hung door of the research station, the musty air filling their lungs, but there was something else—a pungent scent that didn't belong. They paused, eyes scanning the dim interior. Something felt off.

"Ray... do you smell that?" Ross asked, his voice low and cautious.

Ray sniffed the air, his face contorting in confusion. "What is that? It's like..."

Before Ray could finish his thought, a sharp, grating noise came from the small hallway. The sound of hooves scraping against the floor.

Ross's blood ran cold. He motioned for Ray to stay quiet. The hairs on the back of his neck stood up. The noise grew louder—a grunt, followed by a series of snorts, unmistakable and feral.

"Boars," Ross muttered, his voice thick. "They're here." He peered down the short hallway.

Two pairs of glowing eyes turned and were suddenly fixed on him with an almost predatory intensity. Their tusks gleamed in the dim light as they snorted, backing up slightly to size up the intruder.

Ross didn't have time to think. He threw his spear down and slammed his body into the side of the old file cabinet and slid it into the narrow hallway, wedging it into place and creating a barrier between them and the boars. With every ounce of strength, he pushed it as far as he could, the metal screeched across the floor and scraped against the walls. Grunting with effort, he braced his back against it, blocking most of the passage just as the boars slammed into it from the other side. The force rattled the walls, shaking loose dust from the ceiling. The cold steel dug into Ross's skin, preparing himself for the inevitable.

Through a narrow gap on the side—no more than a few inches wide—clawed hooves scraped against the tile. Snouts rammed into the space, the beasts shrieking in frustration. One managed to wedge its tusk through, jerking its head violently, trying to pry the barrier loose. Ross gritted his teeth, pressing his shoulder against the cabinet, feeling the pressure of the creatures pushing back.

The entire research station shuddered with the impact of their violent assault. The boars' grunts and snorts filled the air, a clamor of raw frustration.

They charged. Relentless and furious, slamming into the back of the file cabinet with all their might. Their snorts and grunts echoing through the room. Driven by a primal urge to clear the obstacle that stood between them and their prey, they continued to charge, eager to impale the outsiders.

"This isn't gonna hold forever!" Ross growled.

Ray was already searching for something—anything—to help reinforce the barricade. The metal cabinet groaned under the assault, shifting slightly with each impact.

"No," Ross shouted. "I've got this. You work on the radio." His muscles burned with strain as he shoved back against the cabinet, his body trembling with the effort. Sweat dripped down his face, stinging his eyes, but he didn't dare let up.

Ray rushed toward the antiquated machinery, his pulse hammering as the guttural grunts and frantic clawing of the boars filled the air. The dim light flickered above him. He ripped at wires and yanked free anything that looked useful. His fingers fumbled over rusted bolts and frayed cables, his mind racing. *Think, think!*

"Ray!" Ross shouted, his voice tight with urgency. "How's it coming?"

Ray wiped the sweat from his brow. "Still working on it!" Ray barked, his voice strained as he twisted wires and fumbled with the radio, his hands shaking. He glanced at the phone screen that screamed back at him30%—barely enough to keep hope alive. "Come on, come on..." His fingers moved quickly, desperately trying to get a connection, but the boars pounding against the cabinet threatened to shake the whole building apart.

Ray got the battery pack. It was old but not completely dead. He flipped it over, rubbing some grime off the metal contacts. "It's got some juice left," he muttered. "Enough to give this radio a kickstart, maybe more. He rushed over and dug through more cables, finding one with stripped ends. He could use it to connect the battery pack to the radio. Essentially, hot-wiring it back to life.

The boars grunted loudly then a horrible screech came as they charged at the cabinet again. Ross shoved with all his strength, his shoes sliding against the floor, barely managing to keep the beasts at bay.

"Ray, we've got to hurry." Ross snapped.

"Damn it, Ross! I'm trying!" Ray snapped back, his voice breaking with frustration, trying to concentrate at the same time.

Ray twisted the exposed wires together, bridging the connection. A sharp spark and then nothing.

He needed to figure out a way to use the radio's antenna to amplify the cell phone's weak signal.

He yanked the long, retractable antenna from the back of the radio. He tested its movement.

He rummaged through the cables, then pulled out a coaxial wire—it was frayed but still had some length to it.

He carefully pried off the back cover of his cell phone and found the small internal antenna. He wound the exposed wire around it, then connected the other end to the radio's antenna base.

His thoughts were interrupted by another crash. He looked up in time to see Ross almost fall to the floor. The boars' hooves thundered louder. Ross grunted, pushing the old file cabinet with everything he had. The cabinet barely held together as the boars got stronger – angrier.

"Ray, hurry the hell up! I can't hold them off much longer!" Ross growled; his teeth gritted.

"I know! I know!" Ray hissed through clenched teeth. Ray powered on the radio, adjusting the frequency dial. "I've got to use the radio's transmission capabilities to amplify the phone's outgoing signal."

The boars were relentless, trying to claw their way out again.

"Just hold them back. I'm working as fast as I can!" Ray yelled as he frantically opened his phone's network settings, switching it to manual mode. He started scanning for signals.

Ross gritted his teeth, his back still pressed against the cabinet. "We need that signal, Ray! Or we're screwed!" Another boar lunged at the file cabinet, slamming into it with terrifying force. Ross stumbled again, barely staying upright.

The screen blinked.

For a moment, nothing.

Then—

A single bar.

"Holy shit," Ray breathed. "Got it, my friend."

Ross barely registered the success, his focus entirely on the boars. "Great, now just make it work!" He braced hard against the file cabinet, muscles straining, and yelled as another charge from the boar almost knocked him to the floor again.

Ray's hands shook as he dialed a number—the emergency frequency.

The phone rang once. Twice.

Then—a voice.

"This is the U.S. Coast Guard. Identify yourself."

Ross and Ray locked eyes, disbelief washing over them.

Ray's voice was hoarse when he spoke. "We're survivors of the Emerald Princess. We need help."

The radio buzzed, but before they could confirm the connection—

The cell phone died.

"No, no, no!" Ray cursed, wiping the sweat from his brow. "This can't be happening. You've got to be fucking kidding me!"

"Ray!" Ross yelled as he felt the cabinet crash into his back, another violent strike from the boars. The room shook, and Ross felt his arms grow weaker. "Ray, do something!"

The silence after the call ended was deafening.

Ray let out a string of curses, slamming his hand on the table. "Do you think they heard me? Did the message go through?"

Ray stared at the lifeless phone in his hand, his pulse hammering in his ears. The battery was dead. Completely. The screen wouldn't even flicker.

Then—

A sharp burst of static crackled through the old radio.

He froze and turned to the rusted device, barely daring to breathe as the static rose, dipped, and then—

A voice.

"...Repeat... unidentified signal... anyone receiving this? Over."

Ray's eyes widened. "Holy shit, the radio's working!" He leaned in closer to the radio, voice frantic, "Hello? Hello! We need help! We're survivors of the Emerald Princess Cruise Line. It's been two weeks! Please contact the cruise line office in Florida and let them know we're alive! We're alive!"

The muffled voice crackled again, fading in and out. "...copy... information... repeating... Florida..."

Ray's heart raced. "Yes, yes...Florida. The Emerald Princess Cruise Line."

The radio crackled louder now, static building as Ray adjusted the dial.

The boars pounded at the cabinet again, and Ray's heart raced in his chest.

Ray groaned, panic flooding through him. The voice from the radio stuttered once more, then faded altogether.

He slammed his fist on the table, his voice dark and heavy. "It's dead. There's a chance they heard me, though."

Ross's eyes were wild with desperation. "We need to get the hell out of here. Now!"

Ray stood. His fists clenched in frustration. "I know. But how? If you move from the cabinet, they'll burst through. We won't have a chance."

He ran through the station's door, his heart pounding in his chest — eyes scanning the area frantically until they landed on a large boulder just a few feet away.

He sprinted toward it without hesitation, planting his hands against the rough, unyielding surface. Every muscle in his body screamed in protest as he pushed, his feet digging into the dirt. He strained, gritted his teeth, and with a final desperate heave— the boulder lurched forward.

Inch by inch, he rolled it toward the entrance. His arms trembled; his breaths came in ragged gasps.

Then, he staggered back inside, hands on his knees, chest heaving.

Ross stayed where he was, pushing against the file cabinet one last time as the boars crashed into it. "Hurry, Ray!" Ross shouted. "I can't hold them off any longer!"

"I've got it. But, we're gonna have to move fast. I rolled a boulder to the door. On the count of three, we rush out of here, close the door, and roll the boulder against it, blocking them in. They won't be able to get out until we're long gone. I hope."

Ross nodded quickly, his face focused. "Got it. Just say when."

Ray looked at him, eyes filled with urgency. "Three!" He yelled.

In a flash, the two men rushed through the door. Together, they rolled the boulder against it. They could hear the boars inside. They had crashed through the cabinet barrier. Their hooves thundering, and their snorts growing louder as they tore through the station looking for the invaders.

"Let's move!" Ross shouted, and they bolted into the forest, the sound of the boars' fury behind them. The door held, and the air was thick with terror as they ran, adrenaline pumping through their veins.

"Go, go, go!" Ross yelled again, and they pushed forward, the sound of hooves fading into the distance.

Their escape was a blur of motion—every step driven by the fight for survival. They could hear the boars pounding at the door, but they didn't dare stop to look back.

When they thought it was safe, the two men slowed, their breaths coming in ragged gasps as they stumbled to a stop. With their hands on their knees, they tried to catch their breath, the adrenaline still pumping through them.

Ross stood first, wiping the sweat from his brow, his breathing still uneven and eyes darting around, braced for another wave of danger to crash down upon them. He clenched his jaw, the frustration evident in his face. "Well, what do you think?" he asked, his voice tight.

Ray exhaled slowly; his expression clouded with doubt as he wiped his forehead. "I don't know... we'll see," he replied, his words trailing off as uncertainty crept back in.

They stood in the stillness of the forest, the realization of what they'd just endured pressing heavily on them. The hum of the radio, their only lifeline, had faded, and the surrounding woods—indifferent, relentless—seemed to mock them.

Ross's voice broke the silence, low but steady. "We've done all we can do. Now we wait."

Ray nodded, slipping the dead phone back into his pocket. The little faith they had clung to was now reduced to nothing.

"Damn it. I left my spear."

Ray gave him a look of disbelief. "You want to go back to get it?"

"No, I'm good."

Ray clapped Ross on the back. "Good answer. Now, Let's get back to camp," Ray said, his voice quiet and hollow.

With no more words, they turned and made their way back toward the camp. Their steps were heavy, laden with the uncertainty of what was to come. The question of whether they'd been heard, whether anyone would come for them, lingered in the air between them.

CHAPTER
THIRTY-ONE

B Y THE TIME ROSS and Ray trudged back into the camp, the sun blazed overhead, their faces drawn with exhaustion. The rest of the group looked up. Grace's gaze lingered on Ross, telling a story of relief and restrained emotion. The captain strode toward them, his weathered face etched with concern.

"Well?" the captain asked, his voice low but steady while his eyes betrayed his worry. "What happened?"

Ross glanced at Ray, who nodded silently, gripping the dead phone. Ross took a deep breath and turned back to the captain.

"Whatever Ray did with the radio caused it to come to life for a split second," Ross explained, his voice low. "He told them that we were survivors from the Emerald Princess and also asked them to contact the cruise line office in Florida." We're just not sure if they heard us."

The captain's eyes lit up, his jaw tightening as he processed the information. "Not sure, huh?"

Ray's shoulders slumped. He opened his hand, revealing the dead phone. "We could hear their voices. We're just not sure they heard us. I want to believe they did."

The captain exhaled slowly, rubbing his chin. The lines on his face seemed more profound now, the pressure of responsibility pressing harder. He nodded, a flicker of hope in his eyes regardless of the uncertainty.

"We did everything we could," Ross said, his voice firm but edged with frustration. "Now, we wait."

The captain looked out where the sandy beach met the endless sea. His voice was calm, almost resigned. "We're doing that anyway, so... what's a little more waiting?" He turned back to them, offering a small, weary smile. "At least now, there's a chance."

Ray let out a shaky breath, his fingers running through his hair. "It's better than nothing."

The captain nodded. "It is. And if there's one thing I've learned out here, it's that you have to refuse to give up.

A heavy silence settled over them. The distant sound of the waves lapping against the shore seemed louder now, a reminder of isolation and possibility. Ross looked at the group, at Grace's worried eyes and the exhausted faces of the others.

"We're going to make it through this," he said, more for himself than anyone else.

Grace stood and stepped closer to Ross, her hand brushing his arm briefly. Her voice was soft but steady. "Is everything okay?"

Ross rested his head on hers. "With any luck, yes."

The captain nodded, his expression grim but grateful. "Good work, you two."

Zoe sat on a log near the fire, her arms crossed and her face tight with frustration.

Ray noticed her agitation and walked over, wiping his hands on his shirt.

"You look like you're ready to punch something," Ray said, his voice light but concerned.

Zoe shot him a sharp look. "What's taking them so damn long, Ray? We've been here almost two weeks. No planes, no helicopters, not even a damn flare in the sky. Don't they know we're missing?"

Ray crouched down beside her, his tone soothing. "They know. These things take time, Zoe. It's a big ocean out there."

"So much time has passed, though," she snapped, her voice cracking. "What if they've stopped looking? What if... what if they think we didn't make it and just stop looking altogether?"

Ray placed a hand on her shoulder, his grip gentle. "No one stopped looking, I promise you that. Search and rescue teams are trained for this. They don't give up, and neither can we."

Zoe's eyes glistened as she stared into the fire. "I just... I can't stop thinking about Grace's mom. She must be losing her mind, not knowing if she's alive or dead. And what about the others here? Their families? We can't stay here forever."

Ray nodded, his voice low. "We won't. But you've got to stay strong—for yourself and for everyone else. People look to you, Zoe. You keep this place together."

Zoe sniffed and let out a shaky laugh. "I'm not exactly doing a great job now. Am I?"

"Sure you are," Ray said with a small smile. "You've got the kids laughing and playing games, don't you? That's something."

Not far from the fire, a small group of children played in the sand, their giggles cutting through the tension in the camp. They had fashioned a game using sticks and shells, creating a pretend village that rivaled the adults' makeshift shelters.

One of the younger boys shouted, "I'm the king of the island!" as he balanced precariously on a mound of sand before it collapsed. The others cheered, their laughter infectious.

Grace watched them, a faint smile on her face. "It's amazing how they've adapted," she said softly, glancing at Ross, who had come to stand beside her.

"Kids are resilient," Ross replied, his gaze warm as he observed the scene. "They find joy wherever they can. We could learn a thing or two from them."

Grace chuckled, though her expression turned serious. "Zoe's not handling this well, though. She's barely holding it together."

Ross nodded. "I saw Ray talking to her. He'll pull her out of it."

"He can try," Grace said, folding her arms. "But she's right. It's been almost two weeks. It's hard not to wonder what's taking so long."

The sun was still strong that afternoon, but a cool breeze blew off the water. The camp became quiet as the children began an energetic game. The adults prepared what little food they had, and Ross returned to the fire with a thoughtful expression.

"Tomorrow, we'll start clearing a bigger section of the beach," he said to Grace. "If we can make a signal big enough, it'll be seen better."

Grace nodded. "Okay. I'm willing to do anything to keep from sitting around looking at the sky, hoping for a miracle."

The distant splashing of the ocean filled the silence between them. Grace glanced at Ross, sensing the weight he carried even in moments of stillness.

"You've been quiet since you got back," Grace said gently, breaking the silence. "Are you concerned about the water situation? Or something else?"

Ross hesitated, staring into the fire as if searching for answers in its flickering light. "Something else," he admitted, his voice low.

Grace leaned forward slightly, her expression soft but curious. "You want to talk about it?"

For a moment, Ross said nothing. Then he took a deep breath, his shoulders rising and falling as though bracing himself for impact. "It's not something I've ever told anyone," He began. "But... I think I need to."

Grace nodded, encouraging him with her silence.

Ross looked at her, his gaze steady but filled with pain. "The book you read—the one I wrote—it wasn't just a story. It was my life."

Grace's brows furrowed, and she tilted her head slightly. "Yeah, I know, it was about your relationship. Right?"

He nodded, his jaw tightening. "Right, but the person who died? I changed the name."

Grace creased her brow, "I know."

"Some years ago, I was engaged. Her name was Nicole. She was... everything to me. Or so I thought. And then there was Carl—my best friend since college. We were like brothers. I trusted them both completely."

Grace's stomach tightened as she sensed where the story was heading.

Ross's voice faltered for a moment, but he pressed on. "One night, I noticed things weren't adding up—whispers, odd glances, excuses that didn't make sense. I started putting the pieces together, and when I finally confronted Nicole, she denied it. But deep down, I knew. I knew they were lying to me."

He paused, his hands clenching into fists as he stared at the ground. "That night, I went looking for them. I found them togeth er... in Carl's car. They were kissing. I got out of my car to confront them."

Grace covered her mouth with her hand, her eyes wide.

"Carl saw me," Ross continued, his voice hollow, "He panicked. He hit the gas, trying to get away. I... I got in my car and followed them. I just wanted answers. I wanted to know why. Why the people I trusted most betrayed me."

Ross took another deep breath, his voice breaking slightly. "They were going too fast. I should've stopped. I should've let them go. But I didn't. Carl lost control... They hit a truck, and the car flipped. It burst into flames before I could even get to them. That's how Nicole died."

Grace's hand fell from her mouth, tears brimming in her eyes. "Oh, Ross..."

"I tried to save them," Ross said, his voice cracking. "I ran to the car, but the flames were too hot. I couldn't get close. I could hear them screaming and pleading with me to help them. And I couldn't. I couldn't save either one of them."

The raw pain in Ross's voice made Grace's chest ache.

"I hated them for what they did to me," Ross continued, his tone quieter, almost a whisper. "But I didn't want them to die. I allowed my emotions to drive my actions. I shouldn't have chased them. I just should've let them have each other."

Ross looked up at Grace, his eyes glistening with unshed tears. "That's why I wrote the book. It was the only way I could process it, the only way I could try to make sense of the betrayal and the guilt. I poured everything into it—every ounce of anger, pain, and regret."

Grace reached out, placing her hand gently on his. "Ross, I can't imagine how much that must have hurt. But it was the way you were able to tell the story from both perspectives—the villain's and the two lovers who happened to fall in love at the wrong time. And he dies, leaving them both to grieve."

Ross let out a quiet breath, his gaze fixed on the fire but **seeing** something else entirely—memories, ghosts of the past. "In the book, Celia's husband dies. But in real life, it was my fiancée and my best friend, and they left me here to grieve."

Grace squeezed his hand gently.

"I didn't know how to be angry at them," Ross admitted, his voice rough. "They didn't mean to fall in love. It just... happened."

Grace swallowed, her heart aching for him. "And writing the story helped you understand that?"

"It helped me survive it."

Grace let his words settle, the weight of what he had been through pressing into the space.

"Ross," she whispered, "you didn't just write about grief. You wrote about forgiveness."

Ross finally looked at her, something unreadable in his eyes. "Yeah... I guess I did."

Grace smiled, brushing her fingers lightly against his. "You were not only able to forgive them, you were able to forgive yourself too."

He shook his head. "It was tough coming to terms with what I had done. I wanted to create something that would inspire others to face their own hidden wounds. But I didn't want it to be just another self-help book. So, I turned it into an engaging work of fiction instead."

Grace tightened her grip on his hand. "Your story broke down walls for me, Ross. It made me confront some of my darkest moments."

Ross looked at her, his expression softening. "It means a lot to hear you say that. I've carried this for a long time, alone. I thought if I told anyone what I had done, they'd see me differently."

"I don't see you differently," Grace said firmly. "I see you more clearly. You've been through hell, yet you're still here, trying to help people. That takes strength, Ross."

Ross allowed a faint smile to touch his lips. He brushed her hand with his. "Thank you for saying that."

They sat in silence for a while, the firelight reflecting in their eyes. For Ross, the weight of his secret felt just a little lighter. And for Grace, their connection deepened, built on shared pain and the determination to find peace.

In the distance, Zoe's laughter rang out as Ray told her some ridiculous story, drawing smiles even from those nearby. For a moment stood a small reminder that even in survival, hope could still find a way to shine through.

CHAPTER THIRTY-TWO

T HE RADIO OPERATOR ADJUSTED his headset, his fingers moving quickly over the console. The signal was faint and inter-mittent, but it was there. He leaned toward the microphone, his voice steady and professional in spite of the thrum of excitement building in the room.

"This is Coast Guard Search and Rescue, Sector Seven. We have a possible distress signal coming from an island-based research station that hasn't been used for years. Frequency is steady. Why would it suddenly start signaling? This is a long shot, but I think it might be our missing cruise ship passengers."

The lead officer nodded, his jaw tight. "Patch us through to the cruise line's office. Now."

The sun rose on another day of waiting, longing for answers that refused to come. The air inside Karen Fletcher's office was heavy and thick, with too many unanswered questions. Families trickled into the office, their faces etched with exhaustion, their eyes flickering between desperation and reluctant faith.

The map on her desk was littered with red circles—each one a failed lead, another hope dashed, another door closed. She stared at it, willing something—anything—to make sense. Then, her phone buzzed, shattering the silence. She snatched it up, her pulse spiking as dread and anticipation tangled in her chest.

"Commander?" she said, trying to keep her voice steady.

The voice on the other end was clear, clipped, and professional. "Good morning, Karen, I may have some news you want to hear. We believe we may have found your missing travelers."

Karen's breath caught in her throat. She gripped the edge of her desk, her knuckles white. "You—you found them? Where?"

"We're picking up a distress signal from an old research station on a remote island," Commander Whitmore explained. "The signal is faint but steady. Someone there managed to activate a radio transmitter. Once those are set, they can keep broadcasting on the same frequency."

Karen's mind raced. The possibilities, the hope — it all felt so unstable. "But you're not sure it's them?"

Whitmore's voice softened, but the tension remained. "Not yet. The island wasn't on any of our projected search paths. The storm must've blown the ship completely off course if it is them. We wouldn't have known they were there unless someone managed to get that radio working."

Karen's voice trembled. "Can you reach them? Are they okay?"

"We're enroute right now," Whitmore said firmly. "We'll know more once we make contact. I promise we'll keep you updated."

She swallowed hard, a tear slipping down her cheek. "Please, Commander... bring them home."

"We'll do everything we can, ma'am. You have my word."

The engines roared as the vessel sliced through the waves, the sun sinking lower on the horizon. Commander Whitmore stood at the bow, the wind tugging at his uniform, his eyes fixed on an island's faint, misty outline in the distance.

A junior officer approached, his voice tense. "Signal is holding steady, sir. It's definitely coming from that island where the old research station once was."

Whitmore nodded; his jaw clenched. "Get ready. We might be bringing people home today."

Karen Fletcher sank into her chair, the phone still clutched in her hand. The room felt both unbearably quiet and deafening with the sound of her own heartbeat. The tiniest spark of faith flickered in her chest, fighting the fear that it might be extinguished.

She whispered to herself, barely audible. "Please, let it be them."

The afternoon sun cast a golden glow over the sandy beach that had been their home for two weeks. A welcome breeze drifted in from the water. Above them, the vast blue sky stretched endlessly, melting into the horizon where it met the ocean in a seamless embrace.

But this was just another day of survival—another day of waiting, enduring, and holding onto the hope that rescue would come.

Ross exhaled, bracing himself for the continued routine of the day, but then—he froze.

His body went still, every muscle tensing. A sound cut through the humid air, faint but distinct—a low whirring, distant yet growing. His heart stuttered, a sharp inhale catching in his chest. His pulse pounded as he lifted a hand, shielding his eyes against the glare of the sky. *Was it real? Or just another cruel trick of the mind?*

But no—this was different.

The noise grew louder.

And this time, Ross dared to believe. He squinted at the sky, shielding his eyes with his hand.

"Hey!" he shouted, "I think I hear something!"

Heads turned, eyes widened. A ripple of energy surged through the camp as everyone bolted from their makeshift shelters, feet pounding the sand. They crowded beside Ross at the shoreline, hearts thundering, breath caught in their throats.

Grace grabbed Ross's arm, her eyes wild with anticipation. "What is it? What do you hear?"

Ross didn't answer. His eyes continued to scan the sky; his breath held hostage by the possibility that this was real. The sound grew louder—sharper, the unmistakable thump-thump-thump of rotor blades slicing through the air.

Ray's eyes went wide, his breath catching in his throat. For a second, he was frozen in disbelief. Then, as the realization hit, his voice came out in a hushed, almost reverent whisper."A helicopter." The words barely left his lips before excitement surged through him like a jolt of electricity. He spun around, his face lighting up as he shouted, louder this time, his voice echoing into the open air. **"It's a helicopter! A damn helicopter!"**

Suddenly, the outline of the aircraft emerged from the clouds — a gray bird of salvation, its blades chopping furiously, the sun glinting off its metal frame. The wind from the rotors whipped the trees into a frenzy, sending leaves and debris swirling.

"There!" Zoe screamed, pointing frantically. "Look! There it is!"

A cheer erupted from the group, a sound born of desperation and raw, unfiltered joy. Arms shot skyward, fingers pointing, waving, reaching for the helicopter as if willing it closer.

"They found us!" someone cried, their voice breaking.

Tears streamed down faces, and laughter bubbled up alongside sobs. Grace clung to Ross. "They're here. Oh my God, they're really here."

And then, cutting through the air, came the resounding blare of a horn — the unmistakable call of the Coast Guard vessel.

"Look!" Ross shouted. "The Coast Guard!" His voice ragged with relief.

The horn blasted again, louder, closer, a triumphant declaration that help had arrived. The sleek gray vessel surged into view beyond the breakers, waves crashing against its hull. The sun glimmered off the ship's insignia.

Ray fell to his knees in the sand, his shoulders shaking with laughter and tears. "We did it. We fuckin' did it!" He barely had time to process before his head snapped up, scanning the shoreline for Ross. And then he saw him. Without hesitation, he jumped to his feet and sprinted toward him. When he reached Ross, he grabbed him by the shoulders, his hands trembling with adrenaline, relief, and something more profound—gratitude.

"We did it, man," Ray said, his voice thick with emotion.

Ross clapped a hand to Ray's back before pulling him into a tight, brotherly embrace.

"No," Ross corrected, his voice rough but sure. "You did it. I just held back the damn boars."

Ray laughed hoarsely, shaking his head as he pulled back. "Bullshit, man. I couldn't have done it without you."

He grinned, slapping Ross's palm in a solid, victorious high-five before gripping his hand tightly, silently acknowledging everything they had survived.

The helicopter hovered while the ship's crew waved from the deck, shouting words lost to the wind but carrying the unmistakable tone of, *You're safe now!*

Ross turned to the group; his voice choked. "We're going home."

The air was alive with shouts, cries, and the deafening, beautiful sound of rotor blades and ship horns — a symphony of survival, a song of salvation.

As the rescue teams descended, hands reaching out to pull them from the edge of despair, the world seemed to crack open with light. The nightmare was ending.

Commander Whitmore descended onto the shore, his boots sinking slightly into the damp sand. His sharp eyes scanned the exhausted group before him — disheveled, bruised, but very much alive. He took a deep breath, the salty breeze carrying with it the impact of their ordeal.

He stepped forward, his voice clear and commanding yet warm. "I take it this is the crew from the Emerald Princess Cruise Line?"

For a heartbeat, there was silence. Then, the realization sank in, and the beach erupted with cheers and tears. Arms flew around shoulders, hands clutched together in joy, and relieved sobs mingled with shouts of triumph. The sound was pure, unfiltered elation.

The captain of the Emerald Princess pushed through the crowd, his gait steady despite the weariness in his eyes. He stopped in front of Commander Whitmore, his back straight, the burden of responsibility etched deeply into his face.

"Yes, sir," the captain said, his voice rough but firm. I was the captain of that ship. We hit a maritime storm, and it threw us off course. I lost the ship." His throat tightened. "We lost twelve travelers...eleven at sea and one on the island, but everyone else is accounted for."

A heavy silence settled for a moment, the gravity of those lost lives hanging between them. Commander Whitmore's expression softened, his voice carrying the compassion of someone who knew what it meant to bear such a burden.

""While our hearts go out to those lost, you've saved so many," the commander said, his tone firm. "You kept them safe, and that's what matters."

The captain nodded, his jaw trembling slightly. "Thank you, sir."

Commander Whitmore's eyes swept over the group, taking in the faces lined with exhaustion, relief, and tears of joy. He squared his shoulders and gestured toward the waiting vessel.

"Let's get you aboard. I'm sure you're more than ready to get home."

The words hung in the air for just a second before they registered. Then the beach exploded again — cheers, cries of relief, hands clasping in gratitude.

Ross turned to Grace, his eyes shimmering with relief. "We made it. I told you we would." His voice was steady, but as he looked at her, he sensed something else—something unspoken. Beneath the victory, beneath the long-awaited rescue, there was a trace in her expression. A quiet, almost imperceptible sadness. It wasn't just exhaustion. It was the realization that, after surviving this storm, she now had to return home and face another.

She smiled slowly through her tears, her fingers gripping his hand tightly. She nodded slowly, "Yes, we're really going home."

Ray let out a whoop of triumph, his voice raw with emotion. Zoe hugged Grace so tight that they nearly toppled over, laughter bubbling through the tears.

As they began to move toward the waiting ship, the sun broke through the clouds, its rays spilling over them like a blessing. The sea, once their enemy, now shimmered with promise.

They were found. They were saved. And they were going home.

CHAPTER THIRTY-THREE

THE HUM OF THE phone line felt endless, but finally, the voice on the other end crackled to life. Karen Fletcher clutched the receiver, her fingers trembling slightly. Commander Whitmore's voice was calm, but there was something behind it—something she hadn't dared to hope for.

"Karen, Commander Whitmore here," he said with confidence. "I'm calling with an update. The signal we traced—it led us to the survivors of the Emerald Princess."

Karen's heart stuttered in her chest. "You mean...? Are you sure?"

"I'm positive," Whitmore replied, his voice steady. "We've got Captain Lloyd Parker right here with us. They're safe. They're on their way home."

The words hit her like a tidal wave, and for a moment, Karen couldn't speak. She blinked rapidly to keep the tears at bay, her throat constricting. But the news wasn't over yet. "Are all of the passengers accounted for?" she managed to ask, her voice cracking with the weight of the question.

The commander's silence was brief but heavy, and when he spoke again, his words carried both relief and sorrow. "Unfortunately, not everyone made it. They lost a few, but the majority are safe. They're eager to be reunited with their loved ones."

"Do you have a list of the survivors?"

"No, but we can get that to you within the hour." He bellowed out the command to one of his crew, giving him the task of getting the names of all the survivors.

A sob caught in Karen's throat, but she forced herself to steady. "Thank you, Commander. I'll let the families know," she said, her voice thick with emotion. "We're all grateful. More than you know."

"You're welcome," Whitmore replied softly. "Now, go tell them. It's time for their joy."

"Commander, I'd like you to stay on the phone while I tell them. Rejoice with us." She stood from her chair, the phone in her hand. The weight of what she'd just learned sank in for a heartbeat. She turned toward the door of her office. Her hand hovered over the handle for a moment, then she opened it wide.

"Everyone," Karen called, her voice steady yet thick with emotion as it carried over the anxious crowd gathered in the lobby. The restless murmurs fell into silence in an instant. Eyes locked onto her, filled with exhaustion, desperation, and the kind of hope that felt too fragile to trust.

She swallowed hard, feeling the weight of their expectations pressing in on her. She held the phone high. "I have news."

The air tightened. A heartbeat of silence followed.

"I'm speaking with the Coast Guard."

A ripple of tension spread through the room, every breath held, every expression frozen between fear and longing. Karen inhaled deeply before delivering the words they had been praying for—words that would change everything.

"Your loved ones have been found. The survivors of the Emerald Princess have been located, and they're on their way home."

For a moment, the world stood still.

Then—the dam broke.

A collective intake of breath, followed by an eruption of sound. Cheers, gasps, cries of relief. Disbelief melted into joy, arms flung around one another, tears streaming unchecked. Some sobbed into their hands, others laughed through their tears, gripping onto anyone near them, grounding themselves in the reality of it.

Karen blinked against the sudden blur of her vision as the room transformed from a place of waiting to a place of celebration. Reporters surged forward, cameras flashing, voices shouting over one another. Questions flew, phones rang, but nothing could overshadow the sheer, raw relief pulsing through the room.

Mrs. Davis and Mary Parker locked eyes. With unspoken understanding, they rushed over and wrapped their arms around each other in a fierce, desperate hug. Their sobs mingled, a release of days of torment and grief.

Karen put the phone to her ear. "Thank you, Commander."

"Of course," Whitmore replied. "And Karen... tell them we're celebrating with them."

"I will, Commander," Karen said. "Thank you... thank you so much."

She ended the call and turned to face the room again. Her eyes swept over the faces of the families, the ones who had waited and hoped, sometimes with only the smallest flicker of faith. "I have one last thing to say," Karen called out, her voice breaking with emotion. "It is with a heavy heart that I have to deliver this news. I've been told there have been a few fatalities. However, the majority of the passengers are coming home. We will have the list of survivors within the hour."

In that moment, all the pain, all the suffering, and waiting... it didn't matter anymore. The majority of their loved ones were alive, and they held on to the belief that they were on the list. There was no greater gift than this—no greater relief. The room again burst into celebration.

As promised, the list of survivors was faxed to Karen's office within the hour. She stood in front of the group, the paper trembling slightly in her hands, as she cleared her throat and looked up at the sea of expectant faces. The room had fallen silent, everyone holding their breath, waiting for her to speak.

With a steadying breath, Karen began, her voice wavering only slightly as she called out the names, each one a lifeline to the waiting families.

Mary stood and asked, "Lloyd—Lloyd Parker, Captain of the Emerald Princess?" Karen's eyes scanned the list. Then looked up at Mary Parker, nodding wildly. "He's here. He's on the list." Mary plopped down in her chair, covered her face, and wept. A collective exhale of relief echoed in the room.

"The rest of names were called...each one more poignant than the last. Each name was met with gasps, tears, and silent prayers of gratitude from those who were there.

A sense of disbelief began to soften, replaced by pure joy. Mrs. Davis clutched her chest as she heard Grace's name, a sob breaking free from her as the reality settled in. The ache of uncertainty that had lingered for days was finally gone.

Karen continued, her voice shaking but resolute. "Zoe King." Again, Mrs. Davis clutched her chest, hearing the familiar name of her daughter's best friend.

RJ Henderson, she announced, looking around the room for his loved ones. They weren't present. She moved on to the next name. The list went on and on, with the room erupting in emotion, families reaching out to embrace each other, breaking down in tears of joy and relief. In that moment, the world outside could have fallen away, and it wouldn't have mattered.

Karen allowed the moment to unfold, watching as parents, spouses, and children held each other tightly, the weight of everything they'd lost and everything they'd regained flooding through them all at once.

Finally, Karen lowered the list, her own tears threatening to spill over. She smiled at the room. "I'll let you all gather your things. If you want to go home and freshen up, we have their ETA at 4:00 this evening. It's almost over."

Ethan didn't show up at the cruise office that day. Instead, he stayed with Olivia, avoiding the inevitable awkwardness of facing reporters and the judgment of a world that already saw him as a villain. Another day spent under the harsh lights of the cruise office, another round of questions he didn't want to answer. So, he turned his phone off, unable to face the barrage of calls and messages that had flooded in since his name had appeared in the papers. He couldn't bear to read the comments or listen to people offering their opinions on the latest news, so he shut himself off, retreating into the quiet of Olivia's presence.

But the news of the rescue found him, just as it had found everyone else—flashing across the screen of Olivia's phone and television with a loud BREEEEEP and a headline that cut through the air: BREAKING NEWS: Survivors of the Emerald Princess Found!

The images that followed hit him harder than he expected. The faces of the survivors. And then—Grace's face, alive and unharmed. His heart stalled in his chest. There was no relief, no joy in seeing her. Just a strange, cold emptiness that he couldn't shake. He stared at her face, unblinking.

Life would have been much easier if she hadn't been found. Eventually, the reporters would have drifted off, social media would have latched onto another trending story, and he and Olivia could have quietly lived off the money Grace would have left behind. But now, he had to face the tedious task of pretending, of making people believe he actually gave a damn. He'd have to act concerned and play the part of the grateful husband whose wife had been miraculously rescued and brought home.

He glanced at his watch. They were due at 4:00, giving him enough time to clean himself up and head to the cruise office. He could be there when Grace arrived, waiting to offer the perfect words—the ones that always worked before. He'd convince her that he had been beside himself the whole time she'd been gone, that he hadn't stopped thinking about her, about what may have happened. Making her believe their rough patch was only a misunderstanding that could have been ironed out if she had just stayed. He'd lay low for a week and then go back to being himself. He had done it before. And he'd do it again.

CHAPTER
THIRTY-FOUR

T HE SHIP GLIDED INTO port, its horn echoing like a beacon of
    salvation.The deck buzzed with nervous energy, survivors
peering anxiously over the rails. Below, families and loved ones
crowded the pier, waving wildly. Faces painted with a mixture
of joy, relief, and tears.

The pier was a chaotic frenzy of reporters, photographers,
and curious onlookers. Microphones and cameras jutted forward like weapons as reporters swarmed the disembarking
passengers, shouting over one another with questions. Grace
stepped off the gangway, her heart still heavy with the weight
of the ordeal, only to be met by a wall of flashing lights and a
storm of voices.

"Where's Grace Hargrove?"

The voice boomed over the crowd above the other voices.

Grace froze, her eyes darting across the crowd, confusion flickering across her face as the crowd shifted, an almost unnatural ripple of movement flowing toward her.

"Grace Hargrove? Where can we find her?"

The voices were multiplying, overlapping in a wave of urgency. Grace felt her stomach tighten as she hesitated, her fingers curling around the railing for support.

Slowly, she raised her hand, her voice barely above the noise.

"I'm Grace Hargrove."

The reporters surged forward; Microphones were suddenly thrust toward her face, an onslaught of rapid-fire questions filling the space around her.

"Grace, are you taking Ethan back even after his affair?"

"How long have you known about his mistress?"

"Is that why you went on the cruise?"

Grace blinked, her mouth opening and closing. She stumbled back, the sheer force of the questions slamming into her like a physical blow.

"What... what are you talking about?" she stammered, her voice tinged with panic. "I don't..."

"Do you think Ethan regrets cheating?"

"Are you planning to forgive him, Grace?"

Grace's head whipped from one side to the other, her eyes widening. "I—I don't know what any of this is about," she said, her voice shaking. "I don't..."

Another reporter's voice rose above the others.

"The video of your mother confronting your husband has gone viral. Haven'tyou seen it?"

"Viral video?" she repeated, her voice shaky, trying to wrap her brain around the implications of what they were saying. "What video?"

"It's everywhere," a young journalist said eagerly, thrusting a phone toward her with the clip already playing. "Millions of views."

Grace glanced at the screen, her stomach twisting as she recognized her mother's voice, her sharp words cutting through the noise. Her pulse quickened, and she stepped back, shaking her head.

"I can't..." she started, her voice breaking, but the reporters pushed closer.

"Grace, do you agree with your mother?"

"Do you think he deserves the backlash he's receiving?"

"Was the cruise your way of leaving him?"

The crowd pressed in. Flashes exploded like white-hot lightning. The weight of it all became suffocating.

Then—

"Back off! Give her some space!"

Ross's familiar voice sliced through the air.

He appeared at her side, his tall frame a protective barrier between her and the frenzied crowd of reporters. He held up a hand, his expression stone-hard.

"That's enough. She's been through enough without you hounding her."

Grace followed the voice and met Ross's gaze. "Ross!" her voice broke raw with relief, needing his steady presence.

"Who are you?" a reporter demanded.

Ross ignored the question, focusing on Grace. He placed a reassuring hand on her shoulder. "Let's get you out of here."

Grace could only nod. Her legs moving on autopilot as Ross guided her through the shouting voices. Each step felt heavier than the last. Grace instinctively shrank back, shielding her face with her hand, the flashes searing her vision. She wasn't ready for this— for the world to dissect her suffering, her survival, her secrets. Ross walked just behind her, his jaw tight, eyes scanning the crowd like a hawk. He placed a steadying hand on her back and gently hurried her forward.

The reporters kept shouting questions, their voices trailing after them as Ross rushed her through the doors where family members were waiting for their loved ones.

"Just a few more steps," he said. Regardless of all the frenzy, his voice was calm.

Ross leaned in close, his breath warm against Grace's ear. "Ignore them. Just focus on me."

She nodded, clinging to his words as they pushed forward through the blinding flashes, the shouting voices, and into the uncertain light of freedom.

Around them, others survivors flinched under the relentless assault of lights and questions. The news broadcast in real-time, every moment of their descent captured and transmitted to screens across the country — the lost survivors of theEmerald Princess, found at last.

Zoe's eyes darted from side to side, her lips pressed into a thin line as she tried to block out the noise. A reporter lunged toward her, microphone extended.

"Zoe King! You were also stranded! Can you tell us what happened on the island?"

She shook her head, lifting a hand to shield her face. "Not now," she muttered,trying to slip past.

Ray tugged at his collar, his face pale, exhaustion etched into every line of his expression.

"Ray Franklin! Is it true you helped keep everyone alive?"

"Did you think you'd make it back?"

"What was the worst moment for you out there?"

Ray gritted his teeth, blinking against the harsh flashes. "I'm not answering anything right now."

A few feet away, another survivor looked like she was about to crumble. A reporter cornered her.

"How did it feel being lost at sea?"

"Were you scared you'd never be found?"

She just let out a shaky breath, her arms wrapped around herself.

"I... I just want to see my family."

More survivors were being pulled aside, their exhaustion on full display. The questions kept coming, the voices relentless.

It was madness.

Grace scanned the crowd, her heart pounding in her chest. A familiar voice rang out, cutting through the air.

"Grace!"

She turned toward the sound. There, standing just beyond the ropes, was her mother, arms outstretched, tears streaming down her face.

Grace's voice cracked as she tore away from Ross and bolted forward, stumbling into her mother's embrace. Sobs shook her shoulders as she clung tightly. "I didn't think I was ever going to see you again."

Her mother kissed the top of her head. "You're safe now, baby. You're home."

"What about me?"

Grace recognized the cold voice and stiffened.

"Don't I get a hug?"

She turned to see Ethan standing beside her mother, his eyes narrowing. He spread his arms expectantly, a forced smile curling his lips.

Grace's voice dropped, flat and icy. "Ethan."

Annoyed that he had the audacity to show up after everything he'd done, Grace's mother instinctively stepped between them, as if shielding her daughter from his presence. Her voice was unwavering. "We need to get you home, Grace.

Ethan stepped forward, his hand curling around Grace's arm. "Yes, Grace. I need to get you home."

Her mother's voice turned to a dangerous tone. "Get your hands off my daughter, Ethan. She's not going anywhere with the likes of you."

Ethan's grip tightened, his smile twisting. "Ohhh? She's my wife. She's going home with me."

"No." Her mom's voice was firm, her head shaking in defiance. "Not this time."

From a distance, Ross watched the scene unfold, his heart lodged in his throat. He saw Ethan's hand clamp onto Grace's arm and saw the pain and hesitation in her eyes. Every fiber of his being screamed to act, but his feet felt nailed to the ground.

Zoe's voice sliced through his paralysis. "So, you're just going to stand there and let that happen?"

Ross turned to find her standing beside him, arms crossed, eyes blazing with disbelief.

"She might not want to be with me now that she's home." Ross muttered.

Zoe snorted a sharp, incredulous laugh. "You're actually saying that with a straight face? You know Grace loves you. Everyone on that island knew it. Don't mess around and lose her. Not when she's right there."

"I take it that's the infamous Ethan?" Ethan's name slipped through Ross's tight clenched teeth.

Zoe nodded in disgust, "You'd be right."

"Who's the woman?"

Zoe's voice softened. "That's Mrs. Davis, Grace's mother. She's amazing. Now, go over ther and show her you are, too."

Ethan's grip tightened; his face twisted with frustration. "Grace, come on. Stop making a scene."

Her lips trembled, but she didn't speak. Ethan yanked her harder.

Ross watched Grace's mother try to shield her again, but Ethan was stronger. He yanked her forward, dragging her partway into the crowd.

The pain in her eyes shattered the last of Ross's hesitation. He cut through the crowd and reached them within seconds, his hand clamped down on Ethan's shoulder, stopping him in his tracks. "You're not taking her anywhere," Ross growled, his voice low and deadly. "Get your hands off her."

Ethan spun around, his face contorted with rage. "Who the hell are you? Get away from us!"

Ross didn't flinch. He stared him down. "I won't say it again." He warned. "Grace, you and your mother come with me."

Ethan sneered. "Get your hands off my wife. She's my wife!" He jerked her arm again, and Ross's patience snapped. His fist shot out and connected with Ethan's jaw in a sickening *crack*. Ethan stumbled back, clutching his face. A strangled yell and a string of curses escaped his lips.

Without hesitation, Ross scooped Grace into his arms, his firm, steady grip enveloping her as he turned sharply toward the waiting car at the edge of the pier.

The moment Ross's fist connected with Ethan's jaw, the crack seemed to echo over the pier, louder than the hum of the crowd. For a heartbeat, the world held its breath.

Then all hell broke loose.

Reporters scrambled closer, cameras flashing like wild lightning, microphones thrust forward to capture every angle. Shouts and gasps filled the air, overlapping in a whirlwind of excitement.

"Did you see that?!"

"He punched him! He just punched Ethan Hargrove in the face!"

"Who IS that?"

"Did anyone get a name?"

"I think I heard her call him Ross."

Reporters flipped through the survivor lists.

No 'Ross.'

Grace clung to Ross, her head resting against his shoulder, her face turned away from the relentless flashes. The noise of the world disappeared as Ross's confident strides carried her farther from the scene that erupted behind them.

Mrs. Davis was not too far behind with an expression that was equal parts amusement and curiosity. Her lips curved into a faint smile as she took in Ross's dramatic exit. She didn't move to intervene; instead, she squared her shoulders and followed them as she was told.

Turning briefly, she glanced over her shoulder at Ethan, who was standing frozen amidst the remnants of the media frenzy. His face was a mask of barely concealed humiliation, and he held his jaw as the reporters focused on him.

When they reached the car, Ross gently placed Grace in the front seat, closing the door behind her with a decisive thud. Mrs. Davis opened the backdoor and slipped inside without a word. Her demeanor was calm as if it were just another ordinary day.

Ross turned to her. "You okay, Mrs. Davis?"

"I certainly am young man," she answered.

Ross climbed into the driver's seat, his knuckles gripping the wheel as he glanced at Grace. Her face was buried in her hands, her breathing still uneven. He softened his tone, leaning slightly toward her. "Grace, it's okay. You're safe."

Mrs. Davis looked between them, her eyes narrowing slightly as her curiosity deepened. But she didn't ask questions—not yet. Instead, she rubbed Grace's shoulder from the back seat. "I've never been so relieved and happy to see you, baby. I don't think I'll ever stop touching you. Making sure it's real." She glanced out the window, her lips twitching into a smirk as she caught a glimpse of Ethan still surrounded by reporters.

Meanwhile, social media was already on fire:

@NewsOnTheGo:

"BREAKING: Chaos at the pier! Grace Hargrove, survivor of the *EmeraldPrincess* disaster, is caught in a heated confrontation with her husband, Ethan Hargrove—AND THEN SOME MYSTERY MAN JUST PUNCHED HIM IN THE FACE???" #EmeraldPrincessSurvivors #WhoIsHe

@GossipUnlocked:

"Did anyone else just watch that LIVE?? Who the HELL is the guy that just knocked Ethan Hargrove's teeth loose and then carried Grace away like a damn MOVIE SCENE?! #WhoIsHe #WeNeedAnswers"

@CelebrityChronicles:

A SHOCKING TWIST in the *Emerald Princess* survivor saga! An unidentified man just stepped in, took down Ethan Hargrove, and left the pier with Grace in his arms! WHO IS HE?! Someone find out NOW. #BreakingNews#MysteryMan"

@TrueCrimeFiles:

"Wait... something isn't adding up. NO ONE named *Ross* is on the survivor list. #SomethingIsFishy "

@PopCultureReacts:

"All I know is that Ross-or-whatever-his-name-is just knocked Ethan into next week, grabbed Grace, and peaced out. AND I NEED ANSWERS. #ShipwreckToLoveStory"

CHAPTER
THIRTY-FIVE

R AY JOINED ZOE AT the pier and leaned against a post, arms crossed, watching as Ethan, full of self-importance, grabbed Grace by the arm. Big mistake.

"Oof," Ray muttered, shaking his head. "That guy just made a very poor life decision."

"Oh, this is gonna be good," Zoe whispered, practically bouncing on her toes as she elbowed Ray.

Then it happened—Ross's fist connected with Ethan's face in a perfect, no-nonsense punch, sending the man stumbling backward, clutching his jaw like his whole world had just been rearranged.

Ray's eyebrows shot up, his expression caught somewhere between surprise and approval.

Zoe's lips parted in shock before she stifled a laugh, her eyes gleaming with amusement as she whispered, "Did that really just happen?"

The pier fell silent for a moment, and then... absolute bedlam.

"Hell yeah!" Zoe cheered, throwing her hands up. "Took you long enough, Ross!"

Ray let out a low whistle. "Damn. That was clean. Man's got good form."

They watched Ross scoop Grace up into his arms like some kind of action-movie hero and strode off through the crowd like he owned the damn pier.

"Now, that's what a man deeply in love does," Ray laughed.

They stood there, mouths open, watching Ross march past them with Grace wrapped securely in his arms. Grace's mother trailed behind them.

Zoe snapped out of it first, throwing her arms up again. "Way to go, Ross!"

Ray gave him a nod of approval. "Strong finish, my man. Strong finish."

Ross didn't even glance their way, too focused on the woman in his arms, but Grace, red-faced and wide-eyed, shot them a look over Ross's shoulder that was equal parts mortified and grateful.

"Did that just happen?" Zoe asked again, blinking.

"Yep," Ray confirmed, popping the 'p.' "And I think we just witnessed the best damn exit in the history of breakups."

Zoe grinned. "Tell me you got that on video."

Ray patted his pockets. "Damn it. Missed my shot."

Zoe sighed dramatically. "Guess we'll just have to rewatch the news highlights later."

They stood there for another beat, watching Ross carry Grace away from the pier like he was walking straight into their future.

And with that, the two of them turned, walking away from the pier with the energy that said, 'Well, *that was worth the price of admission.*'

"So, how are you getting home?" Ray asked.

"I left my car here. Thank God I did Valet parking. They had my key and were very understanding. My car is over this way."

The quiet between them was unusually strained and uncomfortable. Zoe broke it when she asked, "What now?

Ray faced her, "What do you mean?"

"I'm not ready to let you go," she admitted, her voice quiet but sure.

Ray looked at her, brows slightly furrowed. "Who says you have to?"

Zoe hesitated, biting her lip. "Well... we're home now. I just thought maybe you'd want to be by yourself for a while. You know, decompress. Get back to your own space."

His gaze locked onto hers, unwavering. "Zoe, when I told you I loved you, I didn't mean 'for as long as we were stranded on an island.'" He shook his head slightly, as if the idea itself was absurd. "'I love you' isn't supposed to be temporary."

A sudden pressure settled in Zoe's chest at the sincerity in his voice.

"You sure?" she asked, forcing a small, uncertain smile. "Because let's be honest—I'm not exactly the easiest person to deal with."

Ray smirked, "Oh, I'm well aware. Stubborn as hell, opinionated, terrible at following directions..."

"Okay, wow, way to sell me on this relationship," Zoe interrupted, rolling her eyes.

Ray chuckled, but when he spoke again, his voice softened. "But you're also fearless, brilliant, and the only person I've ever met who makes me feel like I matter. So yeah, I'm sure."

Zoe swallowed hard, blinking away the sudden burn behind her eyes. "Damn it, Franklin, you always have to be the smooth one, huh?"

Ray grinned. "What can I say? I had a lot of time to practice while waiting for rescue."

Zoe shook her head but was already moving toward him, closing the space between them. She looped her arms around his neck, her forehead resting against his.

"I love you too, you know," she murmured.

Ray brushed his fingers through her hair, tilting her chin up. "Yeah, I know."

And then he kissed her, slow and deep, like they had all the time in the world—because—they did.

"What do we do now?" Zoe asked again. This time a little quieter.

Ray laughed and rolled his eyes. "We're back to that?"

He stretched, rolling his shoulders like a man without a care in the world. "Well, I'm officially a free agent until they assign me to another cruise ship. Pretty sure they'll want me to take some time off, though. You know, recovery from the whole 'lost at sea' situation."

Zoe snorted. "Yeah, because, of course, that's something you just bounce back from. Right?"

Ray smirked. "Exactly. Which means I have a few priorities." He started ticking them off on his fingers. "One, I need a new charging cord for my phone. Two, you need a whole new phone because yours is currently at the bottom of the ocean. Three, I have no ID, no credit cards, and no cash. So unless I plan to take up a lucrative career as a dockside philosopher, I'm basically just a bum loitering on a pier."

Zoe shifted, tapping her fingers against the car door. "Let's go home, Ray."

"I like the sound of that," Ray said, hopping into the passenger side. They drove off.

Zoe laughed, shaking her head. "First things first."

Ray raised an eyebrow. "What's that?"

She shot him a pointed look. "I need a shower. And so do you."

Ray exhaled, running a hand through his messy hair. Salt, sweat, and days of survival clung to him like a second skin. Yeah, she had a point.

"That would be great," he admitted.

Ray holds up four fingers. "Number four. I need a change of clothing."

"Lucky for you, I've got a bag of men's clothes in my trunk."

"That's oddly convenient. You keep emergency outfits for men in the trunk of your car?"

She rolled her eyes. "No, genius. I work with a mission that helps people in need—clothing, shelter, resources. I was going to call someone to come pick up the bag when I returned from the cruise, but it looks like you just became a person in need."

He paused, meeting her gaze. There was something different about Zoe now—not just the sharp-witted woman he fell in love with, but someone who actually gave a damn about others.

CHAPTER THIRTY-SIX

"M OM? WHAT ARE THEY talking about, Viral video? What video?"

"You'll see." Mrs. Davis said, sitting forward, her amusement showing. "Ethan showed his true colors, dear. It's all over social media." Then, concerned, she added, "But don't worry about that right now. Let's just get you somewhere quiet."

Ross started the engine, his jaw still tight as he pulled away from the pier. The car glided into the city streets' relative calm, leaving the reporters' whirlwind and the bright flashes of cameras behind. "I don't live too far from here. Would you want to go to my place?"

"Your place would be fine with me. Zoe's house is an hour away, and I would love a hot shower and a change of clothes." Grace said.

"You're not alone in that department." Ross laughed. You can choose from a couple of my bathrobes." He turned to her. I think

I can get used to watching you walking around in one of my bathrobes," he said with a wink.

Grace gave a slight, sheepish smile and cast an embarrassed glance at her mother, whose eyes sparkled with curiosity. She had no idea who this man was—the one who had swept her daughter off her feet, both literally and figuratively—but there was something about him that she liked. Something solid. Something good and honorable.

As they drove, Grace looked out the window, her mind racing. She felt the weight of Ross's steady presence beside her and her mother's watchful gaze from behind. She allowed herself a moment to exhale, the tension in her chest easing ever so slightly.

Moments later, Ross pulled into a wide driveway in front of a stunning, lavish home. The sun caught the elegant lines of the house, its windows glinting like polished gems. Grace's eyes widened as she took it in.

"Who lives here?" she whispered.

Ross looked at her, his eyes soft. "I do."

Grace turned to him, her brows furrowing. "Ross, you never told me you lived like this."

He smiled faintly. "We weren't exactly in a position to talk about how we lived, wouldn't you agree?"

She nodded, the ghost of a smile touching her lips. He climbed out of the car and opened the door for them. Retrieving an extra key from under a flower pot, he unlocked the door, and they stepped inside the warmth of Ross's home. A stark contrast to the cold one she shared with Ethan. Ross led them to the living room, a space that felt grand but also welcoming, with soft lighting and plush furnishings. He gestured for Mrs. Davis to have a seat, "Make yourself at home," and she did, her eyes scanning the room with quiet approval.

Ross took a deep breath, his gaze fixed on Mrs. Davis. "I know you don't know anything about me, but I need you to understand how much I care about your daughter." His voice trembled slightly, but his eyes were steady. "She's been hurt enough. What she needs now is to know that I love her, that she's safe with me."

He turned to Grace, his eyes softening, his voice dropping to a tender mutter. "But you know that already, don't you, Grace?"

Her eyes shimmered with tears as she nodded, her voice barely a whisper. "I do."

Ross swallowed, his throat tight. "And you love me too, right?"

A tear slipped down her cheek as she nodded again. "Yes, Ross. I love you."

He turned back to Mrs. Davis, his voice stronger now. "I want you to know that Grace is my priority. No one will ever hurt her again. I'd give her the world if she'd stay with me."

Mrs. Davis studied Ross, the heavy silence stretching between them. She finally nodded, a tearful smile breaking through. "You're right. I don't know you, Ross, but I can feel the sincerity in your words. Grace deserves to be happy." Her expression hardened as she turned to her daughter. "I found out what happened with Ethan, Grace. He's not good for you, dear. You've got to get away from him."

Grace's lips trembled, her eyes filled with pain and resolution but when she spoke, her voice was strong and clear. "I have some decisions to make, Ross. Let me get my bearings. I know I love you, but I'm learning that love isn't always enough. I need you to give me time. We can't just jump into this."

Ross's shoulders slumped. He closed the distance between them and pressed his lips to hers in a soft, tender kiss. For those few seconds, everything else slipped into oblivion, leaving only the warmth of his love. When he finally pulled away, their foreheads rested together, sharing the quiet intimacy of the moment. Ross whispered, "Take all the time you need. I'll be here."

When they finally parted, Mrs. Davis's eyes shone with pride and relief. "I had always believed you'd find love, Grace," she said softly. "But more importantly, it looks like you're finding yourself."

Grace smiled, tears streaming freely now. "Thank you, Mom."

Ross took her hand in his, intertwining their fingers. "This is going to be difficult being this far away from you. I've gotten used to knowing I could look over my shoulder, and there you'd be," he whispered. "How do I protect you when you're so far away?"

As they stood together, a sense of peace finally settled over them.

Mrs. Davis smiled, her eyes twinkling with gentle humor. "Now, I'm sure you two are in need of that nice, hot shower you talked about on the way here." She patted Ross on the shoulder. "Ross, point me in the direction of your kitchen. I can whip up a good home-cooked meal for you both if you don't mind. You deserve it after what you've been through."

Ross chuckled, his arm still wrapped around Grace's waist. "Yes, ma'am. I would love to sample the cooking skills I've heard so much about. Grace tortured us by talking about them. The kitchen is through that door. Use whatever you need."

Mrs. Davis clapped her hands. "All right, you two. Go get cleaned up. By the time you're done, something warm and delicious will be waiting for you."

Ross leaned down, pressing a tender kiss to Grace's forehead. "Come on," he whispered. "I'll show you around."

Grace nodded, her heart swelling with love and relief. As they disappeared, Mrs. Davis headed for the kitchen with a satisfied smile.

Ross took Grace's hand, his fingers threading through hers, and led her up the stairs and down the hallway. The rich scent of wood polish and faint traces of his cologne lingered in the air. The floors were dark mahogany, each step softened by a plush runner that muffled their footsteps.

They entered the master bedroom, and Grace's breath caught in her throat. The room was spacious and inviting, bathed in the soft glow of the afternoon sun streaming through tall windows framed by sheer curtains. The walls were a soothing shade of slate gray, accented by tasteful art pieces — abstract forms that hinted at both strength and vulnerability.

A king-sized bed dominated the space, dressed in crisp white linens, a deep navy comforter folded neatly at the foot. The bed offered a promise of comfort. A pair of matching nightstands held minimalist lamps with frosted glass shades, casting pools of warm light. On one side, a framed photo of Ross and an older couple hinted at family ties she hadn't yet learned about.

Her eyes swept over the room, noting the subtle touches of Ross's personality — a pair of running shoes tucked under a bench at the foot of the bed, a leather jacket draped casually over a chair, and a book left open on the nightstand. The space was refined, masculine, yet lived-in — a reflection of the man she was coming to know.

Ross squeezed her hand gently, guiding her toward a set of double doors. He pushed them open, revealing a bathroom that felt like a private spa. The walls were lined with sleek, gray marble streaked with veins of white. Recessed lighting glowed softly, reflecting off the gleaming surfaces and giving the space a serene, almost ethereal quality.

A spacious glass-enclosed shower stood in one corner, equipped with multiple jets and a rainfall showerhead mounted in the ceiling. The water controls were sleek and modern, set into the marble wall. Nearby, a large, freestanding soaking tub sat under a frosted window, inviting and serene.

Grace's eyes lingered on the vanity — a long, elegant marble slab with twin sinks, each framed by a backlit mirror. Plush navy towels hung neatly on a rack, and a small potted plant added a touch of life to the otherwise cool palette.

She caught sight of their reflection in one of the mirrors — Ross standing behind her, his eyes warm, his presence steady and reassuring.

He leaned down and whispered, his voice low and tender. "This is your space now too, whenever you're ready to accept it. Everything you need is right here."

Grace turned to look at him, her eyes shimmering. "Ross, your home is beautiful, but— I."

He smiled, brushing a stray lock of hair from her face. "Shhh. We won't talk about it now. I know you, Grace. You need to figure things out in your own time, in your own way. And as much as it kills me to wait, I will—because you're worth waiting for."

Grace nodded.

"Look in my closet and choose any bathrobe you like. Stay with me tonight, Grace. I'll buy clothes for you tomorrow."

"Believe me, I want to. But I think it's best that I go to my mother's tonight. If you let me wear your bathrobe to her house, I'll make sure you get it back. I have extra clothes there."

"If that's what you want." He kissed her slowly.

"No, it's not at all what I want. I want to be here with you. I want you to make passionate love to me all night."

"I can do that," Ross said with a teasing smile.

"Then what, Ross?" Grace's voice was soft, but her eyes held an intensity that tightened his chest. "Another layer of confusion added to our situation? Give me the space to figure out my life so I can give you all of me."

258

She drew in a breath, her fingers gripping the hem of her shirt as if centering herself. "If you love me, you'll do that for me."

Ross exhaled slowly, running a hand through his hair. Everything in him wanted to fight against this—to hold on, to convince her that she didn't need space, that they could figure it out together.

But that wasn't fair to her.

And damn it, she was right.

His jaw clenched as he nodded, swallowing the lump in his throat. "And if I give you that space... how long do I have to wait?"

Grace's expression softened, her hand instinctively reaching for his before she caught herself and pulled back. "I don't know."

Ross let out a quiet, humorless laugh, shaking his head. "That's not exactly reassuring, Grace."

"I know," she whispered.

They stood there in the charged silence, neither willing to move, neither willing to say what the other wanted to hear.

Finally, Ross sighed and stepped closer, lowering his voice. "Just tell me one thing."

Grace lifted her gaze to his. "What?"

"Are you coming back to me?" His voice was rough, unsteady, raw.

She hesitated for only a moment before nodding. "I hope so."

Ross closed his eyes briefly, letting the weight of her words settle inside him. It wasn't a promise—but he would hold on to hope.

When he opened his eyes, he studied her face, searching for any hesitation, any doubt. But there was none.

"All right," he said finally with a nod.

Grace's lips parted as if she wanted to say something more, but no words came. Instead, she looped her arms around his neck and brought his face down until their lips met, when they pulled apart.

Her eyes lingered on him for a heartbeat longer before he turned and walked out of the room.

Because if giving her space meant having all of her in the end—

Then, he would give her what she needed and wait.

As Grace turned on the shower and watched the steam rise, she realized this wasn't just a place to wash away the grime and exhaustion. It was a place to let herself be reborn in the safety of Ross's world.

The warm water cascaded over her shoulders, and she felt like she was washing away every bit of the tension she had felt on the island. And then a familiar and comforting scent began to drift through the air. The steam of the shower mingled with the rich, savory aroma of something delicious cooking downstairs — roasted herbs, sizzling butter, and a hint of garlic.

Grace paused, took a deep breath through her nose, and smiled softly. The scent stirred memories of childhood and safety all wrapped up in one.

After the shower, Grace tightened the bathrobe and descended the stairs, her footsteps soft against the wooden floor. The red fabric brushed her legs, warm and familiar, though the thought of wearing Ross's robe with nothing underneath made her cheeks flush slightly. She paused at the bottom step, spotting him leaning casually in the kitchen doorway, talking to her mom.

He turned when he heard her approaching and walked to her.

"I knew it would look better on you than me," he said, his voice low and teasing, as his eyes met hers.

Grace raised an eyebrow, feigning indifference, although the warmth rose to her face. "Don't get used to it," she quipped, tugging lightly at the robe's oversized sleeves. "It's a temporary loan."

Ross chuckled, straightening from his relaxed position. "Take all the time you need. I have plenty to spare if you plan on raiding my closet."

Grace crossed her arms, the corner of her mouth twitching with an almost smile. "You think very highly of yourself, don't you?"

His grin widened, stepping closer but stopping short of invading her space. "Only when I'm right." His voice softened, the playful edge fading. "It really does look good on you."

For a moment, Grace didn't know how to respond. The way he looked at her—like she was the only thing in the room that mattered—left her unsteady. She broke the silence with a quiet laugh, shaking her head. "You're impossible."

"And you're stubborn," Ross countered, his eyes twinkling. "Guess that makes us even."

Grace rolled her eyes but couldn't stop the smile that slipped onto her lips. She changed the subject.

"Mom is doing what she does best," Grace said, her voice tinged with emotion.

Ross smiled, a warmth spreading through his chest at the sight of her smile. "It smells amazing."

Grace nodded, her eyes glistening. "She always knows how to make things better with a meal. It's her way of showing love."

Mrs. Davis continued moving about the kitchen, pretending not to hear the playful exchange between her daughter and Ross. Her sharp eyes followed their every move, and a knowing smile crept across her lips. She nodded, fully immersed in the delightful scene unfolding before her.

"Hmm," she said, loud enough to be heard, though her eyes remained fixed on the pot she was stirring. "I can't remember the last time I saw my daughter smile like that."

Grace froze, her head snapping toward her mother. "Mom!"

Mrs. Davis didn't look up and continued to stir with deliberate nonchalance. "What? I'm just saying, it's refreshing to see a little life back in your face."

Ross, standing by the counter with an amused expression, chuckled softly. "I'll take that as a compliment."

Mrs. Davis finally glanced over, her gaze landing on him with a mix of curiosity and approval. "Oh, it was absolutely a compliment. And for the record, Ross, red is her color."

Grace groaned, burying her face in her hands. "Mom, stop!"

Mrs. Davis shrugged, entirely unfazed. "What? I like him. He's charming, funny, and clearly not afraid to call you out on your nonsense. It's about time someone did."

Grace peeked at Ross through her fingers, finding him grinning ear to ear. "Don't encourage him," she mumbled.

"Oh, I don't think he needs encouragement," Mrs. Davis replied smoothly. "He seems to be doing just fine on his own."

Ross leaned against the counter, arms crossed, and shot Grace a playful look. "Your mom's pretty great, you know. I think I'll keep her on my side." He said with a wink.

Mrs. Davis raised a brow, a mischievous twinkle in her eye. "Smart man."

Grace threw her hands in the air in mock exasperation. "You two deserve each other."

Mrs. Davis and Ross exchanged a conspiratorial smile, both clearly enjoying how flustered Grace had become. Mrs. Davis sighed contentedly. It had been a long time since she'd seen her daughter this animated, and she wasn't about to let the moment pass without relishing it.

"On that note," Ross said, his deep voice warm with amusement, "I think it's time for my shower. If you ladies excuse me, I'll return when I'm more presentable."

Grace raised an eyebrow, crossing her arms as he started toward the stairs. "Oh, please. You're already smug enough; a shower won't help."

Ross paused mid-step, turning back with a mock-offended expression. "Smug? You wound me, Grace. I prefer to call it 'quiet confidence.'"

Mrs. Davis chuckled, unable to hide her delight at their banter. "Call it whatever you like, Ross. But I'd say you've earned at least a little of that confidence."

Ross gave her a playful salute. "Thank you, Mrs. Davis. At least someone here appreciates me."

Grace rolled her eyes, but a small smile tugged at her lips. "Just go, Ross. The sooner you leave, the sooner the air in here gets less... insufferable."

He laughed, retreating up the stairs but calling over his shoulder, "Don't miss me too much while I'm gone."

Mrs. Davis waited until he disappeared before turning to Grace with a sly smile. "He's charming, isn't he?"

Grace sighed, shaking her head but unable to suppress her own smile. "He's... something, all right."

Mrs. Davis leaned back, her gaze softening. "He's good for you, Grace. You need someone who keeps you on your toes."

Grace didn't respond right away, her mind lingering on Ross's easy grin and the warmth he brought into the room. "Maybe," she said finally, her voice quiet but filled with thought. "Maybe I do."

"What are your plans for this evening?" Mrs. Davis asked, her eyes studying Grace carefully.

Grace took a deep breath. "Ross said he's taking you back to your car tonight. I'm going home with you, Mom," her tone firm but gentle. "I've got clothes there, and if you can take me to Zoe's tomorrow, I can pick up my car. I'll get Ross's bathrobe back to him soon.

I'd like to visit the pier sometime, too. Grace's voice was soft, almost a whisper as she spoke, her eyes distant. "I feel like I need to experience it quietly, with no reporters and no distractions. Just me and the pier."

Her mother nodded slowly, her expression softening with understanding. "I get it," she said. "Sometimes you need closure on your own terms."

Grace smiled faintly, grateful for her mother's empathy.

"Does Ross know you're coming home with me?" her mom asked, tilting her head slightly.

"Yes, I told him," Grace replied. "He's okay with it."

Mrs. Davis studied her daughter for a moment, a small, approving smile tugging at her lips. "I like him, dear," she said simply, her voice warm with sincerity.

Grace looked down, her cheeks flushing slightly. "I know," she admitted, her voice softer. "Me too."

He was a sight to behold when Ross joined them in the living room. He wore a pair of tailored charcoal slacks that hugged his lean frame just right, paired with a crisp, sky-blue button-down shirt. The top two buttons were left undone, revealing a hint of his tanned collarbone, and the sleeves were rolled casually to his elbows, adding a touch of effortless charm. A leather belt and polished loafers completed the look, exuding an air of sophistication and ease.

Grace glanced up and felt her breath hitch for just a moment. He looked so much like the man she had first seen on the deck of the ship, except this time, he wasn't wearing khaki shorts and slip-on shoes. There was a maturity to his presence now, a depth in his golden brown eyes that hadn't been there before. She smiled softly, her thoughts briefly slipping back to how much had changed since that first encounter.

The three gathered around the dining table, where Mrs. Davis had outdone herself. The meal was a comforting symphony of flavors and warmth: roasted herb chicken, buttery mashed potatoes, and green beans cooked to tender perfection with a hint of garlic. A fresh garden salad adorned with slices of ripe avocado and cherry tomatoes sat in the middle of the table, along with a warm basket of freshly baked rolls.

Grace savored every bite as they ate, her face lighting up with pure delight. "I sure have missed this," she said, her voice filled with appreciation. "Real food. Food that doesn't taste like it was caught or hunted an hour ago."

Ross chuckled, his fork hovering over his plate. "Amen to that," he agreed. "I had all this in my freezer and fridge? I'm going to have to have you come over more often. And that's not just because I've been living off fish, coconuts, and... questionable meats."

Mrs. Davis laughed warmly, clearly pleased by the compliment. "Well, I'm glad to give you both a proper meal," she said. "Though I'm not sure what to make of the fact that my cooking is competing with 'questionable meats.'"

They all laughed, the sound filling the room like a healing balm. The warmth of the food and the company created a sense of normalcy that felt almost surreal.

Later that evening, Ross drove Grace and Mrs. Davis to the pier. The city lights reflected off the calm water, creating a serene backdrop as they arrived. Grace stepped out of the car first, taking a deep breath of the salty air as she looked at the empty pier. It was quiet. Just the lapping of waves against the dock.

As Mrs. Davis got into her car, Ross and Grace stood by her car door, the soft hum of the night wrapping around them. Ross reached out, gently tucking a loose strand of hair behind her ear. "So, this is it?" he asked, his voice low and filled with emotion.

"For now," Grace said softly, her eyes searching his. "Thank you, Ross. For everything."

"You don't have to thank me," he said, his hand laced with hers. "You saved me as much as I saved you, Grace."

Tears pricked at her eyes, and she blinked them away quickly. She leaned in, pressing a soft kiss to his cheek. "Take care of yourself," she whispered.

Ross smiled, though there was a trace of sadness in his eyes. "You too," he said, stepping back as she climbed into the car.

Mrs. Davis started the engine, glancing at Ross with a knowing smile. "You're a good man," she said simply.

"Take care of her," Ross replied, his gaze steady.

As the car pulled away, Grace turned in her seat to look back at him, her heart twisting as his figure grew smaller in the distance. A bittersweet smile crossed her lips as she whispered, "Goodbye, Ross." The words carried conviction and heartache, a promise of something not yet finished.

CHAPTER THIRTY-SEVEN

WEEKS HAD PASSED SINCE the rescue, yet the television remained off. Grace knew exactly what awaited her if she turned it on—the same endless loop, the same damn footage, the same relentless reminders of a day best left behind. The world had latched on to the story and refused to let it go.

Grace slowly reclaimed her life piece by piece. She started with the basics—replacing her phone and her credit cards. She secured a new driver's license and all other missing identification. Each step felt like a small victory—a way of regaining control over what the storm had taken. With every document replaced and every number re-established, she's reminded that, no matter what happens, life can always be rebuilt. The process is methodical, almost therapeutic, but also bittersweet.

She continued to stay with her mother, choosing distance over confrontation, but soon Ethan became the final door she needed to close.

She hadn't seen or spoken to him since the day at the pier.

His number was still blocked on her phone.

At first, it had been necessary—self-preservation. She wasn't ready to deal with his excuses, charm, or manipulation. But now it was time.

After weeks of clarity and rediscovery, she found herself in the kitchen, where it was warm and inviting, filled with the comforting scent of cinnamon and baked apples. Grace's mother stood at the counter, adding the final decorative touches to an apple pie, her hands moving with the ease of someone who had done this a thousand times.

Grace lingered in the doorway for a moment before stepping in. "Mom, can I talk to you?"

Her mother glanced over her shoulder, offering a soft smile. "Of course, dear." She set the pie aside and wiped her hands on a kitchen towel. "What is it?"

Grace hesitated, then took a deep breath. She sat in a chair at the kitchen table. "I just wanted to let you know that I'm going to set up a time to meet with Ethan."

Her mother's hands stilled, her brows knitting together in immediate disapproval. "Why?" she asked, turning to face Grace. "He doesn't deserve it."

"I have to see him, Mom," Grace admitted, folding her arms. "This whole ordeal changed me. I'm curious to find out if it changed him at all."

Her mother let out a weary sigh, shaking her head as she crossed the kitchen and sat in the chair next to Grace. "And when you realize it hasn't, then what?"

"Then I go to the next phase of my life. I move on."

Her mother studied her for a long moment, concern etched into her features. "Sweetheart, you don't need Ethan's permission to move on. That man put you through hell. You don't owe him a conversation, let alone a second thought."

"I know that." She sighed. "But I need to face him. On my terms. No running, no blocking, no pretending like he never existed."

Her mother continued to study her, then leaned back in her chair. "I think it's a mistake, dear. But I know when you set your mind to something, there's no talking you out of it."

Grace gave a small smile. "Wonder where I got that stubborn streak."

Her mother smirked. "Must be genetic." She exhaled through her nose, shaking her head. "I suppose I can't stop you. But I don't want you walking into this thinking you'll find something that isn't there. Men like Ethan don't change, dear. At least, not in the way you want them to."

Grace nodded slowly, though doubt still clouded her expression.

Her mother studied her carefully before asking, "Have you spoken to Ross?"

Grace lowered her gaze. "No."

"Are you going to?"

Grace bit her lip, then shook her head slowly.

Her mother let out an exasperated sigh. "Oh, Grace."

"Mom, it's just... complicated."

"No, sweetheart, it's not," her mother said, her voice low but firm. "I like Ross. I like him *a lot*. That man carried you off that pier like you were the most important thing in the world to him. He fought for you. And I know you love him. So, I need to ask—why are you making Ethan a priority right now when Ross is the one who actually deserves a conversation?"

Grace swallowed hard. "Because I need to close one door before I walk through another."

Her mother reached across the table, taking Grace's hands in hers. "That's fair, but don't take too long standing in that doorway, dear. Because the things that matter most don't wait forever."

Grace felt the weight of those words settle deep in her chest.

Her mother gave her hands a squeeze. "Just promise me this—after you see Ethan, you'll talk to Ross. Because, Grace, if you let him slip away, I think you'll regret it more than anything."

Grace nodded, knowing deep down that her mother was right.

"Okay, Mom."

Her mother smiled, though worry lingered in her eyes. Then she stood and walked back to the pie, running a careful hand over the crust.

"Now, do you want to help me with this pie or just plan to stand there brooding?"

Grace let out a breath of laughter, stepping forward. "Fine. But if the pie turns out lopsided, I'm blaming you."

"Oh, honey," her mother teased, "if this pie turns out lopsided, I'm blaming Ethan."

Grace laughed, shaking her head, but the conversation still weighed on her.

She knew what she had to do. She just hoped she had the courage to follow through.

CHAPTER
THIRTY-EIGHT

Ross stood at the window. The quiet of the house pressed in around him, the absence of Grace's presence settling like a weight in his chest. She had only been there for a day, and it felt like a lifetime. This was her home. He could still see her standing in his robe, the fabric hanging loosely around her frame.

His jaw tightened as he turned away, his footsteps heavy in the empty space. The couch where she had sat, the coffee cup she had held—each small detail felt amplified. A hollow ache spread through him, unexpected yet undeniable.

He ran a hand through his hair. Did he really have the right to feel this way? He had no claim to her beyond the connection they had shared on the island.

He exhaled slowly, rubbing a hand over his face as if trying to shake off the lingering warmth of her being there.

But damn if he didn't miss her.

Ross closed his eyes, the memory of her voice as clear as if she were standing in front of him.

"If I choose to pursue this thing between us, I hurt Ethan. And if I decide to go back to my husband, I hurt you. Either way, somebody gets hurt. I don't want you to get hurt because of me."

His jaw tensed, muscles twitching as his thoughts darkened. Ethan! That pathetic excuse for a man. Damn it. They were not equals when it came to loving Grace.

Ross exhaled sharply, his fingers curling into fists at his sides. He could still feel the satisfaction of that punch—the way his knuckles had connected with Ethan's smug face. But it hadn't just been about the moment. That punch had been fueled by every betrayal, every disloyal situation Ethan had put Grace through.

Ross wasn't afraid of a fight—but this wasn't a fight he could win with his fists.

Ethan didn't deserve her. But it didn't mean that the pull of familiarity wouldn't tempt her back.

Ross paced the length of his living room, his fingers gripping his phone tighter than necessary. He had tried to stay patient, but the not knowing was eating him alive. With a sigh, he scrolled to a number and tapped it.

The phone rang twice before Ray picked up, his voice laced with amusement. "RJ Henderson. To what do I owe the pleasure? Don't tell me the news media finally tracked you down."

"No. It's still been pretty quiet over here, but that's not why I'm calling."

"What's up, man?"

Ross pinched the bridge of his nose. "How is everything? How's Zoe?"

"Zoe's good, man."

"So, the two of you are working out then?"

"Actually, yeah, we are. So, are we going to continue this small talk, or are you going to ask me what you really want to know?"

Ross exhaled, rubbing a hand over his jaw. "Is she back with him?"

There was a pause, and then Ray's voice returned, softer this time. "No, man. She's still staying with her mother. She didn't even go home to get more clothes. She told Zoe she'd rather buy new ones than deal with him."

Ross let out a breath he hadn't realized he was holding.

"From what Zoe says," Ray continued, "Grace hasn't even spoken to Ethan. Hell, I don't think she's even acknowledged his existence. But—"

Ross's lungs constricted. "But what?"

Ray chuckled. "Relax. It's a good 'but.'"

Ross frowned, "Then get to it."

"Zoe says her face lights up whenever your name is mentioned."

The weight in Ross's chest shifted, replaced by a rush of warmth. He smiled. Somehow, knowing that made his mood lighter.

"You serious?" he asked, though his voice had lost some of its tension.

"Dead serious."

Ross ran a hand through his hair, leaning against the wall. "Then what the hell is she waiting for?"

"She's got it in her head that she has to close one chapter before she starts another. She's just trying to figure out how to do it."

Ross let out a frustrated sigh. "How long does it take to close a damn chapter?"

Ray chuckled. "You just have to be patient."

"Yeah, well, patience was never my strong suit."

"Look, I know it sucks, but from what I hear, Grace isn't torn between you and Ethan. She's done with him—she's torn between you and whatever sense of obligation she thinks she has to her past. And trust me, she's gonna realize soon enough that you're her future."

Ross was silent for a moment, absorbing Ray's words. He wanted to believe that—needed to.

"And if she doesn't?" Ross finally asked, his voice quieter.

"Come on, Ross. Grace is no fool." Ray said without hesitation. "Just... hold on a little longer."

Ross exhaled through his nose, staring at the floor.

"Yeah," he murmured. "All right."

"Good. Now stop moping and go do something useful. Chop wood, go to the gym, lift weights, but..." he paused for a second, "keep me posted."

Ross huffed a quiet laugh. "Yeah, yeah. Thanks, Ray."

"Anytime, Henderson. Hang in there."

Ross ended the call, setting his phone on the living room table.

Hold on a little longer.

His fingers drummed against the surface, and he returned to the window. He wasn't sure how much longer he could take it, but if Grace was still thinking about him—*if she still lit up at the mention of his name*—then maybe, just maybe, the wait would be worth it.

Ross let out a slow breath, pressing his palms against the windowsill, staring at nothing in particular. The waiting would be the worst part. Knowing she was out there, wrestling with a decision that felt inevitable to him—but only if she let herself see it.

CHAPTER THIRTY-NINE

TIME STRETCHED BY AND Grace knew she had procrastinated long enough. It was time. She sent the text, the one that would set everything in motion. It was simple and direct—nothing like the fiery confrontation she once thought it would be.

Grace: *We need to talk. Coffee tomorrow at 2?*

Ethan: *It's about time. I'll be there.*

She knew what that meant; it wasn't just about the words. It was the tension she saw beneath them, the echo of someone who still couldn't let go of control. He wasn't giving up, not as long as he thought he still had something to fight for. But this time, she wasn't the woman who could be coerced. She wasn't the woman who stayed in the background, silently suffering, letting him set the pace of their lives. She sent the name of the café and laid her phone down.

The place was small and quiet—a corner café tucked away from the prying eyes of the busy streets, the kind of place where the clink of coffee cups could fill the silence between two people without being awkward. They had spent many hours talking about everything and nothing in places like this. Back when it was easy.

She arrived early, taking a seat by the window. The air outside was cool, the last vestiges of autumn clinging to the trees. She sat thinking about everything she had been through in the past few months. The isolation on the island, the endless quiet. The space she had found to truly listen to herself. And now, here she was, about to face the man who had once been her entire world.

Ethan arrived on time, his usual confident stride, the faint hint of a smirk tugging at his lips as he spotted her. She watched him approach. The man who had once made her heart race, but now, all she could feel was a quiet, simmering detachment. He was still the same—still so sure of himself, trying to twist the world to his needs.

"Grace," he said, his voice smooth but with that edge of entitlement she had come to know too well. "Finally found time to add me to your schedule, huh?"

She didn't respond immediately. Her gaze was steady, but she was calculating. Trying to gauge if he had changed. If there was anything left in him worth salvaging.

He sat across from her, eyes scanning her face as though trying to read her expressions. But Grace wasn't the woman he knew anymore. She wasn't the one he could manipulate with those tender words or sweet promises.

"I'm happy you asked to meet me, Grace," Ethan continued, leaning forward. "We have things to talk about—unfinished business. I thought when you came back, we could, you know, fix things? It's been a hell of a ride, but we're strong. We've always been strong."

Grace felt a bitter laugh rise in her chest but didn't let it out. Instead, she said, "Unfinished business, Ethan? After everything? You think this meeting is about unfinished business?"

Ethan's smirk faltered for a moment, but he quickly recovered. "Come on. We've been through a lot, but we've always made it work, haven't we? You leave, you come back. You always do."

"I came here for closure," Grace said, her voice calm, but the impact of her words hit harder than she intended. "I came here to see if there was anything left of the man I thought I knew. As soon as you walked in, I could see there was nothing."

Ethan's expression shifted, the mask of charm slipping into something more familiar. His voice took on a harder edge. "Grace, what are you doing?"

She ignored his question and asked one of her own. "What are you going to do about Olivia and the baby?"

"I'm going to take care of them. I thought we could fix up the guest bedroom. Add a crib and some, you know, baby things. We could keep the baby with us when Olivia's working."

Grace stared at him in disbelief. "And how do you plan to take care of them when you don't have a job, Ethan?" She asked.

Ethan leaned back in his chair, his arms crossed. "I figured you'd help me. You always do. You know how it goes. You take care of things, Grace. That's how it's always been."

Grace stared at him, her stomach twisted, and heat rose in her chest as she set her coffee down with trembling hands—not with weakness but with barely contained rage.

"Are you actually serious right now? You expect me to *what*—play stepmother to the child you had with another woman?

To clean up *your* mess while you get to pretend everything's fine? Do you even hear yourself?"

She let out a bitter laugh, shaking her head.

"You didn't just betray me, Ethan—you destroyed me. You shattered my trust, my dignity, and my sense of home. And now, you sit here and act like I should *help you* raise proof of that betrayal?"

She leaned forward, her voice trembling with controlled fury." Do you even understand what you're asking? Do you know what it feels like to be *replaced*? To have your world ripped apart while you were busy trying to hold it together? I was fighting for us, and you..." she broke off, blinking back the sting in her eyes, her jaw tightening. "You were out creating a family with someone else. Don't you dare ask me to make it easier for you. Here's what I'm going to do. I'm going to let you and Olivia take care of your own baby. You need to figure out how to live with what you've done. It's called responsibility, Ethan."

Ethan's eyes narrowed, but she could see the doubt flicker behind them. He wasn't used to her being this direct, this sharp. He was used to her being the woman who folded under pressure. "Come on. Where are you going with this? It's not that simple."

"Oh yes, it is. You made it simple by choosing to be disloyal. You walked away from me before you knew you were doing it. Every time you lied to me, every time you chipped away pieces of me with your gaslighting." Grace's voice held the finality of someone who had spent too long running from the truth. "I let you turn me into someone I didn't recognize anymore.

Ethan stood up abruptly, his chair scraping loudly against the floor. "This is insane, Grace. You're making a big mistake!"

Grace stared at him, stunned by the sheer audacity of his words. A bitter laugh escaped her lips, though there was no humor in it. Her eyes burned with fury as she leaned forward, her voice low but lethal.

"Sit your ass down, Ethan."The words cut through the air like a blade, sharp and unforgiving. Her fingers curled around the edge of the table, her knuckles white, her teeth clenched so tight it was a wonder she didn't shatter them.

She didn't raise her voice—she didn't have to. The anger simmering beneath her skin, the quiet authority in her tone, was enough to freeze him in place.

For a second, he hesitated. His jaw clenched, his hands forming fists at his sides. But something in her eyes—something he'd never seen before—made him falter. Slowly, reluctantly, he sank back into his chair. "So, you're just going to throw away everything we built?"

Grace exhaled, steadying herself. Then, with deadly calm, she met his gaze. "The only thing we built was a house of lies. Now listen carefully, Ethan, because I'm only going to say this once. I don't want you calling me, texting, or dropping by. For the record, I'm not throwing anything away. I'm simply handing it back to you. It's time that I choose me for once."

The silence between them stretched long, and Grace felt the full weight of her decision sink deep into her bones. "You'll be hearing from my attorney."

"By the way, I watched the viral videos, Ethan," Grace said quietly, her voice steady even with the storm raging inside her. "I saw the lies. I saw how you tried to spin everything and thought you could manipulate the world into seeing you as the victim. It was humiliating."

Ethan leaned forward, his voice low and tense. "Who was the man, Grace? The one who punched me and carried you away? What's going on there?"

Grace smiled, "That was Ross. He's been there for me in ways you couldn't even begin to understand."

279

"Ross?" Ethan scoffed. "So, now you've got a new knight in shining armor."

"This is not about Ross. It's about you and me."

Ethan's face blanched. "Grace, you're not listening to me. You don't know what you're doing. How am I supposed to live without you?"

She shrugged. "I have no idea. All I know is that... I'm done."

Ethan opened his mouth to speak, but she pushed her chair back. Stood, picked up her purse with a quiet finality, then glared at him one last time.

"I lost enough of myself loving you, Ethan. I won't lose another second cleaning up the wreckage you left behind."And with that, she walked away, leaving him to sit in the mess he created—alone. She didn't need to hear his excuses anymore. She had made her choice. It wasn't out of anger. It wasn't out of revenge. It was a choice made out of self-preservation.

And when Gracee stepped outside, she knew that she was finally free.

CHAPTER FORTY

G RACE SAT IN THE small restaurant, absently twirling her glass of wine between her fingers. Her thoughts had been quieter lately, more structured, but there was still an ache she couldn't quite place. She'd had weeks to think, to process, and to reflect. Social media was still filled with videos of Ethan's public embarrassment. His words replayed like an endless loop of irony and shame. Grace shook her head every time she saw it, her lips twisting with disbelief and pity.

She knew now, with absolute clarity, that Ethan was no longer part of her world—no longer overshadowing her choices. The realization was freeing, but it left her questioning what came next.

Zoe plopped down across from her, her usual energy lighting up the room. She pushed a stray strand of hair behind her ear and gave Grace a knowing smile.

"What's that look for?" Grace asked, raising an eyebrow.

"Oh, nothing," Zoe replied, feigning innocence. "Just wondering when you're going to stop moping around like a tragic heroine in one of those novels you used to read."

Grace rolled her eyes. "I'm not moping. I'm thinking."

"Thinking? Please," Zoe said with a dramatic sigh. "You've been thinking for weeks. You've had plenty of time to figure out that Ethan is trash—thank goodness you're done with him—and now you're just stalling."

Grace frowned. "I'm not stalling."

"Oh, really?" Zoe leaned forward, her eyes narrowing with playful suspicion. "Have you seen Ross lately?"

Grace's heart skipped a beat, and she focused intently on her wine. "No."

Zoe's grin widened. "Why not? What are you waiting for? Another storm to throw you two together?"

Grace looked up, startled by the accuracy of Zoe's words. "It's not that simple, Zoe."

"Sure, it is," Zoe said with a shrug. "You're in love with him, aren't you?"

Grace blinked, her cheeks flushing. "I..."

"Don't even try to deny it," Zoe interrupted, pointing her finger at Grace. "I see it all over your face. You light up when you talk about or even think about him. Ethan's out of the picture. What's stopping you?"

Grace sighed, leaning back in her chair. "I guess I'm scared. What if it doesn't work out? What if I get hurt again?"

Zoe reached across the table and took Grace's hand, her voice softening. "Grace, you've already been through hell. You've survived more than most people ever will. Don't let fear stop you from being happy. Ross isn't Ethan. He's one of the good ones. You know that."

Grace nodded slowly and changed the subject. "I was thinking of visiting the pier tomorrow morning. She said, keeping her voice casual. "You wanna come with me?"

Zoe froze mid-sip, then slowly set her glass down, her eyes narrowing like Grace had just suggested jumping into shark-infested waters.

"Not a chance," Zoe said flatly. "I've had enough of that place to last me a lifetime."

Grace smirked, picking up her wine. "Come on. No cameras, no chaos. Just... quiet."

"Yeah, well, I like my quiet with walls and a working thermostat now." Zoe crossed her arms. "Seriously, what's the appeal? Haven't we suffered enough near large bodies of water?"

"It's not about the water," Grace admitted, staring at her hands. "I just... need to go back. Experience it without all the noise. Just clear my head and..." she hesitated, "...just be."

Zoe exhaled, her expression softening.

"You sure this isn't about Ross?"

Grace blinked, caught off guard. "What? No. I mean... maybe? I don't know."

Zoe gave her a knowing look. "Mmhmm."

Grace sighed, rubbing the back of her neck. "I feel like I've been stuck between who I was before and who I'm supposed to be now. And everything was a blur the last time I was at that pier. I just want to stand there and feel it—on my own terms."

Zoe studied her for a moment, then smirked. "You're really set on this, huh?"

"I am."

Zoe let out a huff and picked up her wine. "What time are you going? If I change my mind, I'll meet you there."

Grace chuckled. "Fair enough. I'm thinking about 9:00. You think I'm crazy, don't you?"

Zoe grinned. "Oh, without a doubt. But hey, you wouldn't be you if you weren't."

Grace laughed. "So, what about you, Zoe? What's going on with you and Ray?"

A dreamy look crossed Zoe's face, and she smiled. "I'm in love with him."

Grace's eyes widened in surprise and delight. "That's wonderful news, Zoe."

Zoe's smile turned mischievous. "Yeah, it is. But don't think you're off the hook. You need to figure things out about Ross. You deserve to be happy, Grace. Really happy."

Grace nodded, her heart lighter than it had been in weeks. "I'll think about it, Zoe. I promise."

Grace sat curled up on the couch in her mother's living room, staring at the untouched cup of tea in her hands. The steam curled lazily into the air, the faint scent of chamomile filling the quiet space. It should have been calming. It wasn't.

Her mother sat across from her, watching her carefully, waiting.

"You're thinking about him."

It wasn't a question.

Grace let out a slow breath, running her fingers along the rim of her mug. She had been thinking about him. Every day. Every night. Ross.

"I don't know what I'm waiting for," she admitted, her voice barely above a whisper.

Her mother tilted her head. "I think you do."

Grace swallowed.

She had already left Ethan. Not just physically but emotionally.

And she had already chosen Ross.

The realization hit her like a rush of wind, swift and undeniable.

"I love him." The words slipped out before she could stop them, and once they were spoken, she felt them settle deep inside her. "I love Ross."

Her mother smiled softly, reaching over to squeeze her hand. "Then why are you still here?"

Grace blinked, her fingers absentmindedly twisting the gold band around her finger. The weight of it had once felt like security, like a promise—but now, it was nothing more than a reminder of everything she had outgrown.

The morning sun cast a golden glow over the pier, its warmth cutting through the cool, salty air. Grace stepped out of her car and breathed deeply, letting the sea breeze fill her lungs. The scene was serene, almost surreal. There were no reporters or desperate cries for answers—just the quiet lapping of waves and the occasional call of a seagull—a sense of peace.

She stood at the edge of the pier, savoring it. Listening to the gentle ebb of the waves below her feet creating a soothing hum. The salty breeze tousled her hair, carrying the scent of the ocean and memories she couldn't shake. She closed her eyes. It was so quiet here now, unlike the day they'd returned.

Her fingers lightly traced the wooden railing as she walked, her footsteps soft and unhurried. In her mind, she replayed the craziness of that day—the flashing cameras, the reporters shouting her name, and then the moment she'd watched a fire ignite in Ross's eyes. That punch landed perfectly and deservedly, and her heart still raced at the memory.

She smiled faintly, her cheeks warming at the thought of how he had scooped her up like she weighed nothing, his protective strength shielding her from the world. She had replayed that clip a thousand times, every detail etched into her mind—the stunned gasp of the crowd, Ethan's bewildered expression, and the way Ross's arms felt around her.

But it wasn't just the physical act that stuck with her. It was the declaration beneath it, the implied promise in his actions: *I will always protect you. You're worth it.*

Grace sighed, leaning over the railing to watch the waves lap at the pier's support. Her chest swelled with conflicting emotions. She'd spent weeks untangling her feelings, sorting through the wreckage of her marriage and the unexpected, undeniable connection she felt with Ross. And now, here she was—standing where it had all come to a head.

Her demeanor was calm, but her eyes betrayed the turmoil within. They carried a quiet intensity, reflecting the determination she'd slowly built during her time alone. Now, she wondered if she had taken too long.

She straightened, brushing a strand of hair behind her ear as her lips curled into a soft, bittersweet smile. "That day changed everything," she admitted, her voice almost lost in the wind.

Her heart tugged as she thought of Ross—not just the man who defended her, but the man who saw her, challenged her, and who, in spite of everything, had stayed close in his own quiet way. She couldn't ignore it anymore. Every memory of him carried a warmth that settled deep in her chest, a quiet assurance that this—whatever it was—was real.

"Wow," came a low voice behind her. "Fancy meeting you here."

Startled, Grace whipped around to see Ross standing a few feet away, his hands casually in his pockets, a soft smile playing on his lips. Her heart skipped a beat, her breath catching in her throat.

"Ross?" she said, barely believing her eyes. "What are you doing here?"

"I could ask you the same," he replied, his voice steady but warm. "But since you asked first... I needed to come back. The last time we were here, it was pure pandemonium. I wanted to experience it in the quiet and light of day."

Grace tilted her head, studying him. "You didn't know I'd be here?"

Ross shook his head, stepping closer. "It feels right that you would be."

Her lips parted slightly in surprise, and she glanced down, suddenly self-conscious. "My mom didn't tell you I was coming?"

Ross chuckled softly. "I don't have your mom's number, and I don't think she has mine. Unless..." he arched an eyebrow, teasing, "you?"

"I didn't," Grace said quickly, a faint blush rising to her cheeks. "So... this is just a coincidence?"

"I wouldn't call it a coincidence," Ross said, his gaze holding hers. "I believe it's fate—fate and a friend named Zoe."

She nodded, "Zoe." She took a small step toward him, her voice soft. "It's good to see you, Ross."

He opened his arms slightly, his smile deepening. "Come here, woman."

Grace hesitated only for a moment before running into his embrace. As Ross's arms wrapped around her, warmth spread through every inch of her being, melting the tension that had gone unnoticed until now. This was a sanctuary, a space where letting go felt natural. His hold didn't just offer safety; it felt like home, like something long sought after without ever realizing the absence.

She closed her eyes, sinking into the steady rhythm of his heartbeat, a quiet lullaby against her crazy thoughts. His hand moved gently along her back, soothing and anchoring her, as if silently promising, *I've got you.*

And... she believed it.

"You belong here," Ross said, his voice low."

Grace pulled back slightly to look up at him. "Did the reporters ever catch up with you?"

He shook his head. "Nope. But, It's just a matter of time."

"Do you care?"

"Not at all. I'd tell the world I love you."

She rested her ear back against his chest. "I love you too."

Her heart was full yet aching, "This feels so good. I feel like I'm at home when I'm with you," she admitted.

"That's because you are."

"Sometimes I wonder if I deserve that."

Ross cupped her face in his hands, his eyes searching hers. "You know you do, Grace. You deserve especially that."

Their lips met in a slow, tender kiss that erased every doubt and fear. Everything outside that moment felt irrelevant, leaving only the two of them.

When they finally pulled away, Grace smiled softly, her eyes brimming with unshed tears. "Oh, I have something for you."

Ross arched a curious eyebrow.

She walked to her car and pulled a small bag from the back seat. Returning to him, she held it out with a shy smile. "Your bathrobe. I've been carrying it with me in case I got—I thought you might want it back."

Ross laughed, taking the bag but keeping his eyes on her. "You didn't have to. Unless you're coming home with me. In that case, you can wear it in the morning."

Her cheeks flushed at his words, but she didn't look away. "Ross..."

He dipped his head and gave her a wink. "When you're ready."

Grace turned back toward the ocean, her gaze drawn to the horizon. She slipped her hand into her pocket and pulled out her wedding ring, the small band of gold glinting in the sunlight. She just stared at it for a moment, her emotions swirling—pain, hope, freedom.

"What are you doing? You okay?" Ross asked gently, sensing her hesitation.

Grace met his gaze, her eyes steady. "I'm finally letting go."

With a flick of her wrist, she tossed the ring into the water. The tiny splash it made seemed insignificant, but to Grace, it was monumental. She exhaled deeply, a weight lifting from her shoulders.

Ross reached for her hand, intertwining his fingers with hers. "You okay?"

She nodded, her lips curving into a genuine smile. "Yeah. I am now."

He squeezed her hand. The sound of their footsteps was the only noise, a quiet rhythm that matched the steady beat of her heart.

As they reached his car, Ross turned to her one last time, kissing her and placing a light kiss against her forehead. "I'll see you soon?"

Grace smiled, her heart full of something she hadn't dared to hope for. "You'd better."

He slid behind the wheel of his car and started the engine. She watched as he pulled away, his taillights disappearing into the distance. Then, with a deep breath and a final decision, she slid into her own car and followed him. She was still running, but this time, she was running toward the only thing that had ever truly felt right.

Ross glanced in his rearview mirror, his gaze softening as he saw Grace's car following close behind. A knowing, satisfying smile crept across his face. She hadn't turned away or let the fears or doubts hold her back. She was with him in every sense of the word.

He powered down his window with a quiet chuckle, letting the warm breeze tousle his hair. He extended his arm, giving a subtle wave of acknowledgment. It was his way of letting her know he understood her decision and it was the right one.

CHAPTER
FORTY-ONE

"SURVIVORS OF THE EMERALD *Princess shipwreck are still adjusting to life after their harrowing ordeal. Among them, Ray Franklin and Zoe King—two unlikely allies who braved the wilderness together and lived to tell the tale.*"

Zoe groaned and smacked the mute button on the remote, tossing it onto the couch beside her. She slumped back against the cushions, rubbing her temples as if that would erase the ridiculous phrasing from existence.

"I swear if I hear them call us 'unlikely allies' one more time..."

Ray, sprawled comfortably in the recliner across from her, smirked as he took a slow sip of his beer. "At least they didn't call us 'heroes' this time. That title comes with expectations."

Zoe rolled her eyes and laughed. On the screen, the clip rolled for the millionth time—Ethan grabbing Grace, Ross stepping in, bam, Ethan stumbling back, clutching his face in shock. The camera zoomed in on Grace's stunned expression before Ross scooped her up like some kind of old Hollywood romance hero and marched off into the crowd, not even acknowledging the chaotic scene he left behind.

Zoe nearly choked on her drink. "I swear, Ross is going to need a publicist to handle this. The entire world is freaking out, and not one reporter managed to get a clear shot of his face. How is that even possible?"

Ray laughed, shaking his head. "Hey, I say let him enjoy it, because once they find out who he is, they're not going to leave him alone. He's gonna get promoted from shipwreck survivor to best-selling author, and then legend."

Zoe sighed dramatically, rubbing her temples. "I wonder how Grace and Ross deal with this every day. You think they get as tired as we do watching it?"

Ray smirked. "Are you kidding? Speak for yourself. That punch is legendary. They should frame it and play it on a loop at their wedding reception."

Zoe snorted. "Right, because nothing says 'happily ever after' like replaying your husband knocking out your toxic ex."

Ray shrugged. "I'd watch it."

"You have watched it. Multiple times." Zoe laughed, shaking her head.

"Can you blame me? That was some fine work. Perfect form, great follow-through—Ross should get a damn sports endorsement deal."

"You're way too invested in this."

Ray leaned forward, mock-serious. "Look, all I'm saying is if you're gonna have your personal drama broadcasted to the world, at least make it entertaining. And Ross? He delivered."

Zoe groaned and flopped back against the couch. "I swear, I don't know how Grace puts up with either of you."

Ray winked. "When she marries Ross. She'll be signed up for life."

"Guess that means I'll be signed up too." Zoe sighed.

Ray grinned. "You'll love it."

Zoe muttered something under her breath, but she didn't deny it.

What are they going to say next? "Survival was such a leisurely vacation? Or that we 'bonded over a shared love of the great outdoors'?"

"You gotta admit, we were pretty badass out there." Ray said, resting his beer on the table. "Especially when Ross held off the boars while I rigged the radio."

Zoe chuckled, shaking her head. "Fine. I'll give you that one."

Ray leaned forward. Feels weird being back in the real world."

Zoe sighed, her gaze drifting to the muted news broadcast where images of the shipwreck flashed across the screen. "Yeah, everything feels off. It's like we're expected to return to normal, but normal doesn't feel the same anymore."

Ray studied her for a moment before nodding. "Especially when you spend the first few nights sleeping on the floor instead of the bed because the mattress felt too soft. Too... fake."

Zoe turned to him, "I know. I wake up, expecting to hear the waves or the wind in the trees. And then I remember—oh right, I have four walls and a working shower again."

Ray gave her a small smile. "Luxury is weird, huh?"

"Luxury is overrated," Zoe muttered, "although the hot showers are a perk."

A comfortable silence settled between them. Outside, the city hummed—car horns, distant chatter, life moving forward like nothing had happened. But for them, everything had changed.

Ray finally broke the silence, stood, and closed the distance between them. "So... how long do you think it will be before we lose our 'unlikely allies' status?"

Zoe smirked. "The second they realize we actually love each other."

Ray grinned. "It's up to you if you want to keep 'em guessing."

"I honestly don't care who knows."

Ray leaned down and kissed her softly. The glow of the city lights streamed in through the window, casting gentle patterns across the room. Zoe exhaled, stealing a glance at Ray. "I love you."

"I fell in love with you the first time you tried to tell me how much lime to add to a drink."

He smiled and pulled her closer.

CHAPTER
FORTY-TWO

T HE DINING ROOM GLOWED with the warmth of flickering candles and the golden afternoon light filtering through the tall windows. The scent of roasted turkey, cinnamon, and fresh herbs filled the air, mingling with soft laughter and clinking glasses. The table, set with gleaming china and a rich autumn centerpiece, was surrounded by faces that now felt more like family than friends.

Ross looked around the room, his heart full. This house — their home — was lavish, sure, but the real richness was in the people gathered there. Grace caught his eye and smiled, her fingers brushing his hand beneath the table.

Grace's mom, sitting beside her, beamed with a joy that had been hard-won. Across from her, Zoe and Ray whispered and laughed together.

Zoe leaned toward Ross, twirling her wine glass between her fingers. "Have you heard from anyone?" she asked, her voice light but curious.

Ross, seated at the head of the table beside Grace, nodded. "Yeah, I still hear from the captain from time to time." He paused, taking a sip from his glass. "I invited him and his wife to join us for Thanksgiving dinner, but his family already had plans."

"That's a shame," Grace said, glancing toward Ross. "I would've loved to see him again."

"Same," Ray added, carving himself another piece of turkey. "The guy saved our asses. Would've been nice to feed him for once."

Laughter rippled around the table.

"Well, he told me they're just as thankful as we are to be able to enjoy this time together with family," Ross said, setting his glass down. "After everything... I think we all appreciate the little things a lot more now."

Zoe nodded thoughtfully, glancing around the table at the people who had become her family. "Yeah," she said softly, "I think we do."

A comfortable silence settled over the group, broken only by the soft pop of a champagne cork and the distant hum of music playing in the background.

A lot had changed in a year.

One of the biggest changes—one that still left Grace breathless when she thought about it—was that she was now *married* to Ross. What once felt impossible, what once seemed like a distant dream buried under years of heartbreak and self-doubt, had become her reality.

For the first time in her life, Grace was experiencing what it truly meant to be *loved*. Not just in words, not just in fleeting moments, but in every touch, every glance, every quiet reassurance that she was safe, cherished, and chosen.

Ross loved her. It was shown in even the little things. The way his fingers traced lazy circles on her back when he thought she was asleep, the way he listened—*really listened*—when she spoke, as if every word mattered. It was in the way he reached for her hand, even when they were just walking from one room to another, as if some part of him always needed to feel her close.

He was *thriving* in loving her. Every moment with Grace was a reminder of what it meant to truly share a life with someone—to *choose* them, day after day. He had waited for her, fought for her, and now, as he watched her move through their home, her laughter filling the space they had built together, he knew with absolute certainty—she was it. *She had always been it.*

Their love was *real*. It was the kind of love built on late-night conversations and sleepy morning kisses, on shared dreams and unwavering trust. It was the kind of love neither of them had dared to believe in before—one they now held onto with everything they had.

Because after everything they had been through, everything they had lost, *they had finally found each other.*

And neither of them would ever take that for granted.

Zoe leaned back in her chair, sipping her wine as she took in the familiar faces around the table. A year ago, the four of them had been survivors, clinging to each other in the wake of disaster. Now, they were embracing life unburdened by the past.

"All right, Franklin," she teased, nudging Ray beside her. "Tell them the big news."

Ray smirked, setting down his glass and stretching his arms as if he were about to make a grand speech.

"Well," he started, "for those of you who somehow missed the fireworks and the screaming of my loud and excited mother, Zoe and I are officially engaged."

Cheers and applause erupted around the table. Ross gave him a solid clap on the back while Grace reached across the table to squeeze Zoe's hand.

"About time!" Ross said with a grin.

"Took you long enough," Grace added with a wink.

Zoe rolled her eyes. "He was the one dragging his feet."

"Hey," Ray said, holding up his hands in mock offense. "I was waiting for the right moment."

"And the right ring," Zoe teased, flashing her left hand where a stunning engagement ring glittered in the candlelight.

"I had to make sure it was worthy of you," Ray said smoothly, pulling her close and kissing her.

Ross smirked. "So, what's next? Are we planning a tropical wedding? Maybe on an island? You know, since you two are such pros at surviving on one."

Laughter filled the room.

"Please," Zoe groaned, shaking her head. "I am never setting foot on an island again unless it has a five-star resort and room service."

"Noted," Ray chuckled, squeezing her hand.

Grace smiled. "But seriously, we're all so happy for you both."

"Thanks," Ray said, his expression softening. "And in other news, the captain put in a good word for me, and I'm officially back as head bartender on another cruise ship. No shipwrecks this time, hopefully."

"Hopefully," Zoe muttered, earning another round of laughter.

"I know I joke," Zoe continued, "but honestly, I'm so proud of you, Ray. You're doing what you love and worked your way back to it."

Ray turned to her, his expression warm. "And the best part? No matter where I go, I know exactly where home is."

Zoe's heart squeezed, and she smiled. "Yeah?"

"Yeah," he said with a wink."

A collective *awww* rippled around the table, and Zoe groaned. "Great. Now I *have* to marry him. He just locked it in."

Ray grinned. "Smart choice, babe.

Grace's mom smiled warmly, her eyes shining with pride. She set down her glass and reached for Grace's hand. "I'm so thankful that my daughter is home. I'm thankful for her strength." Her voice wavered slightly, the memories of the past year glimmering in her eyes. "It took so much courage to leave a life that wasn't serving you. And now, seeing you with Ross..." She turned to Ross, her smile deepening. "I'm grateful for a son-in-law who loves my daughter the way she deserves to be loved."

Ross's eyes softened, and he nodded, his voice husky. "Thanks, Mom. That means the world to me."

Grace squeezed her mother's hand. "I love you, Mom."

"I love you too, dear."

Ross stood, pulling Grace up beside him. The room fell quiet, the anticipation thickening in the air. He looked out at the faces around the table, his heart pounding with the weight of what he was about to say.

"We've been through so much this past year," Ross began, his voice steady but full of emotion. "From being lost at sea, to finding hope where we least expected it. We have all faced fears we never thought we'd overcome."

Grace smiled, her eyes glistening. "But we're thankful for it. Because without all of that frenzy and fear, we wouldn't be here. We wouldn't have found the people who make our lives worth living."

Ross's voice softened as he glanced at Grace, his eyes full of love. "And now, we have something else to be thankful for."

Grace took a deep breath, her smile radiant. "Ross and I are expecting a baby in the spring."

The room was utterly silent for a moment, the words sinking in. Then, the room exploded with joy.

"Oh my God!" Zoe squealed, nearly knocking over her chair as she leaped up to hug Grace. "I knew it! I knew something was up when you didn't toast with us!"

Ray clapped Ross on the back, grinning ear to ear. "Congratulations, man. That's incredible."

Grace's mom's hands flew to her mouth, tears streaming down her cheeks. "A grandbaby?" Her voice cracked. "Oh, Grace, I am so happy." She pulled her daughter into a fierce embrace, then hugged Ross tightly. "You're going to be wonderful parents."

Ross laughed, a mixture of joy and disbelief in his eyes. "We'd like to believe that."

Grace wrapped her arms around his waist, leaning into him as the celebration swirled around them. "We've got everything we need right here," she whispered.

Ross kissed the top of her head, his heart overflowing. "And a little one on the way."

The clinking of glasses, laughter, and tears of joy filled the room, a testament to love, survival, and the unbreakable bonds forged beyond the reach of the storm.

CHAPTER
FORTY-THREE

EPILOGUE

THE BOOKSTORE WAS PACKED, the energy in the air thick with antic- ipation. Rows of people filled the seats, holding crisp copies of RJ Henderson's new book, *Choosing Grace: A Story of Love and Survival*. The title gleamed in bold gold lettering against a deep ocean-blue cover—a quiet nod to the storm that had changed his life forever.

Cameras clicked rapidly, flashes illuminating the stage where RJ stood, ready to speak. As far as the media was concerned, this event wasn't just about his book—it was a reflection of survival, a glimpse into how those who had endured the Emerald Princess tragedy were moving forward. Reporters whispered among them- selves, some scribbling notes, others adjusting their cameras to capture the moment. The audience leaned in, eager to hear from the best-selling author who had lived through the unimaginable and come out on the other side with a story worth telling.

RJ stood at the podium, his presence commanding yet humble, his fingers lightly resting on the edges of the book in front of him. He scanned the faces in the audience—people who had come not just to hear his words but to feel them.

His gaze settled on her.

Grace sat in the front row, quiet but radiant, her hands gently resting over the curve of her belly. Their child. Their future. She wasn't just part of this story. She was the story.

RJ cleared his throat, shifting his focus back to the crowd. When he finally spoke, his voice was deep, steady, and filled with something unshakable.

"When I started writing this book, I thought I was telling a story about survival."

He let the words sink in, his eyes sweeping the audience.

"But survival is about more than just making it through the storm. It's about the choices we make when no one is watching. When the cameras are gone, and all that's left is you—and the truth of who you are."

The room was silent, hanging onto every word.

"I thought I understood strength. I thought I knew what it meant to love. But then I met someone who redefined everything I thought I knew. Someone who showed me that real strength isn't just surviving—it's *choosing* to live. It's choosing to love, even after the worst storms."

His gaze flicked back to Grace, something unspoken passed between them. And then back to the audience.

"Symbolically, the word grace is often associated with poise, beauty, and strength under pressure. It can also represent resilience and the ability to endure hardships with dignity and courage. Choosing Grace was never difficult for me.

302

I watched her find her way through the darkness, through the fear, through the weight of everything that tried to break her. Yet she survived.

I was there as Grace stumbled and fought through the wreckage of her past as she pieced herself back together with nothing but sheer determination and a heart too strong to be defeated.

I saw the moments when doubt crept in, when the pain nearly swallowed her whole. I saw the nights when she thought no one was watching, when she let the tears fall, when she questioned if she was enough.

But she never gave up.

She kept standing back up. She pushed forward. She found a way through it all—not because it was easy, not because she wasn't afraid, but because she refused to let the darkness win.

I have never seen anything more beautiful.

This book is a love story about resiliance—a kind of survival, not just surviving a tragedy but overcoming heartbreak, doubt, and fear... and choosing love anyway.

He took a breath, then stepped away from the podium, smiling at Grace glowing in the front row. He walked to her. At that moment he thought of the night he carried her away from the pier. As fate would have it, she was never meant to be a fleeting part of his life.

He held his hand out to her.

She smiled at him, love shining in her eyes, before placing her hand in his. He gently pulled her to her feet.

A ripple of murmurs spread through the crowd, eyes darting to the very pregnant woman beside him.

Confusion spread through the room like a slow-burning fuse. Reporters exchanged glances, flipping through notes and scrolling through archived footage on their phones, piecing together what had been right in front of them all along.

RJ continued, "I went on a cruise thinking I was going to find inspiration for my next novel—and I did.

Ladies and gentlemen, meet my wife, Grace.

The woman who changed my life. The woman who fought through the storm—both the one that crashed around us and the one that had been raging inside her for far too long.

And by choosing her, I found myself too.

She was the inspiration for the novel and the reason I believe in love again.

For the first time, the audience saw the whole picture—the love story and the future they were building together.

The crowd erupted—thunderous applause, standing ovations, and murmurs of realization spreading like wildfire. This was the woman who had inspired the pages of the book they held in their hands. The moment was electric.

Under the bright lights of the bookstore, it all began to come together. The best-selling author, RJ Henderson, was Ross, the man who had shielded Grace from the cameras. And now, another memory slammed into place—RJ was the mystery man who had punched Ethan Hargrove that day and carried Grace away in his arms, leaving the media scrambling for answers. The reporters had searched, dug through records, chased leads—yet none of them had been able to track Ross down. RJ Henderson and Ross are one and the same. Right in front of them, the truth was undeniable. The cameras flashed wildly as the weight of the revelation settled over the room. Cameras clicked frantically, pens scratched against notepads, the weight of the discovery sending a ripple of energy through the press. Not only was RJ Henderson married—he was married to *Grace, and they were having a child.* Survival may be the beginning of the story, but love is the reason it's worth telling.

Grace turned to Ross, leaning in just enough so only he could hear.

"I'm so proud of you."

Ross pressed a kiss to her forehead, his hand instinctively resting over her belly.

"We did it together."

As they stood before the crowd, hand in hand, past behind them and future ahead—Ross knew one thing with absolute certainty.

They hadn't merely survived the storm; they had forged a new life from the ordeal, something far deeper and more meaningful than they'd ever imagined.

The following morning, major headlines exploded across news outlets:

- "The Mystery Man Revealed: RJ Henderson is Ross, the Hero who saved Grace on the Emerald Princess."

- "Shipwreck Survivor's Turned Soulmates: RJ Henderson and Grace's Unbelievable Love Story."

The tabloids had a field day:

- Author, Fighter, Husband — RJ Henderson's Secret Identity Shocks The World

- Grace's Mystery Savior Revealed—And He's The One Who Punched Ethan Hargrove.

Social media was on fire.

- *The Internet is losing it's mind, and rightfully so. The real story was staring us in the face the whole time, and we never saw it coming. RJ Henderson, you magnificent secret genius.*

- *Wait...RJ Henderson is Ross?! TikTok is in meltdown mode right now. It isn't just a book—it's a real-life love story.*

- *Choosing Grace is not just a title, it's what Ross chose to do in every possible way.*

- *Ethan Hargrove somewhere scrolling through the news like: "WHAT?!"*

- *Not me thinking Choosing Grace was fiction when the whole time it was a real-life epic romance that involved a shipwreck, a rescue, a public scandal, and a literal fight for love.*

- *RJ Henderson had the craziest PR strategy EVER: write the book, casually reveal it's actually his love story, and leave us all screaming in the void.*

- *Hollywood, don't mess this up. We need this adaptation.*

But while the world celebrated the love story that had captivated millions, not everyone was applauding.

When reporters reached out to Ethan Hargrove for a statement, they were met with a clipped response:

"No comment."

Yet, according to sources close to him, the news had caught him completely off guard.

Some claimed he had seen the headlines while waiting in the lobby of a high-profile firm for a job interview.

Witnesses recalled the moment his expression twisted in disbelief, his grip tightening around his phone as he skimmed the article.

Seconds later, he had stormed out of the building, leaving behind a stunned receptionist and an interview slot that would now go to someone else.

Others said he had been silent, brooding—realizing that the chapter he once controlled was no longer his to rewrite.

Ross flipped open the newspaper and slid it across the table toward Grace, the bold headline staring up at them.

"Well?" Ross asked, watching her reaction. "What do you think?"

Grace smiled, running her fingers over the words, shaking her head in amazement. "I think the world just fell in love with you."

He let out a chuckle, shaking his head. "I don't care about the world, Grace. I care about you. Did I do our story justice?"

She met his gaze, warmth in her eyes. "From the looks of this and what's trending on social media, I'd say you didn't just tell our story, Ross... you gave it life."

About the author

Adele Hewett Veal: Author, Storyteller, Dreamer

Adele Hewett Veal, a graduate with a BA of Science in Business, specializing in Communication (2012), has nurtured a deep-rooted passion for writing since her childhood. Her early endeavors in crafting short stories, plays, and poetry laid the foundation for her creative journey. In 2003, she embarked on an ambitious project, releasing a CD titled "From a Whisper to a Touch, An Inspirational Moment with Adele Hewett," where her theatrical poetry, enriched with music and sound effects, captivated audiences with its unique blend of inspiration and artistry.

Adele's passion for storytelling has been the driving force behind her compelling novels. Her works, including a trilogy, "Shadow in the Mirror," "Reflections from Within," and "Range of Darkness," are testaments to her ability to weave intricate tales that engage and enthrall readers. Each novel is a showcase of her talent for creating vivid, immersive worlds and complex, relatable characters. Adele introduced her novel, "The Jigsaw Effect: On the Edge of Trust", in 2024

Today, she is thrilled to introduce her latest masterpiece, "Beyond the Storm's Reach." This novel, like her previous works, is a testament to her evolution as a writer and her commitment to providing her readers with an exhilarating literary experience.

Adele's aspiration extends beyond the pages; her dream is to see her novels transition from the written word to the silver screen, bringing her stories to life in a new dimension. Her journey as an author is a beacon of inspiration.

Also By Adele Hewett Veal
Shadow In the Mirror
Reflections From Within
Range of Darkness
The Jigsaw Effect: On the Edge of Trust
Now, Not Later: Harnessing the Mindset to Transcend Procrasti-
nation

www.ingramcontent.com/pod-product-compliance
Lightning Source LLC
Chambersburg PA
CBHW030341020726
47493CB00003B/626